"Sweet . . . You're sweet emerald fire."

Cat forced her lashes open, hotly aware of the naked desire in Slade's face. His eyes held her captive with a look that went straight to the heart. Suddenly aware they were in a new location, she glanced around.

"Where are we?" she asked.

Slade moved slowly out of his crouched position, knowing that if he didn't, he'd be sorely tempted to kiss Cat again.

"We've landed at Mourning Dove Ranch in time to see the sun set in a couple of hours." Slade grinned and lifted a hand in welcome as his ranch manager came down the long, narrow dirt strip in a beat-up Jeep. "Our chariot has arrived, my lady. Are you ready to go to your castle?"

Yes, she realized with eagerness—she was more than ready to see this extraordinary man's hideaway. "Lead on, my prince."

Dear Reader,

Spellbinders! That's what we're striving for. The editors at Silhouette are determined to capture your imagination and win your heart with every single book we publish. Each month, six Special Editions are chosen with *you* in mind.

Our authors are our inspiration. Writers such as Nora Roberts, Tracy Sinclair, Kathleen Eagle, Carole Halston and Linda Howard—to name but a few—are masters at creating endearing characters and heartrending love stories. Their characters are everyday people—just like you and me—whose lives have been touched by love, whose dreams and desires suddenly come true!

So find a cozy, quiet place to read, and create your own special moment with a Silhouette Special Edition.

Sincerely,

The Editors
SILHOUETTE BOOKS

LINDSAY McKENNA
Solitaire

Silhouette Special Edition

Published by Silhouette Books New York

America's Publisher of Contemporary Romance

SILHOUETTE BOOKS
300 East 42nd St., New York, N.Y. 10017

Copyright © 1987 by Lindsay McKenna

ISBN: 0-373-09397-7

First Silhouette Books printing August 1987

America's Publisher of Contemporary Romance

Printed in the U.S.A.

Books by Lindsay McKenna

Silhouette Intimate Moments

Love Me Before Dawn #44

Silhouette Desire

Chase the Clouds #75
Wilderness Passion #134
Too Near the Fire #165
Texas Wildcat #184
Red Tail #298

Silhouette Special Edition

Captive of Fate #82
Heart of the Eagle #338
A Measure of Love #377
Solitaire #397

LINDSAY McKENNA

enjoys the unusual and has pursued such varied interests as fire fighting and raising purebred Arabian horses, as well as her writing. "I believe in living life to the fullest," she declares, "and I enjoy dangerous situations because I'm at my best during those times."

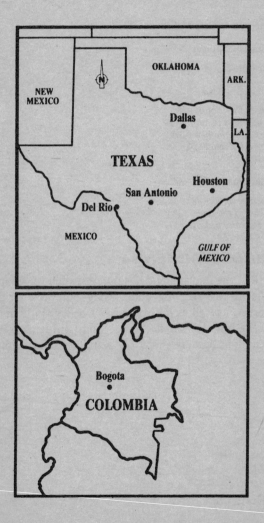

Chapter One

Don't go in there. It's too dangerous." A large hand splayed across on the blueprint of the emerald mine in Hampton, Maine, that Cat was studying. Her concentration broken, she blinked. Thinking it was the owner of the gem mine, she slowly stood up and turned.

Normally, she barely had to lift her eyes to look into those of a man, so she was momentarily disconcerted to find herself eye to eye with a khaki-covered chest. She brought her gaze up and looked into dark blue eyes the color of midnight sapphire and equally breathtaking. The man's stubborn jaw accentuated the intensity of his gaze, and if it weren't for the laugh lines bracketing his mouth and the crinkles at the corners of his eyes, she would have bet he never smiled.

"I beg your pardon," Cat said coolly.

"I've already been in that mine. It isn't safe."

Her mouth curved into a knowing smile. "What mine is?"

Impatience flared in his eyes. "This is no time for jokes, Ms. Kincaid. I was in that dump this morning and the owner is crazy to ask anyone to actually inspect that worthless pit. The timbers are not only rotted, but there's water in the sedimentary manging wall above those timbers that's weakened the entire crosscut."

"You're obviously not Mr. Graham," Cat returned testily. "So perhaps you'd be good enough to tell me who you are, and how you know my name."

"No, I'm not the owner of this worthless excuse for a mine. And everyone in our business knows the name Cat Kincaid." His eyes grew warm and he extended his hand. "My name is Slade Donovan. I'm a geologist."

Cat shook his hand, finding his grip firm but not overpowering. "I don't understand, Mr. Donovan. Has Mr. Graham hired you to help assess the condition of the Emerald Lady Mine?" She stole a look at her watch. She didn't have much time and she couldn't waste what she had on social amenities.

Slade had the good grace to look sheepish. "Well, not exactly, Ms. Kincaid. Oh, hell, do you mind if I call you Cat? That's what most people call you, right? I don't like standing on formality any more than I have to."

Wariness returned to Cat's eyes. "Slade Donovan. Where have I heard that name before?"

He colored slightly, heightening the ruddy glow already in his cheeks. "Mining engineers and geologists are a pretty close group on the international circuit," he parried. "I've worked a few gem mines in Africa and South America."

Cat pushed a few dark brown strands of hair from her forehead and took a step back, gauging him closely in the interim. "I know I've heard of you..."

"That's not really important right now; you are." He pointed out the grimy window of the old shack. "Lionel Graham has a poor reputation among geologists. You can't trust him." His voice, naturally low and with an obvious

Texas accent, deepened with urgency. "He's waited too long for a mine inspection into that crosscut. Those post and stull timbers would crack if someone were to breathe on them the wrong way, Cat."

"Ms. Kincaid, please, Mr. Donovan. If the owner hasn't hired you, then what are you doing here?" It was on the tip of her tongue to ask just who he thought he was to be telling her, a mining engineer, whether she should go into a mine or not. Staring at him critically, she guessed his age to be around her own thirty-three years. He managed to look both rugged and boyish, a combination helped by the lock of rebellious brown hair lying on his broad brow.

He suddenly offered her a devastating smile, obviously meant to melt the heart of any woman he wanted to charm. The smile, however, had the opposite effect on her. Placing her hands on her hips, she stood waiting for an explanation.

"Actually, I flew in from Bogota when I heard you were coming here." Slade brushed the errant lock back in one quick motion. "I've been trying to track you down for days. I got in last night and—"

"Ah, there you are, Ms. Kincaid." Lionel Graham, a portly man dressed impeccably in a gray suit, entered the office. His balding head shone beneath the naked light bulb suspended above them, and his brow wrinkled as he turned to the tall man standing beside her. "What are you doing here, Donovan? I thought you were still in South America."

Slade scowled back at Graham and drew himself up to his full six-foot-four. "I was in Tunnel B this morning, Graham, the crosscut. I can't say I liked what I saw."

Graham frowned, sucking in his potbelly. "Now see here, Donovan, I don't know what you're doing here, but no one is allowed inside the Emerald Lady unless I authorize it."

"I can see why," Slade shot back. "That mine's back is broken. Someone hasn't been following proper pumping practices, and you've got nothing but rotting posts and stulls weighed down by a ceiling ready to collapse on anyone stupid enough to go in there.''

Graham colored fiercely. "What does a geologist know about engineering matters?" he challenged.

"A damn good geologist, Graham." Slade glanced over his shoulder toward Cat. "I know emerald mines, Graham, and you have no business sending anyone down in that shaft."

Cat moved forward, her anger finally at the boiling point. She didn't have time to stand there listening to these two. "Mr. Donovan, your opinion is not wanted or needed. That's why I'm here. I troubleshoot bad mines for a living. Do you?"

Struggling to contain his temper, Slade asked, "Ever hear of taking a bath, Ms. Kincaid?" Although not a common practice, some unscrupulous mine owners would put very little money into a supposedly rich gem site, then declare it a catastrophic business loss to collect a healthy tax return. Well, the Emerald Lady was a lost cause and both Slade and Graham knew it. The only one who didn't was Cat Kincaid, and he wasn't going to let her find out the hard way if he had anything to say about it.

"I fail to see what that has to do with this situation, Mr.—"

"My friends call me Slade. And the Emerald Lady is nothing more than a nice, juicy business loss just waiting to be picked up by Graham."

Graham flushed scarlet. "You've gone too far this time, Donovan," he sputtered. "Unless you're suddenly working with the U.S. Mine Safety—"

Slade turned conspiratorially to Cat for a moment. "That's who ought to be called in to handle this situation. Tunnel B is just begging to fall. But then, Graham—" he turned to the red-faced man "—you wouldn't stand to get as much of a tax loss if you didn't have someone of Ms.

Kincaid's stature sign on the bottom line, stating that your mine is not only inoperable, but a disaster of the first degree."

"Look, Donovan, you've no right," began a riled Graham.

Slade, ignoring him, swung his attention back to Cat. "You've been a mining engineer for over ten years. And there isn't anyone in our business who doesn't respect or admire your work in constructing mines under almost impossible circumstances." Slade jabbed a finger toward the Emerald Lady mine. "But your life and your knowledge, not to mention your neck, aren't worth risking for that pit. I'm telling you, that shaft is deadly. Don't go in there. Let Graham get the U.S. mining officials to do it instead."

Cat was momentarily swayed by the fervor of his request; Donovan's deep Texas accent flowed through her like a cool breeze on a hot jungle night. Then she blinked, realizing that he had literally spun her into his web with his husky, coaxing voice. Irritated that she had let him affect her at all, she said, "Mr. Donovan, I think Mr. Graham and I can handle this. In case you forgot, mine inspection is part of being a mining engineer."

Graham pulled out a white silk handkerchief and mopped his perspiring brow. "It most certainly is! Ms. Kincaid's specialty is troublesome mines; that's why I called her. And I resent your inference, Donovan, that I'm doing this for a business loss. Nothing could be further from my mind. The Emerald Lady is the best, and we'll hire only the best if we get into trouble."

Slade snorted. Graham was lying through his perfectly capped teeth. Slade wondered briefly why Cat couldn't see through Graham's ploy. Who had raised her to never question another person's motives?

"Please—" he opened both his callused hands out toward Cat in a final, pleading gesture "—don't go in there. There was a heavy rain here last night. Give the mine another day to settle down. Water's leaking like a sieve in there, and in the crosscut. The supporting timbers are rotted. A day. Just one.''

There simply wasn't enough time for this, and Cat stepped up to Donovan, her jaw set. ''My schedule doesn't permit the luxury of an extra day. I intend to inspect this mine right now, Mr. Donovan. I don't have time to stand here and discuss this issue. By this afternoon—'' she looked at the gold Rolex watch on her darkly tanned left wrist ''—at 2:00 p.m., to be precise, I have a flight back to New York City. I have to be in Australia by tomorrow evening.''

Rain began falling at a steady clip, spreading a gray pall over the heavily forested area that surrounded the mine. Slade interpreted this as a warning. Cat merely regarded it as an inconvenience.

She picked up her white miner's hard hat, which had accumulated scratches and dents from many years of use. Each depression was from a rock large enough to have injured her. Cat tested the light strapped to the front of the hat before settling it on her sable-colored hair. Then she plugged the jack into a battery pack that she carried on a web belt around her waist. As she finished her preparations, Cat tried to ignore Donovan, whose tightly throttled energy had the room in a state of electric tension.

''Donovan,'' Graham began, ''I don't care who you think you are. You're trespassing on private property.'' He glanced around. ''If you don't leave, I'll call the sheriff on my car telephone and have you booted out of here on your—''

''Save your threats, Graham. I'm staying until Ms. Kincaid is safely out of that mine.'' His blue eyes narrowed on Graham's porcine face. ''And there's not a damn thing you can do about it unless you think you're big enough to throw me out of here.''

Cat shook her head and picked up a safety lamp. Lighting the regulation-size lantern, she watched with satisfaction as the yellow flame grew. She straightened up.

"You going in with her, Graham?" Slade prodded savagely.

"Of course not. She's the mining expert."

Slade's mouth twisted into a lethal line. "You wouldn't be caught dead in there because you know just how unsafe that pit is."

Cat opened the door and nailed both men with a look of authority. "You two can stay here and argue about the mine's merits, but I'm going into it." She looked directly at Slade. "And don't follow me in. Understand?"

He grimaced and nodded. "Whatever you say, lady." Then his icy composure gave way to concern. "But I'd like to see you come back in one piece."

Cat tilted her head, a question in her eyes. What had the scuttlebutt been about the man named Slade Donovan? Later, after the mine inspection was over, she'd search her memory. The name sounded familiar, but was he tied to good news or bad? Judging from his bull-in-the-china-shop tactics, it probably wasn't very good.

"I'll be out in about an hour, Mr. Graham, unless I find something, then it will take a bit longer."

"Fine, fine. Take your time. I'll be waiting."

Slade took a step toward her. "Get in and then get the hell out. Any miner with an ounce of brains could tell twenty minutes after entering it that the mine's broken."

Cat gave him a cool look, then pulled the miner's hat brim a little lower across her eyes. "In about an hour, Mr. Graham..."

Helplessly Slade watched her leave and move out into the downpour. The lightweight pale blue canvas jacket she wore darkened immediately with splotches of rain. Muttering a curse, Slade elbowed past Graham. Cat was halfway across the empty, muddy expanse, heading toward the yawning dark hole of the mine shaft, when Slade caught up with her.

"Ms. Kincaid—Cat—here, take this with you." He thrust a portable radio into her hand. "It's waterproof," he quickly explained. The rain slashed across his face, and his hair darkened as it became plastered against his skull. "Just in case, okay? Don't give me that look, either. This is a safety measure. There's no one here to help you in case something does go wrong." He drew to a halt just inside the shaft. Slade gave her a pleading look, knowing he couldn't intimidate or push Cat into doing what he wanted. He'd heard she had a mind of her own and now he had to deal with that.

Cat stuffed the radio inside her jacket to protect it. The damp, stale air flowing out of the mine swept around them and a chill worked its way up her back. "Okay," she said, "I'll take it with me. But you stay here. I've had enough of your strong-arm tactics, Mr. Donovan. You're just lucky Mr. Graham didn't call the sheriff. You could be in a lot of hot water. He's a fairly influential man in mining, even if his reputation is less than virtuous."

"Lady," Slade confirmed, grinning, "Graham's sunk more worthless pits around the world than I've sampled ore."

"Let me get on with my business, Donovan."

"Yeah, go ahead. How about if I buy you a steak for lunch when you're done?"

There was something intriguing about Slade Donovan that Cat couldn't quite put her finger on; her sixth sense— or was it female curiosity—urged her to accept. "Lunch," she grudgingly agreed. "But a short one."

"I know, you've got a plane to catch." He smiled, the tension in his face easing momentarily.

Cat flipped on her helmet light, holding the safety lamp out in front of her. "See you later, Donovan." Watching where she placed her rubber-booted feet, Cat began her trek down the gentle incline of the adit, or main shaft. Darkness closed around her like a consuming embrace, and the only light was the muted yellow glow of the safety lamp. She inhaled the dankness of the silent shaft. Like most emerald mines, it wasn't deep; it ran shallow, following either sedimentary or pegmatite veins that hid the green rock in calcite nests. The floor was littered profusely with limestone slabs, evidence that the mine hadn't been worked in quite a while.

Cat stopped at every few timbers and studied them carefully with her practiced eye. The overhead roof, or manging wall, of pale green limestone dripped constantly. Most of it was due to the dampness inherent in a mine. But Slade had been right: trickles of water had followed fissures in the sediment and wound their way down into the mine itself. Rock bolts should have been placed in the wall to strengthen it. Without them the wetness would weaken the wall. As Cat ran practiced fingers across the stull, or timbers, supporting the limestone roof, she saw that the main shoring points would have to be immediately replaced and new ones installed.

The thin beam of light from her helmet probed the blackness as Cat raised her head to assess the damage to each post and stull. The adit split into a Y, known to miners as a crosscut. This was the beginning of Tunnel B. The air leaving the shaft was desultory and pregnant with a stale, musty odor. Cat wondered if the dew point was high enough for it to actually rain within the mine. Again, Slade had been right: Graham hadn't even begun to put the necessary care into this mine to make it a decent place to work. If Graham was as knowledgeable as Donovan had said he was, he had no excuse to have skimped on proper ventilation and pumping equipment. Moisture was eating away at the powerful oak and hardwood beams that kept the walls from collapsing and the roof from dropping, and some unlucky miner could lose his life beneath it. She turned down the

crosscut, a secondary tunnel off the main adit, and carefully inspected each support. The limestone had turned a
rust color where water had leaked through from above, indicating iron in the sediment above the exposed vein. Cat
smiled grimly. Slade had accurately predicted the condition
of the shaft: there was no way emeralds were going to be
found in this kind of rock. The only type that held emeralds was calcite limestone, and none was in evidence here.
Even though she wasn't a geologist, she'd seen plenty of
rock, and she was knowledgeable enough to make the assessment on her own.

The deeper she went, the more oppressive the air became. The incline became vertical—what miners called a
winze. Cat halted at the lip of the winze. She held the safety
lamp high, looking for the reason for the vertical descent of
the shaft. Normally, it was because the vein of calcite or
pegmatite went off in an unexpected direction. But judging
from the iron-marked limestone, Cat could see no discern-
ible reason for it. She ran her fingers lightly over the hardwood timber; the surface was slick with algae and wet from
the constant leakage of water. Above, the main horizontal
stull was fully cracked and sagging. Again, Slade's words
came to her about the back of the mine being broken.

Cat's lips tightened and she stood quietly. All around her,
she could hear the plunk, plunk, plunk of water. The pas-
sage gleamed from the liquid seeping in through the walls.
Should she go on? Chances were, if one timber was cracked,
the others would be, too, indicating that the entire roof was
caving in. It was only a matter of time until the limestone,
weakened by water flow through the natural fissures, would
collapse. Why did Graham want her to investigate the wor-
thiness of this mine? It was a total loss. So much money
would have to be poured into shoring up the crosscut alone,
she wondered if the mine's calculated yield was worth that
kind of expense. Cat thought not, but that wasn't any of her
business; that was Graham's decision to make.

The floor of the mine was slippery with mud and slime. Cat took each step carefully, for she had no wish to cause any undue vibration that might further weaken the supports. Automatically, she pressed her wet fingers against her jacket where the radio lay next to her heart. Slade was turning out to be a pretty decent person after all; his advice had been good, and the radio was a definite asset.

Pushing thoughts of Slade aside, Cat concentrated on the overhead stulls. She stopped every ten feet and examined each one thoroughly. About three hundred feet into the winze, Cat crouched by the left wall. The limestone had cracked, and a healthy spring of water gushed through the opening, running down into the shaft. That wasn't good. It indicated a major structural weakness in the rock wall glistening beneath her fingertips. Slowly rising, Cat cautiously moved to the other side of the mine and continued her inspection.

She had gone another two hundred feet, almost to the end of Tunnel B according to the map, when a sickening crack echoed through the shaft. In one motion, Cat turned, sprinting back toward the beginning of the crosscut. Suddenly, a rumbling sound began. The hollow, drumlike roar rolled through the shaft like mounting thunder. She couldn't tell whether the winze was caving in behind or in front of her. Water several inches deep rushed down the shaft, and she splashed through it. She leaped to the lip that signaled an end to the winze. Slipping, Cat skidded to her knees in the muck and mud of the crosscut. The safety lamp bounced twice and then the flame went out.

Loud snapping and groaning noises followed. Cat's breath tore from her as she scrambled to her feet; the only light left was the one on her helmet. Water was rapidly rising from foot to ankle level; she knew a crack in the wall up ahead had given way. Had the entire wall caved in, leaving her no escape?

Behind her, Cat heard the limestone manging wall grate, and she automatically ducked her head, keeping one hand on her helmet as she raced toward the intersection of the adit. Only two hundred feet more, she guessed, gasping for breath. A crash caromed beside her, and rocks began falling. She halted, breathing hard. Should she retreat or—fist-size pieces of limestone began raining down around her. She was trapped! Cat shielded her face and lurched forward, dust and rock hailing down as she slogged forward, staggering and stumbling.

Suffocating dust filled Cat's mouth, nose and lungs. She coughed violently, unable to breathe. Blinded by the dust, which was thicker than smoke, she tripped. As she did, the manging wall where she had stood seconds before dropped to the floor. A rock the size of a baseball crashed onto her hard hat, knocking it off her head. The hat and light bounced crazily, sending a skittering beam of light through the dense grayness. Another rock struck her shoulder, spinning her around. Cat threw her hands up to protect her head as she pitched backward. She slammed into the jagged rocks, the breath ripped out of her. Seconds later, more than a ton of rock and soil filled the chamber where she was trapped. A cry tore from her as the rest of the other wall collapsed, nearly burying her. Pain lanced up her right side and Cat sank back, unconscious.

With a violent oath, Slade raced down the mine shaft. He had heard the ominous crack of timbers, sounding one after another like breaking matchsticks. He shouted for Cat, but his voice was drowned out by a deep roar that sent icy fear up his spine. A rolling cloud of dust engulfed him and he turned back, hacking and coughing, his hand across his nose and mouth as he stumbled out.

Lionel Graham came lumbering out of the mine shack, his eyes round with shock. Slade ran toward him and grabbed him by the lapel of his expensive English raincoat.

"Damn you, Graham, it's happened! Now you get on that car phone and call for help. Now!"

"Y-yes, of course. Of course," he sputtered, and hurried toward his car.

Slade spun around and ran back to the mine opening, pulling out the radio he kept in a leather carrying case on his hip. The red light blinked on, indicating that the battery was sufficiently charged and ready to be used.

"Cat? Cat, can you hear me? This is Slade. Over." He released the button. All he could hear was static. His mind whirled. Was she dead? Buried alive? Or had she been given a reprieve, and been trapped in a chamber? If so, how much air was left? He knew from his own grim experience that dust could suffocate a person. He ran into the mine and went as far as he could before the choking wall of limestone dust stopped him. Again, he called her. Again, no answer. Damn it to hell! He wanted to wrap his fingers around Graham's fleshy throat and strangle the bastard. He might as well have set Cat up to be murdered. But right now, Slade needed Graham's influence to get local miners together to begin excavating the mine to search for Cat.

Slade wasn't one to pray often, not that he didn't believe in God, but he more or less used Him in emergencies only. Well, this was an emergency, and as he pressed the radio's On button once again, he prayed that Cat would hear him this time.

"Cat? Cat Kincaid, can you hear me? This is Slade Donovan. If you can hear me, depress the handset. Show me you're alive. Over."

The constant static of the portable radio now lodged between her rib cage and the wall of rocks slowly brought Cat back to consciousness. Blood trickled from her nose and down her lips. She tried to lick them, but her tongue met a thick caking of dust. Suddenly a sharp, riveting pain brought her fully conscious; it felt as if her right side were on fire. Dully, Cat tried to take stock of herself. She was

buried up to her thighs in rubble. The weak light from her
helmet lay to the left, barely visible through the curtain of
dust that hung in the chamber.

The radio static continued, and dazedly Cat reached into
her jacket. It hurt to breathe. It hurt to move. Dizziness
washed over her and she knew that she was injured. How
badly she didn't know. Not yet. And maybe never. She had
no idea how large or small was the chamber where she was
buried. If it was too small, and there wasn't sufficient oxygen, she would die of suffocation sooner, rather than later.
If she was lucky, oxygen might be trickling through the walls
blocking her escape, and she wouldn't suffocate.

Her fingers closed over the radio. Twisting slightly, she
pulled it out of her jacket. A gasp tore from her and a tidal
wave of pain caused her to black out for several seconds.
When she came to, she took light, shallow breaths of the
murky air. To breathe deep meant suffering a knifelike pain
ripping up her right side. Busted ribs, she thought, slowly
pulling the radio out of the jacket.

The light from her hard hat was slowly dimming, but she
focused on first things first: the radio. Would it work? Was
Donovan still out there? Her hand trembled badly as she
fumbled to turn the radio on. The red light blinked on, and
a rough, scratchy noise greeted her. Finally, she fine-tuned
it with the other dial.

Her fingers, now bruised and bloodied, slipped on the
button she hoped would link her with the outside world. Cat
depressed it and tried to speak, but the only sound that came
from her throat was a low croak. If only she could have
some water! She could hear it all around her, the same
rushing sound as before. Had that wall collapsed behind her
where the limestone had cracked and separated?

"D-Donovan..." Her voice was barely a hoarse whisper. Dust clogged her throat and she wanted to cough, but
didn't dare for fear of disturbing her broken ribs. Then the
radio crackled and an incredible surge of relief flowed

through her as she heard Donovan's Texas baritone come scratchily over the handset.

"Cat! I can barely hear you. Give me a report on your condition."

"I—I'm trapped between a double cave-in. My legs are under rubble, but if I can move off my belly, I can free myself. Chamber is—dust too thick to tell how small or large it is yet."

"Injuries?"

"Right lung hurts...can't breathe very well. Legs are numb but I think if I get the rocks off, they'll be okay."

Terror leaked through Slade's voice. "Head injury?"

Cat had to wait a minute to assess herself. She slowly raised her hand, feeling her dust-laden hair, and met warm stickiness as she felt across her scalp. Her head was throbbing as if it might split into a hundred pieces, like the limestone around her. "Maybe a mild concussion. Dizzy—"

"Oxygen?"

"Let me radio back. Got to try and reach my hard hat."

"All right, just take it easy. We're going to get you out of there. Just hang on. Graham's phoned for help. We expect miners and excavation equipment within the next hour. Get back to me on the size of the place you're trapped in. Over."

Just the reassuring sound of Slade's voice kept her panic from exploding. There was something about him that instilled faith in his promise to get her out of there. Gently, Cat set down the radio. What she would do for some water now! Dizziness came and went and Cat felt nausea clawing up her throat—she had all the symptoms of a concussion. Stretching her left hand out, fingers extended, she reached for her hard hat. There! Her fingers closed over the hat and she pulled it back to her.

As the dust slowly settled around her, Cat got an idea of the chamber's size. Rocks ranging from the size of her fist to huge sheets that easily weighed half a ton were lodged all around her. She had been lucky: if she had not tripped and fallen where she now lay, a sheet of limestone nearby would have sheared right through her. She'd be dead. The drenching reality washed through her and she closed her eyes, exhausted. *I shouldn't be tired. Got to get these rocks off my legs and move around. Maybe I can find some water...* Then drowsiness overwhelmed her.

Slade paced back and forth in front of the mine like an infuriated lion. He gripped the radio tightly in his fist. The rain was continuing to fall at a steady rate; the sky had become a dismal gray. Angrily, he shook off the thought and the feeling. Cat was alive, and that was all that mattered. No one should die alone in that godforsaken place. He wanted to vent his anger on Graham, who sat in his silver Mercedes looking pasty from the turn of events. The frightened mine owner had gone to extraordinary measures to call in local workers who had once toiled in the worthless mine, and to order heavy equipment from a nearby town. The local fire department would arrive shortly with oxygen tanks, masks and rescue apparatus. As soon as they came, Slade was going to borrow a tank and mask and make his way down the shaft to locate Cat's chamber. He halted. Cat should have called in by now.

Slade called her five times and there was no answer. Was Cat unconscious? Had she died because of oxygen deprivation? Torn between staying and going deeper, he stared down the black maw of the shaft. Maybe her radio was on the blink. He tried to ignore his memory of the slur of Cat's words and the pain he'd heard with each breath she had taken. He had a gut feeling she was in a lot more serious condition than she was revealing.

He called again. This time, he got an answer. "Cat, how are you?"

"Uhh, dizzy. Sorry, didn't mean to black out."

Slade's mouth thinned, his eyes reflecting his anxiety, but he kept it out of his voice as he depressed the On button. "You're doing fine. Did you get a look at the chamber?"

"Twenty feet long and ten feet wide. The manging wall is holding. I'm under a stull that's stopping it from falling on top of me."

Relief flowed through him. "Great. Any indication of air supply?"

"Dust still too thick. I'm turning off my light to conserve it. Need water worse."

"I know. Look, you just rest."

"C-can't. Got to try and get rocks off legs."

Slade nodded. "The fire department is coming with oxygen gear. As soon as they arrive, I'm going to find you, Cat. For now, just conserve your energy."

She knew Slade was right, but she was shivering from the overwhelming dampness around her. As dry as her mouth and throat were, the moisture was seeping through to her bones. She shut off the light and slowly began to remove one rock at a time from the back of her legs. Only her left hand was undamaged. Movement of her right arm sent such a spasm of pain up Cat's side that she lost consciousness.

Cat was used to darkness; when she constructed a mine shaft, she was constantly in the darkened earth with only a safety lamp and lighted hard hat to illuminate her way. But rarely had she gone without any light at all, and now the dark was as suffocating as the dust that hung around her. A shiver rippled through her, the darkness like fingers of fear closing around her throat. Cat tasted her panic and concentrated on removing the rocks from her thigh, gradually releasing herself from the entrapment.

Minutes dragged by. *And each minute seems like a lifetime,* Cat realized. She clung to the hope that Slade would call again. Just to hear another human voice eased the terror that was intensified by the dark. Her breath came in painful, ragged gasps; each one feeling as if a knife was being plunged through her lungs. Sweat mingled with dust as it trickled down her face, stinging her eyes. Resting until the dizziness passed, Cat knew she would have to use her right hand to start removing the debris from her right leg. An involuntary cry tore from her contorted lips as she pushed the first rock off her thigh. Blackness closed in on her and she rested her brow against her left arm, sobbing.

"Over here!" Slade motioned the first of two arriving volunteer fire department pumpers toward the opening of the mine. Graham reluctantly got out of his car and met the chief, who was dressed in a white helmet and turnout gear. *Finally,* Slade thought, moving toward the fire chief. In moments he had established his identity and was given an air pack and mask. He took a safety lamp and settled the hard hat on his head, then entered the mine. His heart rate picked up. How far down the crosscut had the cave-in taken place? He mentally began to calculate the possible scenarios he might find. If there was a huge wall of debris, it might take days before they could reach Cat. He prayed it was the opposite—that the bulk of the cave-in had occurred behind her and only a thin wall stood between her and freedom.

Chapter Two

Slade found the wall of rock near the second timber support in the crosscut and carefully examined the timbers around him. They were sturdy and did not appear stressed. That meant mining equipment such as drills and augers could be moved into the mine to begin removing the debris without fear of another avalanche. The dust was still thick as Slade breathed in the sweet flow of oxygen through his face mask. Sweat trickled down his temples, following the line of his jaw. Some of his fear for Cat slipped away; most of the rock and dirt that had fallen was in small chunks, and easily handled by picks, shovels and wheelbarrows. Rescue would come more quickly.

Slade crouched by one wall of the crosscut, watching as a constant stream of water disappeared into the wall. He knew that if it was getting through, life-bearing oxygen could also be carried into the chamber where Cat was trapped. Pulling out the radio, Slade attempted contact with her. He waited patiently, repeating his call three times before she answered. Cat's voice was tight and hoarse, and Slade knew she was in a hell of a lot of pain.

"How's my girl doing?"

A choked sound came over the radio. "Hanging—in there."

"Mining engineers always did have more guts than brains," he told her wryly. "I'm outside the wall where you're trapped, Cat. Give me a status report."

"Oxygen level seems the same. There's—running water to my left."

"Outstanding. How about you?"

"Would it do any good to tell you?"

"Don't play that game with me. I know I can't get to you yet, but I want to know the extent of your injuries and if you're feeling worse."

"I'll bet you use that line on every woman you meet, Donovan."

He grinned, but it didn't reach his narrowed eyes as he continued to appraise the wall of debris before him. "With you, I wouldn't use a line. Come on, level with me. How are you doing?"

"I've got the rocks off my legs and I managed to turn over. The right side of the tunnel wall looks weak and the stull above my head keeps creaking and groaning."

Slade scowled. That meant that even Cat's chamber could cave in, burying her under tons of rubble. Urgency thrummed through him. "How's that concussion you're sporting?"

"Not—good. I keep passing out. Very sleepy when I shouldn't be. I was sleeping until you called. The scratchy sounds from the radio woke me up."

Damn it! She had suffered a worse head injury than he had first thought. "Okay," Slade soothed, keeping his voice steady. "How's your ribs?"

"If I don't breathe, I feel great."

She had spunk, he'd give her that. "And when you do?"

"Feels like someone's shoved a knife up under my right rib cage."

"Think you've got compound fractures?" If she did, the broken bone could conceivably puncture the lung if she moved around too much.

"I can feel blood there. I don't know. It hurts too much to touch the area and find out."

"Stay still if you can." It was either busted ribs or a punctured lung. Or both.

"Right."

"Do you have a water source?" If she had oxygen and water, Cat could last a long time. But if she had undetected internal injuries, time could prove to be their enemy. Cat needed immediate medical attention.

"Y-yes, a small stream along the left wall. All the amenities, Donovan."

"Except you don't have me. And I intend to remedy that situation shortly. Tell me, how many posts are in your chamber?" There was a post for every ten feet of spacing.

"One, Donovan. And it's not looking very healthy."

"You know enough to place yourself under it, with your back up against it, don't you?"

"Y-yes. Once I feel up to crawling over there, I'll do it."

"Can't you walk over to it?"

"Too dizzy. I'd fall and skin my knees."

He almost smiled. "Wouldn't want you to skin up those pretty knees."

"You're full of Texas baloney, Donovan."

He laughed. "I told you before, Cat, with you, I'm honest."

"Sure, an honest geologist. That'll be the day."

"Guess I'll have to prove it to you, won't I?"

"Right now I need a knight on a white charger. Come and get me, Donovan."

"Would you settle for thirty firemen, fifty miners and some drilling equipment instead?"

"Sounds wonderful."

He heard the sudden wobble in Cat's voice, as if she were close to tears. Slade tightened his grip around the radio. "Look, it appears that about ten feet of earth and rock are separating us, Cat. Unless we run into some limestone sheets weighing a ton or more, we ought to be able to reach you within twenty-four hours."

"Slade?"

Slade blinked the sweat from his eyes, hearing the fear in Cat's voice for the first time. "What is it, sweetheart?"

"C-could you contact my parents? Tell them what's happened? Especially my brother Rafe? They live in Colorado. The Triple K Ranch. If I give you the phone number, could you call them? Please?"

"Sure, anything you want."

Relief cracked her voice. "T-thanks. Here's the number."

Slade committed it to memory. "I'm signing off, Cat. The miners will be here any minute. I've got Graham's permission to organize and run this rescue operation. If you need anything, call. Otherwise I'll contact you in about an hour."

"Just let me know if you can reach my family."

"I'll personally make the call. Graham's got a phone in his car."

"Thanks, Slade. It means a lot to me...."

"I can tell." As he left the dankness of the mine, his mind shifted to another matter. Slade knew very few geologists or mining engineers who had sunk roots and had a family or children. He also knew from reading articles on Cat Kincaid that she wasn't married. As Slade got to his feet and began his trek to the adit, he wondered what man in his right mind would let someone as rare as Cat Kincaid out of his sight, much less out of his life. There was a special quality about her that he longed to explore. She was like an emerald mine waiting to be discovered: enticing, mysterious and filled with rich promise.

Gray light filtered through the adit, telling him he was near the opening. Well, he'd discovered one thing about Cat: family meant a great deal to her. Rafe was obviously a brother she could look up to, admire and lean on in times of trouble. Lucky guy, he told himself enviously.

As Slade walked out into the pall of rain, he glared at the gray sky overhead. They didn't need more water; it would loosen more dirt and the rain would trickle through the weakened limestone, making the rescue effort even more precarious than before. Slade had good instincts, and his gut sense had often saved his life in the past. Now, that voice screamed out that another cave-in was near. His instincts also warned him that if this was Cat's first cave-in, she would need emotional support to get back the courage to someday walk into the darkness of another mine.

Cat could barely move her head. She sat with her back against the rough, splintered surface of the post. Five hours had elapsed. Slade had called once an hour and sweet God in heaven, how she came to rely on him; he was her support system against the fear that threatened to consume her. Each passing hour made it become harder to control her rising panic.

Her spirits had plummeted when Slade had not been able to raise anyone at her parents' ranch right away. Cat felt alone and vulnerable in a way she'd never before experienced. Rafe—she needed Rafe's steadying presence. He was always the one to get them out of a jam when they were kids growing up in the Rocky Mountain wilderness. There had been times when she was scared to death, but because Rafe reassured her that it would be all right, she took dangerous chances with him. When Slade informed her he couldn't reach anyone at the Triple K, her fears loomed up again.

Slade had told her he had the first shift with the miners clearing away the debris. Cat couldn't hear the strike of pickaxs or the grind of huge auger drill bits boring holes to

loosen the soft base so it could be shoveled away. The wall,
Slade had said, was at least ten feet thick, perhaps twenty.
It could, at worst, be days before she could be rescued.

At 10:00 a.m., Slade was able to make contact with the
Kincaid Ranch. After a tense conversation, he made his way
to the wall and called Cat. After four tries, she still didn't
answer and Slade grew worried. Another five calls. Nothing. Had Cat passed out? Was she sleeping because of the
concussion? Slade tried to contain his apprehension.

Cat finally floated out of unconsciousness and weakly
raised her left arm. The luminous dials on her Rolex told her
she had been asleep for nearly six hours. She lay on the hard
pebbled floor on her left side to ease the pressure on her
right. Experimentally, Cat lightly ran her fingers over her
ribs, feeling how swollen her flesh had become beneath her
damp canvas jacket. Not good, she thought blearily. The
radio clicked, telling her that Slade was trying to contact her.

The radio lay near her head and she depressed the button. "S-Slade?"

"Cat? My God, are you all right?"

A grimace pulled at her lips. "Fine. Went to sleep, didn't
I?"

"Yeah. Six hours. You scared the hell out of me."

"S-sorry."

"Don't worry about it. Listen, I got hold of your family
and everyone's flying out here to see you. They'll be landing soon and I've arranged to have someone meet them at
the nearest airport. Your parents, brother, sister and her
husband are coming."

Tears leaked down her face and she couldn't trust her
voice.

"The whole family's coming?"

He laughed. "Yeah. I'm impressed. Not many families
would fly to the rescue."

"We're close."

"How are you holding up?"

"I've had better days, Donovan. How are things out there?"

"We've got thirty men on line for you, sweetheart. We're hauling about a ton of dirt and rock an hour. I'm shoring the shaft up with new post and stull every three feet as we go."

Cat nodded, trying to lick her dry lips. "How many tons do you figure is between you and me?"

Slade's voice was apologetic. "About fifty tons of material. If we can keep up the pace I've set, we'll have you out of there in roughly fifty hours."

Fifty more hours in the damp darkness. It seemed like an eternity. Could she control her fear? It was so black, she couldn't even see her hand if she held it up in front of her nose. And she was thirsty. Her tongue felt swollen, her throat rough as sandpaper. She would have to crawl the width of the footwall to sip that trickle of life-giving water along the opposite wall.

"You're doing a good job, Donovan. I'm going to owe you a lot by the time you get me out of here."

"Don't worry, I intend to collect for my services, lady."

Cat smiled, allowing his voice to cover her like a blanket of balm. "Whatever you want, Donovan, within reason."

Slade chuckled indulgently. "Don't worry, the price won't be so high you won't want to pay it. Look, I'll check in on you an hour from now."

Panic nibbled at her crumbling control and Cat gripped the radio, dreading the return to silence. "For some reason, I trust you, Donovan. I shouldn't, but I do."

His voice came back, husky but velvet to soothe her shattered composure. "Hold that thought, Cat. I'll be here for you, that's a promise."

Two things happened in the next hour. The entire Kincaid family arrived at the Emerald Lady, and Slade could not raise Cat again on his radio. Rafe Kincaid, the brother, was close to exploding, firing questions faster than Slade could answer them. The tall, strapping Colorado rancher took off his Stetson, rolled up his sleeves, grabbed a hard hat and went into the mine to help in the rescue effort. So did Jim Tremain, Dal's husband. Slade liked Cat's family; Sam and Inez Kincaid, Cat's parents, and Dal Tremain, Cat's younger sister, helped to set up a place where coffee could be dispensed in the nearby shack and sandwiches could be made for the hardworking rescue crews. Millie, the Kincaid's housekeeper, who was apparently an integral part of the family, watched Dal's months-old baby, Alessandra, while Dal worked.

Within an hour of their arrival, the Kincaid family had organized chow lines for the hungry miners. Meanwhile, Slade had returned to the mine to continue directing the rescue. Slade tried to reassure Rafe that his sister had probably lost consciousness again due to her concussion. Rafe glowered at him, as if it were his fault, but Slade shrugged it off. Let the rancher expend his anger on the pickax he was wielding, instead of blowing up at him.

Cat tasted blood. She lay on her left side, shivering. What time was it? How many hours had passed since she had last lost consciousness? The luminous dials of her watch blurred and she blinked. Her vision was being affected and that frightened her. The radio was pressed protectively to her breast and she shakily turned it on, the red light glowing brightly in the darkness. Almost immediately, Slade's voice came through, soothing her fragmented nerves.

"Cat?"

She heard the anxiety in Slade's voice and was grateful for his undiminished caring.

"I'm alive," she announced, her voice weaker than it had been earlier.

"Thank God. What happened? You've been out ten hours."

"I can't hang on to consciousness, Slade. Keep blacking out."

"Don't worry about it. Let me go get your parents. Your family arrived some time ago. They're helping in the relief efforts. Rafe and Jim Tremain have been using a pickax and shovel the last ten hours. That's quite a family you've got. Hold on . . ."

Tears began to stream down her grimy cheeks when she heard her father's gruff voice, and then her mother's. Cat tried not to cry. She tried to sound brave and calm and steady, everything she wasn't. But when Rafe was put on, her voice cracked, betraying her real emotions. Whether it was the avalanche of tightly withheld feelings or the strain of her entrapment, Cat was barely coherent. There was so much she wanted to say; instead tears flowed in a warm stream down her cheeks, and her voice was wobbly and fragmented.

"S-Slade . . ." she choked.

"He's done a fine job, Cat," Rafe came back. "He knows what he's doing. Look, you just hang on. We've got an ambulance and paramedic crew standing by to take you to the closest hospital. Keep your chin up, Baby Sis. We all love you. Just remember all the times you and I dared danger and won. It'll be the same this time. I promise you."

Rafe grimly handed the radio back to Donovan. Neither man looked at the other; if they had, they would have seen tears forming in the corners of their eyes. Slade's face was slack with exhaustion and streaked with dirt and mud. He took the radio from Rafe.

"Cat?"

"Y-yes?"

"Thirty-five hours to go, sweetheart. You've got a passel of people out here who love you. Just remember that."

* * *

Grim, unshaven men, their eyes bloodshot and red-rimmed from too much dust, their hands bruised and bloodied with scrapes and cuts, continued on. Day had turned to night and then day again. The rain had stopped and so had Cat's infrequent radio exchanges. Yet, the Kincaids' courage inspired the rescuers, and there wasn't a man among them who slept more than a few hours between the mandatory six-hour shifts at the end of a shovel, a wheelbarrow or pickax. No one complained, and Slade found that phenomenal.

Rubbing his bleary eyes, Slade held up his watch. A portable generator provided light in the damp expanse of the mine. Five hours . . . five hours before they broke through and made contact. Was Cat on the left wall near the stream? No stranger to cave-ins, he worried about her dehydrating. The people who knew of his escapes had said he'd had nine lives. Well, Cat had better have nine lives; she'd need them to survive this one.

Cat wasn't sure what pulled her from her floating state. Was it the whoosh of fresh air into the staleness of the chamber or the frantic sound of steel-bladed shovels tearing a hole through the last of the wall that held her captive? Or was it actually recognizing Rafe's hushed voice, and Slade's? Whatever it was, she pulled on the last of her reserves and turned her head, which was now lying in a trickle of water, toward the men's urgent voices.

The light from Slade's helmet slashed through the thick silence of the chamber. His eyes widened as he found Cat covered with filth and dust, her hair caked with mud around her pale, translucent face. She lay on her left side, stretched out across the stream of water. Thank God she'd had the foresight to move to the water; all she had to do was turn her face and sip from the shallow stream. His admiration for her survival instincts rose. Next, Rafe came through the six-foot opening, followed by a paramedic with a thin oak body board and a neck brace.

Slade reached her first, his hand closing protectively over Cat's shoulder. He leaned over from his kneeling position, his face close to hers. He whispered her name twice before he saw her long dark lashes flutter and barely open.

Cat saw a lopsided smile pull at Slade's mouth; his face was tense, his eyes burned out with bone-deep exhaustion. She saw a flame of hope in them, too. She tried to form his name on her parched, cracked lips, but only a hoarse sound issued forth.

"Shh, sweetheart. Your knights in shining armor have arrived. All I want you to do is lie very still while we get you on this body board and truss you up like a Christmas goose."

She wasn't able to comprehend all that Slade said as he leaned over her. The warmth of his breath coupled with his husky voice flowed like balm across her, filling her with new strength. A small smile tugged at Cat's mouth. She felt Slade's long fingers close gently across her shoulder, and she knew he understood.

An incredible aura of care surrounded Cat during those twenty minutes when the three men worked on her. She was conscious for minutes at a time, lapsing in and out of the arms of darkness. Rafe's voice or his familiar touch on her hair would draw her back to consciousness. She began to anticipate Slade's knowing, professional touch as he and the paramedic turned her over, placing her on the body board. She had grown used to the pain in her right side, but the callused pressure of Slade's fingers as he fitted the brace around her neck brought tears to her eyes.

The jab of a needle brought her to greater awareness, but once they had her strapped securely to the thin oak board Cat lost consciousness again.

Slade handed Sam Kincaid another cup of coffee as they

stood in the waiting room of the surgical floor of the hospital. He wasn't sure who looked worse: he or Rafe. They were muddy, their hair plastered down from untold hours of sweat. Every muscle in Slade's body screamed for rest and the luxury of a hot shower. He wrinkled his nose; the brackish odor of the mine and his sour sweat smell surrounded him. He glanced at his watch. An hour ago Cat had been taken to the emergency room, attended by a number of physicians and nurses. None of the family had been allowed to go with her. Why didn't someone come out and tell them how she was?

Slade hadn't tried to hide his own emotions as he'd sat alongside Rafe in the ambulance. Cat had been chalk white; even her freckles had looked washed out. Her once-beautiful sable-brown hair was a stringy mat of mud and blood. There'd been a three-inch gash across her scalp, and she had bled heavily, but he was more worried about the skull beneath her scalp. Just how bad was her concussion? Judging from Cat's pallor and her prolonged bouts of unconsciousness, it was serious.

A doctor came through the double swinging doors, his face unreadable. He headed for the elder Kincaid. The entire family, with Millie and Slade, surrounded the doctor before he drew to a stop.

"Mr. Kincaid?"

Sam Kincaid nodded. "Doctor? How's my girl?"

"I'm Dr. Scott," he said, extending his hand. "Cathy is in serious condition, Mr. Kincaid. She's suffered two broken ribs. She's extremely dehydrated and we've got her on two I.V.s to restabilize her."

Slade closed his fist. His voice was strained. "And her head injury, Dr. Scott?"

Scott's narrow face became impassive. "Severe concussion. She keeps lapsing in and out of consciousness." His brow furrowed. "Is your name Slade?"

"Yes. Slade Donovan."

"Cathy is asking for you. We need to try and keep her awake. I want to keep her from going into a coma."

Inez Kincaid's thin face grew still. "A coma, doctor?"

"Yes. If I can keep Slade with her, she might rally enough to fight back and stay awake. We've got that portion of her head packed in dry ice to reduce the swelling." He looked up at Slade. "Let's get you cleaned up a little, son, and then, if you don't mind, I'd like you to remain with Cathy for a while."

Slade nodded. He followed Dr. Scott down the immaculate hall to a lounge. A nurse gave him a green surgical shirt and a pair of trousers to replace his filthy clothes. Slade took a quick hot shower and fought the deep drowsiness that tried to claim him. It wasn't yet time to sleep off the past forty-eight hours he'd been awake.

The nurse, a petite blonde with blue eyes, smiled once he emerged from the lounge. "Now you look like a doctor, Mr. Donovan. Follow me, please." She took him to the intensive-care unit, where each patient's room was enclosed on three sides with glass panels. Cathy looked dead. She matched the color of her sheets. Her hair had been washed clean and an ice pack placed carefully against her skull. The sigh of oxygen and the beeps of the cardiac unit made Slade grow wary. So many machines to monitor her fragile hold on life, he thought.

The nurse drew up a chair alongside Cat's bed. "You can sit here, Mr. Donovan."

Slade thanked her, but moved to the bed. He reached out and slipped his hand across Cat's limp, cool fingers. They had washed her free of all the filth.

"You look a little on the thin side, Mr. Donovan. They said you and the Kincaids worked but didn't eat. I'll have someone run down to the cafeteria and bring you dinner."

Slade smiled, grateful for the nurse's thoughtfulness. "Thanks," he replied. Then he shifted his attention to Cat. Funny, Slade told Cat silently as he cupped her fingers between his to warm them, you were a stranger to me three days ago. A lump rose in his throat. What is it about you that touches me so?

Perhaps it was the vulnerability of her features. Or the lips that reminded him of a lush, exotic jungle orchid he'd seen in Brazil—cherry red, even now in her present condition. Or perhaps it was her heart-shaped face, or the wide cheekbones that gave her eyes an almost tilted look. A smile eased the taut planes of Slade's face as he followed the coverlet of freckles from one cheek across her broken nose to the other cheek.

Slade reached over, lightly tracing the bump on her nose. How did she break such a pretty nose? And when had she broken it? He had so many questions to ask her, so much he didn't know about her that he wanted to know. "Cat?" he said softly. "Can you hear me? It's Slade. I've come for you. I want you to fight back." His fingers tightened against hers as he reluctantly straightened up. He blinked. Was he imagining things, or had her lashes fluttered in response to his hushed request?

When Cat awoke, she was clear at once as to where she was. The murmuring of the equipment caught her attention first. Then she forced open her weighted lids. She became aware of the broken snore of a man nearby. And then she felt the warm, callused fingers that enclosed her hand. Despite the pain, Cat turned her head to the right. Her eyes widened. Slade Donovan lay slumped in a chair, snoring, his chin sagging toward his chest and his hand gripping hers. A flood of warmth coursed through her and Cat closed her eyes. She was alive. Slade had dragged her back from the depths of the mine.

Her voice cracked when she tried to call his name. Cat used what little strength she had in her hand and squeezed Slade's fingers. She watched him awaken from the heavy sleep. Her heart wrenched as she saw the darkness shadowing his red-rimmed eyes. His face was gaunt and she saw the stress plainly carved on the stubbled, angular planes of his face.

Slade blinked, his hand tightening on her fingers. "Cat?" He whispered her name unbelievingly. Standing, he leaned over the bed, one hand cupping her cheek as he gazed disbelievingly into her barely opened eyes. "I'll be damned, you're awake."

She gave him a weak smile. "I-is this a dream?"

Slade laughed unsurely, his blue eyes burning fiercely with happiness. "If it is, sweetheart, then we're dreaming together." He reached over and pressed a buzzer to alert the nurse's desk. "Hold on, there's a whole passel of doctors who are anxious to see you awake."

Cat was thirsty, her mouth gummy. "What about my family?"

"They're here, waiting for you to open those beautiful emerald eyes of yours." He pressed a kiss to her cool, damp brow. "Welcome back to the world of the living. This calls for one hell of a celebration."

In the next two days, Slade was absorbed into the Kincaid clan. He ate with the family and shared rooms with them at a local motel. At breakfast on the third morning, Sam Kincaid sat with his family, a frown marring his features.

"Dr. Scott says Cat will need a place to recuperate. He's worried about her concussion and thinks she ought to be under some kind of supervision for at least eight weeks." Sam gave his wife a tender look. "With your hip operation coming up in two weeks, we won't be able to give Cat the care she needs."

Rafe's mouth twisted. "I've got the room; it's just the timing, Dad. We've had these Bureau of Land Mines investigations going on for the past few months, and they've thrown off our schedule for a while. Family comes first. I'll take Cat in; she's more important. If I made the time for the BLM, I can sure as hell make time for my sister."

Slade suddenly brightened. "I can help. I think, under the circumstances, Cat would be better off with me." The corners of Rafe's mouth turned down and Slade knew instinctively that Rafe felt this was strictly a family matter; outsiders weren't needed. Slade directed the remainder of his proposal to Rafe to win his approval, knowing the family would then agree to Cat's staying with him. He folded his large hands on the table. This reminded Slade of poker games. Some he had lost; others he had won. This time, the stakes were high, and he had never wanted to win more. Slade didn't question why he wanted Cat on his ranch to recuperate. Since the beginning, Cat had touched some inner chord of his. He wanted—no—demanded the opportunity to get to know her. His reasons for meeting her in the first place would take secondary importance. He put on his most serious expression and spoke in a low voice.

"I know you've only been allowed fifteen minutes at a time to visit with Cat. And she may or may not have been conscious enough to mention our relationship. I have a small ranch in southwest Texas. Del Rio, to be exact. In addition, my next-door neighbors, Matt and Kai Travis, can be of great help, if we need them. Kai's a physiotherapist and a nurse for the local grade school. I have a qualified nurse three miles down the road from my ranch and the perfect place for Cat to stay." Slade's voice dropped. "I think Cat's going to take a lot of attention in order to get back on her feet. I've been in three mine cave-ins myself and I know what they do up here," he said, pointing to his head.

"I care a hell of a lot for Cat. Those hours spent with her while she was buried were some of the worst of my life." He felt a tinge of guilt for implying that he and Cat had a relationship. But it wasn't a total lie, he rationalized. "Having been buried myself, I'm in a pretty good position to help Cat." His voice grew tight with undisguised emotion. "I can help her. I can get her up and over some of the reactions she's going to have because of this experience."

Rafe rubbed his recently shaven jaw. "Kinda like falling off a horse and getting scared to mount up afterward?"

Slade nodded, sensing the subtle shift of acceptance to his proposal. "Yes, only worse. Cave-ins affect everyone differently. Nightmares are common, and with her concussion, someone is going to have to monitor her closely so she doesn't sleepwalk or something. And that does happen." He looked at father and son. "I realize this is a family matter, but in this case, I think I can provide the type of care Cat is going to need."

Sam glanced over at his son. "Why don't we let Cat have a say in this before we decide for her?"

Slade held up his hand. "I really don't think that's necessary. I'm positive Cat will want to come home with me. Besides, I've got my twin-engine plane at the airport ten miles from here. I could fly her back in comfort while you'd have to make an awful lot of special arrangements to try the same thing. I'm sure Cat would like to be with me. I know how close she is with the family, but each of you have a lot of things going on right now. Hell, I'm between job assignments. And even if I wasn't, I'd drop what I was doing to come and take care of Cat."

Rafe looked hesitant, but shrugged his powerful shoulders. "Sounds like it may be the best thing for Cat, and that's the most important thing right now, Dad."

Sam Kincaid stared at Slade for a long time, mulling over the request. "It's settled then. Cat will go home with you, Slade."

Slade felt heat rise in his cheeks as he grasped the rancher's hand. "Thanks, Sam. None of you will regret your decision, believe me." A fierce wave of protectiveness nearly overwhelmed Slade as he rose from the table. He was shocked by his offer to care for Cat, yet nothing he'd ever done had ever felt so right. Gratefully, he shook each man's hand.

Inez kissed her daughter's cheek. Cat had been transferred to a private room and the entire family, minus Millie, who, since the baby wasn't allowed in the room, was in the lounge, stood around her bed.

"You take care, honey," Inez said. She patted Cat's hand gently.

Cat blinked up at her mother. "You're all leaving?" There was a catch in her voice. She saw Rafe nod, his cowboy hat clasped between his roughened fingers.

Slade went to the other side of the bed and grasped Cat's left hand, while giving her a devastating smile meant to neutralize her questions. He hadn't talked to her about the arrangements and he knew the Kincaids hadn't either. Cat wasn't even aware of the agreement, but in all honesty, Slade felt Cat would thrive in the environment he could provide her. His initial reason for contacting her had been to offer her a lucrative business deal. Now, that all seemed unimportant.

"Everything's been taken care of, Cat. All you have to do is just lie there, look beautiful and heal up." He patted her hand, giving her a conspiratorial wink. Her green eyes widened as she stared blankly up at him.

Rafe leaned down, kissing her hair. "I'll be in touch, Cat. Slade's given us your phone number and I'll give you a call every couple of days to see how you're coming along." He smiled. "I'll keep you posted on what Goodyear and Nar are up to. They've had a lot of run-ins with each other lately."

Sam Kincaid was next, giving his daughter a slight smile. "You're in the best of hands, Cat."

"But—"

"Now, now," Slade soothed, "just relax, Cat." He wished they would hurry through their farewells and leave before Cat upset his carefully constructed applecart. Dal and Jim Tremain came over, saying goodbye.

"Slade promised us you'd be in good hands," Dal told her sister. "We'd love to have you stay with us, but I don't think you'd get any rest with the baby around. I hope you understand."

Cat looked from Dal to Slade. His features looked suspiciously beatific.

"Well, uh, sure I understand. And Alessandra probably takes up all your time, anyway."

Dal looked relieved that she understood and pressed another kiss on Cat's waxen cheek. "Listen, we'll call you once you get to Texas. Slade's ranch sounds perfect for you."

Slade's ranch? Cat turned too quickly, pain causing her to gasp. She shut her eyes, all the questions purged from her mind. Slade gave her a game smile and waved goodbye to the departing family.

"Well, we'll be seeing you, Cat," her dad said, opening the door. "We'll call you once a week and see how you're comin' along. Bye, honey..."

Cat tried to speak, to beg them to stay. When the pain finally subsided, the door had shut and silence filled the void. She looked up at Slade, her eyes narrowed. Slade was still holding her left hand, his fingers warming her cooler ones. She wanted to jerk out of his grasp but had better sense than to try it, knowing what the movement would cost her in terms of pain.

"All right, Donovan, what is going down?"

"Donovan? You were calling me Slade before."

Cat compressed her lips, and set her jaw in a well-known Kincaid line that spelled trouble. "What cards do you have up that sleeve of yours? Everyone thinks I'm going to your ranch. No one's asked me. If you think you can shanghai me, you've got another thing coming."

Slade tried to look properly chastised and continued to run his thumb in a feather-light circle on the back of her hand. "Shanghai you?" He groaned and raised his eyes dramatically to the ceiling. "Cat, I simply volunteered my plane and my ranch as a place where you can properly recuperate." He stole a glance at her to see what effect his teasing was having. Absolutely none, he realized with a lurch. Slade girded himself for battle as spots of color came to Cat's cheeks and an emerald flame leaped to life in her eyes. She might be sick, but she wasn't helpless.

Slade tried to nip her reaction in the bud. "Listen to me, this is no time to get upset, Cat. I told your family that a nurse is three miles away from my ranch. Kai Travis and her husband, Matt, are good friends of mine. Dr. Scott said you'd need a warm, dry climate and the help of a nurse from time to time. Plus," he went on quickly, trying to stay ahead of her opposition, "your brother, Rafe, has been under a BLM investigation for the past few months and he's got his hands full trying to catch up on the ranch work. He wouldn't be able to devote enough time to you. Your mother's hip operation is in two weeks." Slade shrugged and managed a hopeful smile. "I offered my ranch because I can take good care of you, Cat, while you convalesce. I did what I felt was best for us at the time."

"Us?" came the strangled response. "There is no 'us'!"

Looking contrite, Slade released her hand and walked to the end of the bed, holding her outraged stare. "Yes, us."

Cat's mouth dropped open. And then she quickly closed it into a thin line. "You and I are complete strangers."

Slade had the good grace to look embarrassed. "Maybe we were a week ago, but I don't feel that way about you now. Not after everything we've gone through together." His voice became husky. "Before, I respected your work as a mining engineer. And then, when you were trapped, I saw and felt your courage. We both know the chances of your surviving that cave-in were pretty slim."

At the mention of the cave-in, a chill wound through Cat. She tried to throw it off, but a suffocating fear rose up into her throat, choking her. Panic followed on its heels and Cat struggled to pretend nothing was wrong. My God, she was breaking out in a cold sweat! What was wrong with her? The fear she felt was all-consuming as it flowed darkly through her. Shakily, she wiped her sweaty brow, refusing to look at Slade.

Finally back in control, she spoke. "That still doesn't give you any right to tell my family that they aren't needed, Donovan!" Her voice cracked. "I want my family, not you."

His face softened and Slade came to her side, brushing his knuckles lightly against her tear-stained cheek. "I know how fragile you really are, Cat, remember? I've been in cave-ins myself and lived to tell about it. I told your family that I knew what you were going to go through and I felt I was the best one for the job."

"I'm not your responsibility, damn it!"

"Don't get excited, Cat. The doctors want you to rest."

"Then you shouldn't have bullied your way into a family situation and taken over like you did!" She was breathing hard, each expansion of her ribs a fiery agony. Sweat glistened on her taut features and she lay back, her fists clenched. She turned her stormy green gaze on him. "You're not doing this out of the kindness of your heart. I wish I could remember where I'd heard your name before. Then, I could put this together."

Slade winced. He wasn't sure himself why he was doing it. Sure, there was his business proposition, but that wasn't his primary reason for wanting her nearby. He felt like a greedy robber, stealing time to get to know Cat on a personal level. "You've a right to be upset and angry," Slade said, choosing his words carefully. "Rafe wanted to ask you if you wanted to go with me or come to the Triple K. For that, we owe you an apology. Rather, I do. Because I persuaded them that you'd be happy to come to Del Rio, Texas, with me." He held her angry gaze. "I may kick around the world, Cat, but I do have some roots. The ranch is nothing fancy, but it's nice. You're not out of the woods yet with your injuries, and I convinced your family that with qualified medical help nearby, my ranch would be better for you. Besides, when you get better, there's a business deal I'd like to discuss with you."

Cat eyed him suspiciously, somewhat mollified by his explanation. "I don't know... Let me think for a moment, Donovan."

He shrugged shyly. "All I'm asking is to be allowed to help you for eight weeks, Cat. Hey, this isn't a jail sentence. If you don't like the place, you can leave. No hard feelings. It's just that you can't be by yourself and I have the time plus the room."

Cat could have cried with frustration, but she had to admit that Slade was right. He had saved her life, and if she hadn't been so arrogant, she'd have listened to his warning.

"All right, Donovan," she muttered, "you saved my life. I didn't realize my mother was going to have an operation so soon." She rubbed the tears out of her eyes. "I hate feeling like an invalid! I don't like to be a burden on anyone, especially you. I don't call getting a crabby, sick mining engineer just payment for all that you've done for me."

His serious face creased in a boyish smile. "I happen to like crabby, sick mining engineers. For the next few months you're going to rest and get plied with a lot of stories told by one of the best storytellers in west Texas: me. You're to be a guest at my ranch, Cat. I just hope you like my company as much as I'm going to enjoy yours."

Cat refused to look at him. "I'm not a small child that needs to be told bedtime stories."

Slade's grin was wide, revealing white teeth. "We'll see," was all he said. He glanced at his watch. "Time for a nap. You close those beautiful eyes, and I'm going to talk with Dr. Scott about what time we can get you out of this godforsaken cell."

Cat wrinkled her nose. "Why should I be so anxious to trade one kind of prison for another?"

Slade came around and pressed a quick kiss to her fragrant hair. "It's really me who is your prisoner."

"Want to bet?" And yet, another part of her relaxed. If nothing else, the cave-in had taught Cat how alone a person could really be. Slade had reached her during those terrible hours, and her heart knew it even if her mind tried to tell her differently. "Don't mind me," she muttered in apology. "I'm not normally this crabby. I do appreciate your offer to take me in."

Slade enjoyed her pout; her lower lip was full and petulant. The urge to capture her mouth and gentle it beneath his was growing, but Slade gently tucked the desire aside. "I understand your apprehension, Cat. Things have moved mighty fast today. But you sit back and concentrate on getting well. Let me take care of you for a while."

With a merry look, Slade opened her door. "Rest. You're getting dark shadows beneath those lovely eyes of yours. Just dream of the Mourning Dove Ranch."

Cat watched Slade leave, enjoying his irrepressible, little-boy spirit that magically coaxed her out of her darkest moments. She shut her eyes, aware that the monstrous fear she had wanted to bury had miraculously vanished. Was it because of Slade? With a groan, Cat tried to look objectively at her motives for capitulating to him. He had vaguely mentioned discussing a business deal with her when she was better. Cat clung to that bare-branch offering and turned away from other feelings toward him.

Since when had she ever backed down from the demands of life? Only once. When she and geologist Greg Anderson had called off their relationship. But this was different, a voice whispered to Cat. Not only that, she reluctantly conceded, she didn't have the emotional fortitude it took to wage the necessary battle to get out of Donovan's clutches. And clutches they were, Cat thought grimly. Or were they?

She couldn't ignore the tender light that burned in his sapphire eyes every time he looked at her. Right now, as never before in her life, Cat needed help from someone other than herself. And Slade had offered that help to her. Instinctively, Cat knew that Slade could help rebuild her strength from the rubble of the mine cave-in.

Chapter Three

"Well, Cathy, you're certainly going to be in good hands."
Dr. Scott smiled as he looked through the release forms,
while Cat sat patiently on the edge of the bed. With the help
of one of the nurses, she had awkwardly pulled on a pair of
cinnamon-colored slacks and a white tank top. Maine's
summer weather was usually on the cool side, but at eight
o'clock this bright August morning, it was already a sunny
seventy degrees.

"We'll see about that, doctor," she told him dryly. Cat
automatically touched her tightly taped ribs. Two of the
lowest had been broken and if the break had been any
higher, her breasts would have prevented the elastic torso
wrap from being applied.

"Mr. Donovan's a paramedic, you know," the physician
said, hurriedly scribbling his signature on the last paper.

"Is he?" Cat looked up with interest.

"Yes, a very capable one. I've given him a list of all the
prescriptions you might need, Cathy. He's going to be

watching you rather closely for the next couple of weeks because of your head injury. Let him know if you ever get dizzy.''

Dizzy? The first time she'd sat up, she'd nearly keeled over. If it hadn't been for Slade's quick action, she would have fallen off the bed. At first, Cat had retreated from his watchfulness; she was unused to being confined by an ailing body and resented being taken care of. But after three days, Slade had remained his cheerful, positive self and Cat had had to beg him not to tell any more jokes. She had feared she would laugh out loud, and that awful, ripping pain would take her breath away. Slade's normally ebullient personality had sobered slightly, then shifted into a new gear—that of charming conversationalist.

A nurse arrived with the wheelchair for Cat's ride to the front doors of the hospital. ''The dizziness may or may not be permanent,'' Dr. Scott warned, helping her into the chair. ''The next two weeks will tell us quite a lot. Off you go, now. I understand you've an air trip ahead. Mr. Donovan's quite a good pilot.''

Cat couldn't resist a smile. ''Did he tell you that?''

''No, I saw his flight logbook sitting with some other items. Being a pilot myself, I got him talking. He's not only multiengine rated, he's up on all the instrumentation demands, too. Judging from the hours he's flown, I'll lay you odds he flies around the world. He certainly has a lot of stories to tell.''

''Slade Donovan is a born storyteller, I suspect. Thank you, doctor, for everything.''

''Have a good flight, Cathy. We'll be eager to hear how you're progressing.''

At the curbside outside the hospital, the nurse eased the wheelchair to a halt. Slade was waiting next to the rental car for her. He was dressed in a freshly pressed blue shirt with epaulets on each shoulder. The shirt matched the color of his eyes, Cat thought. She had to stop herself from staring as if she were a gawky teenager instead of a woman older than thirty. His hair was dark and shining from a recent shower, his skin smooth of the stubble that always gave him a five o'clock shadow by four o'clock.

As Cat took his large hand and stood up, she suddenly saw Slade in a new light. His touch, as always, sent a warm rush through her. He had brought sunshine to her during her recent exile to Hades. She closed her eyes, allowing a fleeting feeling of dizziness to pass. Slade, observing her hesitation, moved closer to her left side, in case she should fall. Cat opened her eyes and raised her face to the sun.

"Do you know how good it feels to be outside again?" she asked, drawing in a deep breath of fresh air.

"Spoken like a true tunneler," Slade replied. His fingers tightened on her elbow. "Ready? I've got Maggie all fueled and waiting."

"Maggie?" Cat looked up at Slade tentatively.

Slade helped her into the front seat of the rental car and then shut the door. "Yeah, Maggie's my twin-engine Cessna. And she's as pretty as her name."

The sun shone warmly through the windows and a fragrant scent of pine drifted in, making the day magical for Cat. As Slade eased into the car, he flashed her a heart-stopping smile. "You'll like Maggie. She's built like a sleek greyhound. Red and white, lean and mean."

"The way you like your women, Donovan?" Now why had she made that remark? He had looked absolutely elated, as if flying were going to release him from his captive state on earth. Cat felt like a genuine wet blanket, but Donovan cheerfully snapped the safety belt across his lap and chest.

"Jealousy will get you nowhere. Maggie's big-hearted enough to embrace both of us. Now, young lady, we've got a light westerly wind and clear skies waiting for us. Ready?"

Yes, she was ready, Cat realized. Perhaps it was partly relief that they were putting miles between her and the mine that had almost claimed her life, but another part of her was

ready for a new adventure. Cat closed her eyes, allowing the
wind to flow across her, moving her hair languidly against
her temple and neck. Slade's hand settled momentarily on
her own.

"Okay?"

The concern in his voice soothed her. "I'm fine. Just enjoying my freedom, Donovan."

There was hurt evident in his voice. "My friends call me
Slade."

Cat opened her eyes and studied his clean profile, from
his straight brows to his finely shaped nose and mobile
mouth. "After all we've been through together, I guess
friend is a good word to use for us."

His hand left her fingers and he concentrated on his driving. Friend was only one term he applied to Cat. He also
wanted to explore other possibilities. She affected him as no
woman ever had before. "Friends," Slade murmured.
"That's a good place for us to start."

"I hope you have a lot of patience," she warned, feeling
suddenly awkward.

Slade pinned her with an intense look. "Why?"

"Because I'm not myself, Slade. I'm jumpy and I snap
when I don't mean to."

He smiled. "Lady, I've been snapped at by the best of
them. I regard our two-month vacation at my ranch as just
one more adventure."

"Normally I'd agree with you. But I'm afraid you're
getting the raw end of this deal, Slade. I'll give you one more
chance to back off from your offer to let me use your ranch
as my hospital for two months."

The road spilled out of the small town, a narrow gray as-
phalt ribbon among the pine-clad hills. "Not on your life,
Cat. I like a woman who has wanderlust in her soul!"

A smile shadowed Cat's mouth as she met Slade's merry
glance. "Folks like us have it in their blood, don't we?

What's so surprising about finding someone like yourself?"

"You try so hard to hide what's deep inside you, Cat Kincaid. I keep trying to figure out who closed you up like a book under lock and key. But I know you're not like those rocks I hunt, without feeling." He laughed, a deep, resonant laugh. "You're like an elusive emerald: hard to find, dangerous to extract and fragile when being cut and polished into a gem."

Cat felt the heat rise in her cheeks. "It's the nature of my work that makes me quiet. You're a geologist, you should know that."

Slade knew, but he couldn't resist teasing her. She responded so quickly to the slightest amount of goading. He really shouldn't, because she was far from well and Dr. Scott had warned him about overtaxing Cat. "I know what you're saying, Cat, but I like to see that green fire leap into your eyes. I'll let you off the hook, though. Dr. Scott gave me a stern lecture about not picking on you ... for now."

Cat closed her eyes, resting comfortably despite the tightness of the rib wrap. "That's big of you," she parried. "I suppose I ought to count my lucky stars for the reprieve."

"It's going to be a short one," he warned, shooting her a mischievous look.

Cat smiled. She knew he was baiting her again. He's good for me, she suddenly realized. But if the big, arrogant Texan knew that, he'd gloat. "What kind of pilot are you?" she asked, changing the subject.

"I got my license at Disneyland. Does that impress you?"

Laughter bubbled up in her throat but she squelched it, trying to avoid the subsequent pain. "You're so full of baloney. Come on, level with me."

"And if I did, would it make any difference?"

"My level of comfort would increase markedly if I knew more of your nefarious credentials." She suspected his credentials were far from nefarious, but enjoyed turning the tables on him for a change.

Slade appeared momentarily wounded. "Well, I have exactly 3,212 hours on my multiengine and I.F.R. ratings and have been qualified in twelve different aircraft during my short experience of flying."

"My comfort level is increasing," she admitted with a smile.

"Let's see. What else? The pilot is thirty-five, six feet four inches tall, single, roguishly handsome, makes a decent living, doesn't have any outstanding debts to speak of and currently is unattached." He looked squarely at her. "How's your comfort level now?"

"It just nosedived."

"Oh."

"I'd have felt better if you'd told me that you've flown around the world and are an excellent navigator."

"Well, I'm that, too."

"But for some reason, you thought your personal stats would be of more interest to me?"

"I don't want you to worry that you'd be a third wheel at the Mourning Dove Ranch. You're lucky—you'll be the only woman there besides Pilar, my manager's wife."

"Somehow, I don't quite know if that's lucky or unlucky, Donovan."

He grinned. "It's definitely lucky, Ms. Kincaid. Wait and see."

"Is that a threat or a promise?"

"Your choice. Which do you want it to be?"

"You're impossible, Slade, certifiably impossible."

"Yeah, that's what I've been told. But then, because of my impossible qualities, I did discover a couple of gem deposits over in Brazil." His voice grew softer. "Ever heard of the El Camino Mine, Ms. Kincaid?"

Cat blinked. The El Camino Mine had been splashed across all the mining and geology magazines two years earlier. It was, according to most geologists, one of the finest tourmaline discoveries in the world. The quality of the precious stones was almost flawless, and had sent excitement through the gem community. One fine deposit of watermelon tourmaline had set everyone on their ears. The pink stones without fractures were as rare as emeralds without flaws. She saw Slade's smile widen.

"Don't tell me...wait...you discovered that deposit! That's where I've heard your name before." Her thumping heart underscored her awe. "I almost ended up working at that site," Cat added in disbelief.

"I know. I was the one who tried to persuade the owners to hire you to sink the shafts." Slade shrugged. "But contracts are contracts; you were still building a mine shaft in Austria at the time. Just think, we almost rubbed elbows two years ago."

Cat was still shaking her head. "You discovered El Camino. I can't believe it."

"You'll wound my poetic soul with barbs like that."

"Somehow, I think very little penetrates that thick skin of yours."

"Mmm, careful. The right woman has open access to my tender heart and loving soul."

"You're going to make me laugh whether I want to or not, Slade. Now stop it."

He saw the faint smile at the corners of her lush mouth, an unspoiled mouth that needed taming. Cat wasn't like most women, he suspected. But then, he didn't expect her to be. She lived in a world of brawny miners, skilled in the reshaping of the earth, but resistant to women who chose to be more than bed partners and housekeepers. Slade knew by the set of Cat's jaw that she had endured much to succeed in her career, and he admired her for that. Like the roses that grew wild behind his ranch house, Cat had not only flowered, she had blossomed in the harsh environment.

Slade cornered the car gently, turning into the flight-service area of the airport. He pointed toward the tarmac. "Say hello to my number-two gal, Maggie."

Cat's eyes widened in appreciation as she stared at the sleek, aerodynamically designed Cessna. Slade might appear laid back, but he took good care of his airplane. Its gleaming white surface looked recently waxed, and the graceful red stripe running from the tail to the nose was a dark ruby color. The name on the fuselage read: Donovan's Services, Inc.

"Just what services do you perform?" she couldn't resist asking.

Slade put the car in park and pulled the key from the ignition. His grin was infuriating. "What service would you like rendered?"

Cat clamped her mouth shut, fiercely aware of the innuendo in his voice.

"If Maggie's number two, who's number one?" she persisted.

Slade released his seat belt and opened his door. Still grinning, he replied, "I'm holding that position open for a woman who wants to share my name and put her shoes under my bed and has as much wanderlust in her soul as I do."

"Chances are, like every other engineer and geologist I've met, you've got a woman in every port."

Donovan winked. "Maybe," was all he said, before he walked off to the flight office. Within ten minutes he had returned with his flight plan in hand. Then he helped Cat out of the car, remaining close beside her, their bodies almost touching.

"Maggie's beautiful," Cat told him admiringly.

"I knew you had a fine eye for beauty. Ready?"

Cat was as excited as if she were heading off to a new mining site in a new land. Slade's smile told her he understood the tremor of excitement in her voice when she said, "Yes, I'm ready."

Some of Cat's initial exuberance turned to gratitude when she entered the spacious cabin of the aircraft. Slade had taken out three seats on the starboard side. In their place was a comfortable-looking cot, complete with a pillow, blankets and sheets. He motioned her toward it.

"Dr. Scott said that you wouldn't be able to withstand a trip sitting up all the time. It's going to take us ten hours to reach the ranch."

She slid him a glance. "Do you spoil all your women this way? So much attention to detail?"

"Just for you, Cat. Just you."

"One part of me believes you; the other doesn't," she said lightly. Her expression, however, was thoughtful.

"You wound my Texas spirit," Slade complained. "Perhaps I'm your knight in shining armor carrying you off to my castle to live happily ever after. Would that be so bad?"

His wistfulness moved through her like a lover's caress. My God, the man could weave a spell with his intimate talk—something Cat had not often found in men she'd met during her travels. She'd been handed most of their lines, but Slade was different. The feeling was good, however, so she didn't really want to fight it.

"You have been my knight, Slade," she admitted shyly. "You saved my life."

He preened beneath her compliment, his careless grin spreading across his face. "Well, my lady, you have a choice: sit up in the copilot's seat for a while and keep me company, or lie down and enjoy the scenery."

"I'd like to sit up in the cockpit."

"Ah, to be with me. Good choice."

"No, I want to see how you handle this plane." Mustn't let him get too cocky, she reminded herself.

"Oh." A shadow crossed his face.

Cat had never run into a man who showed such a range of feelings so easily. Most men stonewalled their emotions and responses, which was why she had found little incentive to establish an enduring relationship with any of them. With Slade, it was just the opposite. He was so obviously rattled by her reason for coming into the cockpit. Feeling more than a little guilty, Cat muttered, "I don't feel like being relegated to the rear just yet. I'm hungry for some good conversation."

Slade brightened and motioned her to move in front of him. "So, you'll even settle for me, hmm?"

Choosing not to reply, Cat sat down and observed Slade's attention to detail as he checked her seat belt before revving up the aircraft's two engines. Once he put on the headset, with the slender mike close to his lips, Slade was in another world. But even then, he made Cat feel as though they were a team, putting a headset on her and showing her where the volume dial was located.

She was entranced by Slade's hands: despite their size and roughness, there was a touching grace to their movements as they went through the preflight check. Heat unexpectedly moved through her. Slade was affecting her on levels she hadn't anticipated.

Meanwhile, Slade was receiving clearance to take off, and launched into a nonstop commentary about how Maggie was just as alive as they were, in her own way. Cat noticed how his fingers wrapped gently around the twin throttles positioned on the console between them, and she wondered what it would be like to be similarly stroked by this man. A slight smile hovered around her mouth as a fantasy began to take shape.

Suddenly, they were lifting off. All else was forgotten as Slade shot her a joyous look. She smiled back. Maggie sliced through the blue skies of Maine, her nose pointed in a southwesterly direction, toward Texas. Slade adjusted the fuel mixture and the engines began their deep, throbbing growl. Then the vibration minimized and peace blanketed the cabin.

"Maggie's crew will now ask their esteemed and illustrious passenger if she would like some coffee."

"I don't know about the esteemed and illustrious part—" she grinned "—but yes, the passenger would love a cup of coffee. Where is it? I can get it."

Slade held up his hand. "No, don't move." He reached down and retrieved a battered aluminum thermos from behind his seat. Setting the plane on autopilot, he expertly poured a cup and handed it to her. Cat's otherwise pale cheeks flamed as their fingertips met and touched. "You look more relaxed," Slade commented. "Is it because we didn't crash on takeoff or because you're on another adventure?"

"You have the disturbing ability to read my mind," she muttered, disconcerted.

Slade poured himself some coffee and recapped the thermos. Then, taking Maggie off autopilot, he wrapped his fingers lightly around the yoke. "Why does that bother you?"

"In my experience," she said thoughtfully, "few men look farther than the wrapping."

"You can't blame any of us poor males for looking, after spending months in some foreign jungle or godforsaken desert. Especially when someone as exotic-looking as you comes along."

Heat flowed up her neck. "I'm hardly exotic." Cat held up her left hand, showing him the calluses on her palm. "That's not exotic, Donovan. I've got hands like millions of women in Third World countries who wash and beat their family's clothes on some rock in a stream. I've got more muscle than women who work out daily at a health spa." She touched her hair. "I have to wear my hair so short that sometimes I'm mistaken for a man from the rear." She grimaced. "I'm hardly exotic, as you put it."

"So you think I'm handing you a line?"

Cat sighed, then admitted warily, "The way you talk, I almost believe you mean it."

Slade gave her a smoldering look. "I do mean it. Someday," he drawled in his thick Texan accent, "I'll show you why you're such an incredibly exotic woman."

Cat avoided his gaze as molten weakness again flowed through her like light refracting through a diamond. "If there is an enigma here," she said, laughing, "it's you. Tell me about yourself. And none of your Texas tall tales."

Slade laughed good-naturedly, then finished off his coffee and set the cup aside. "Now, there isn't a Texan alive who can resist embellishing the truth a bit."

"Try."

Slade scanned the instrument panel. They had climbed to fifteen thousand feet, the skies were azure and the sunlight bright. He pulled a pair of aviator's sunglasses from the pocket of his shirt and put them on. "I was born in Galveston, Texas, thirty-five years ago. My Irish father emigrated to the U.S. when he was a lad and he's still a fisherman in Galveston. My mother—she's the native-born Texan—owns a small shop at an exclusive mall, importing products from Ireland."

"Sisters? Brothers?"

"Seven. I'm the fifth-oldest, with three brothers and three beautiful sisters."

"Not exotic sisters?"

He tilted his head toward her and his voice lowered to an intimate tone. "No, you're exotic. They aren't."

He had such a convincing line, Cat thought, secretly delighted with his opinion that she was exotic and, of course, keeping in mind that it was just that. "I see. How did you get into geology?"

"I decided I didn't want to fish for a living like the rest of my family. I used to stand in the boat and watch the waves and wonder where they had come from. What far shore had they left? What ships did they encounter on their journey?

Or what fish or mammals had graced them with their presence?" Slade shook his head. "No, my father told me when I was only this high—" he pointed to his knee "—that I was like my great-grandfather, who was the family adventurer. He could never stay in one place more than a few months at a time, either."

"And you have that same restlessness?" Cat offered. She handed him her empty cup.

Slade shrugged. "Restlessness? No. Life to me is one constant, nonstop adventure. I always want to know what lies over the next hill or wander through the next valley to see what and who is living there."

"Why the fascination with geology then? You could have been in the merchant marine instead, sailing the seas."

Slade smiled at her question. "Rocks held a special fascination for me. As a kid, when I finished my fishing chores, I used to pick stones up from the beach and study them. I'd wonder why one was black and another striated with pink and white. I used to hold them in my hand, trying to communicate with them and asking them their names and where they had come from."

Cat closed her eyes, resting against the seat. She could imagine a dark-haired boy crouched on the ground, holding in his palm a rock that stirred his curiosity, staring at it with intense fascination. Slade was like a child who had never closed off his ability to dream and spin stories. He was special, Cat admitted, a rare being who still had the ability to fantasize, to ignore the limitations in a rationally constructed society. "And did any of them talk to you?" she asked softly.

"Of course they did," he said with a laugh. "That was what led me to ask my teachers about the life of a rock. Eventually they got tired of all my questions and ordered special books on rock hunting for me."

"And are you still like that little boy, always asking questions?"

"I haven't changed at all," Slade confirmed with satisfaction. "Today, I drive mining engineers to the edge of distraction."

"Where did you take your geology schooling?" she asked, curious to know more about his past.

"Is there any other place? Colorado."

"Like me. I'm impressed."

He feigned drama, his hand across his heart. "Finally! We have something in common."

"Oh, come on, it's not that bad."

"You made it seem that way, Ms. Kincaid."

She shot him a wry glance. "Despite any possible ulterior motives, you did save my life. The least I could be is a decent guest."

"Did I slip something into the coffee?"

Cat chortled. "Come on, I'm not always a stick-in-the-mud."

"Did I accuse you of that? No way, sweetheart. You're a risk taker because your career demands it. It makes you an interesting and exotic woman. One of a kind."

"Oh, please! Get off the exotic kick, Slade."

"I can't help it if you're not a regular hothouse flower. That's your fault."

"Let's steer the conversation back to you. A four-year degree out of Colorado and then what?"

"Just kicked around the world prospecting like any other crazy rock hound."

"What kind of rocks? Is your specialty igneous?" she asked, remembering his tourmaline discovery.

"Why? Do I remind you of an igneous type?"

She smiled. Geologists usually chose one of three of the different rock types to specialize in: igneous, metamorphic or sedimentary. "You know what they say about the igneous type: they run hot and molten."

"So that's how you see me, eh?"

"I see you being bored by sedimentary exploration. You're strong and robust; you're the sort who would challenge igneous rock and tackle it with ease. Although we both know sinking mine shafts into rock that doesn't want to be penetrated isn't easy."

"Granted. Or should I say: granite."

"Slade, I'm not even going to laugh because that's a sick rock joke you'd use on a freshman in geology."

"Nobody said my humor was always in top form." He gave her his innocent little-boy look.

"Do people always forgive your transgressions?"

"More importantly, will you?"

"I don't hold grudges."

"But you'll remember."

Her voice grew soft. "I'll remember."

"Well, enough of me," Slade countered. "How about yourself? I had the pleasure of meeting your entire family, so I got an idea of what you're like."

"I'm sure Dal and Rafe gave you an earful about me."

"Don't sound so wary."

With a grimace, Cat pretended to pay more attention to the sky around them. "All right, you tell me what they said."

"Let's see, what adjectives should I use?"

"If you use exotic, I'm going to take everything you're saying as one-hundred percent baloney, Donovan," she warned him.

"Texans can be serious at times, too," he reassured her, attempting a somber look.

"We'll see. So what do you think of me, now that you've learned all from my family?"

"You're a daredevil. Rafe told me how you two jumped your horses between two cliffs."

"Did he also tell you that my horse stumbled on the other side and fell? I broke my arm and nose."

Slade shook his head. He saw and felt Cat relaxing. She had been so long in isolation with men that she was closed up. He saw the softening of her lips, heard new life in her voice and saw more color stain her cheeks. If nothing else, during the next eight weeks of recuperation, Slade would remind Cat of her decidedly female side, gently drawing all of it to the surface. He knew he could do it; there was a chemistry between them.

"Rafe said you and he made the jump, but that Dal had chickened out. I'd probably be with Dal." Slade paused and looked at her. "What you did matches the kind of career you chose. Mining engineers have to be a blend of conservatism and daring."

"What I did didn't take much brains—is that what you're saying?"

"Hey, we were all young once and we all pulled our share of foolish stunts. I'm chalking up your wild ride to youth."

"If the truth be known, I was scared spitless. Rafe was angry because Dal wouldn't go and he—well, I let him coerce me into doing it."

"But you didn't want to?"

"Are you kidding me? That was an eight-foot leap. I was riding a green four-year-old quarter horse who'd never seen a cliff, much less jumped one. I didn't know if he was going to jump it, skid to the edge, fall into it or what."

Slade pursed his lips, going for a second cup of coffee and offering her some. She declined. "Interesting," he murmured.

"Oh?"

Slade put the plane back on autopilot and sipped his coffee. "That gives me a useful piece of information about you."

"Uh-oh . . ."

He grinned. "It's not bad. What it tells me is that despite an overwhelming fear, you did what had to be done and carried it out successfully. I call that courage."

"That particular stunt was called stupid. What took courage was to tell Dad how I broke my arm and nose. Rafe got the belt on his behind. I would've gotten a licking, too, if I hadn't gotten broken bones."

Savoring the hot liquid before he spoke, Slade commented, "You can still take that basic premise about yourself and apply it like a formula to any other type of situation. No, there's a basic vein of courage in you. I like that."

Cat warmed beneath Slade's compliment; the obvious pleasure in his voice was like a physical caress. She rarely enjoyed men in the field. But she wasn't in the field; her contract assignment had been delayed because of her injury. Cat's brows dipped.

"What's bothering you?" Slade asked.

"Hmm? Oh, I was just thinking that because of this accident, I've blown my next assignment." She had talked briefly to Ian Connors, the man who had hired her. Technically, because of her unexpected injuries, she didn't have to honor the contract. Cat had managed to hold off giving him an answer on whether she'd fulfill the contract or not. Just the bare thought of entering another mine made her break into a cold sweat.

"In Australia?"

"Yes. A two-year contract."

"You needed a vacation anyway, Cat."

He was right. She hadn't walked away from work for five years now. "Work is play for me," she tried without enthusiasm. How could one mine cave-in turn her lifelong love into a terrorizing nightmare she never wanted to experience again?

"Still, we all need time away, Cat."

"Do you?" Cat asked, trying to deflect talk of her going back to work. Specifically, into a mine.

"Sure, I'm only human. I can stand the jungle or being a sand rat for only so long and then I have to get back to civilization and get human again."

"Are you between assignments?"

"Yeah. I was heading home to Texas for a couple of months."

"How long since you were home?"

"One year. I think you'll like Mourning Dove. For west Texas, it's a nice spot."

"A lot of sand, scrub brush, jackrabbit and deer?"

"That, too."

"Tell me about the ranch. Is it a working one?"

"Not anymore. I've more or less created a deer preserve out of it and sold off all the cattle. I have a Mexican family who lives nearby who takes care of it during my absences. Carlos and his wife, Pilar, are the caretakers." His voice grew warmer. "Pilar is the best cook this side of the Mexican border. I can hardly wait to get home and fatten up on her cooking." He patted his hard, lean stomach meaningfully.

Cat understood; she was underweight as well. Perhaps the Mourning Dove Ranch wasn't going to be all that bad after all. Slade wasn't the womanizer she had first thought. As a matter of fact, she was going to have to reevaluate many things about Slade. Cat couldn't apply her earlier experiences to him because he didn't fit into the categories of men she had known before. She slid him a warm look.

"Has anyone ever accused you of being different?"

Slade laughed solidly, flipped a switch to take the plane off autopilot and resumed the task of flying. "Many times. Why? Does it bother you?"

"You are a bit disconcerting." And disturbing. Every movement he made reminded Cat that Slade was a consummate athlete; there was never a wasted motion and he had a coordination that at times took her breath away.

"But not threatening?"

She paused a moment before answering, "No."

"What took you so long to answer my question?"

Cat refused to be baited by him. "Nothing."

"You were trying to decide whether to be wary of me or not, weren't you?"

"Quit being such a know-it-all."

"Your brother, Rafe, spoke a lot about you." He added in a gentler voice, "Good things. How you love the land and the animals. How easily you were moved by a sunset. Or by a foal being born. I like my woman to be easily touched by everything around her."

A tremor vibrated through her and Cat discreetly did not ask what Slade meant when he called her his woman. His ability to put everything, including their conversation, on intensely personal terms rattled her. "Life, to me, is a continual blossoming," she admitted, her eyes darkening with fervor. "All we have to do is keep our hearts and minds open to receive its gifts."

Slade's mouth curved into a knowing smile. "Why are you so afraid to show that side of yourself?"

"I think all of us hide parts of ourselves," Cat said defensively.

"I'm an open book."

"Sure you are. That's why you unexpectedly dropped into my life."

Slade glanced quickly at her. "Best thing I ever did."

Cat shook her head. "So, if you aren't an igneous type, what are you?" she asked, ignoring his innuendo.

"I'm a sedimentary man. Ah, the eyebrows lift and the eyes go wide. What do you know, I finally got a rise out of you."

"You get a rise out of me every time we spar," Cat parried.

"I don't see us as sparring."

"Call it whatever you want."

Slade scratched his head. "Somehow, I'm going to have to instill some trust into our relationship."

Cat almost blurted out, "What relationship?" But she bit back the response. "Why sedimentary rock? Most geologists are bored stiff by that type."

"You find a fair amount of gem-quality stone in sediment, that's why."

"Ah, now you're beginning to make sense. You're more a gem hunter than a geologist." Cat eyed him speculatively. "You're a prospector in search of the mother lode, aren't you?"

Slade checked the instruments, a smile pulling at his mouth. "You mean a treasure hunter? A modern-day gold miner?"

"You said it; I didn't."

"I hear distaste in your voice." Slade's voice was deceptively noncommittal.

Cat tried to evade his comment. Greg had done this to her; he had placed the mining of precious gems over their love for one another. And it had killed their relationship. Struggling not to let her past experience taint her idea of Slade, she said, "There's nothing wrong with finding the world's major tourmaline deposits. It can make you a very rich man."

Slade looked at her a long time. He saw the discomfort in every line of Cat's mobile face. "And you think that's why I go chasing after gem mines?" he probed.

"I don't know. Why do you? You don't strike me as the typical treasure hunter." Which was true. Slade was unlike Greg in many ways, and for the better.

Slade was glad that Cat had asked instead of just assumed why he specialized in precious stones. Even he had to admit that most of the gem hunters he knew were like the old-timers during the gold rush. They were loners to begin with, shaped by the roughness of their life-style. Most of the men he knew carried pistols on their hips and knives in their belts. And they all had one driving force in common: they wanted to get rich. Money took precedence over anything else that life might offer them.

"Gems hold a special fascination for me, Cat. In a way, they're like people: when you first discover them, put a miner's light on them, they're rough and unpolished. Then, as you take the time to gently loosen them from the matrix of pegmatite or sediment, you can carry them to the surface. It's exciting to realize that what you carry in the palm of your hand hasn't ever seen sunlight. As you bring it to the surface to watch the light refract through it for the first time, you're the first one to ever witness it." Slade gave her a soft smile. "It's much like watching a person unfold in front of you, watching how they react and respond. Later, a jeweler will look at that rough specimen with a knowing eye, spot its inclusions and watch how the light refracts through it. He'll cut it to bring out all of the natural fire and brilliance that has waited millions of years to be brought to life."

"That's an inspiring view." At least he hadn't mentioned money as his prime goal, Cat thought.

The corners of his eyes crinkled and he shared a look with her. "I'm comfortable with it. Although there are some people who are always going to be as impenetrable as iron ore."

"How many diamonds have you met in your life, as opposed to plain old iron ore?" she asked curiously.

Slade laughed, enjoying her easy acceptance of how he saw the world. "I've met many an uncut gemstone in both men and women."

"And a few iron-ore types?"

"Sometimes. In my business, as you already know, we're a pretty interesting lot to begin with."

Cat closed her eyes, suddenly exhausted for no reason.

"Tired?" Slade guessed. "Or bored with this piece of iron ore?"

"You're hardly iron ore, Slade Donovan. But right now I think I'd better get some sleep before my opinions get me in trouble. I feel so tired all of a sudden."

"Maybe it's the company you've been keeping."

"Now, Slade," she reassured him, her eyes sparkling mischievously, "you're hardly a bore, and you know it."

A slow smile touched his strong mouth. "Just wanted to make sure."

"You're such an egotist," Cat said, yawning, and slowly rose, then made her way from the cockpit to the cot in the cabin. Carefully, she lay down on her left side, then closed her eyes and spiraled into sleep.

Chapter Four

There was a mild bumping. Cat heard a change in the aircraft's engines and stirred. She had fallen asleep just as they had flown over Pennsylvania's border. Now they seemed to be landing. Probably refueling, she thought groggily, closing her eyes once again. With a sigh, she slid back into sleep.

Slade quietly made his way from the cockpit. It was early evening and the shadows were long as the sun edged toward the western horizon. Cat lay on her back, still sleeping soundly. He'd made a feather-light landing, the wheels gently kissing the parched Texas airstrip. Now they were home. Home... The feeling moved powerfully through him as he gazed down at Cat. Yes, they were home.

He approached the cot, noting that Cat's skin was stretched tautly across her cheekbones and dark shadows lay beneath her thick lashes. It was her mouth, however, that made his body tighten with sudden, almost painful awareness of just how much this woman affected him. He felt the same kind of excitement that thrummed through him when he was close to finding the one rock leading him to a vein of hidden treasure.

Cat was a treasure, Slade had decided. He crouched down, one hand resting near her head and the other on her slender arm. Hungrily, he brought her close to him, breathing in her sweet scent. How vulnerable she was. Leaning over, Slade gently caressed her parted lips with his.

Cat's lashes fluttered as she felt the warmth and pressure of Slade's mouth molding to hers. Heat spiraled through her like a ribbon, flooding upward on its dizzying course. Slade's breath fanned lightly across her cheek. Her heart pounded as his mouth coaxed her lips open, and she responded to him unquestioningly.

The instant Slade felt her returning pressure, his mouth worshipped her as if she were a fragile gift that would shatter if mishandled.

Cat drowned in Slade's honeyed invitation, her nipples hardening against the confines of her blouse. He was strong and good and tasted wonderful. Her nostrils flared as she drank in the scent of his special blend of male aroma combined with a slight hint of shaving cream.

"Sweet," he whispered against her wet, responsive lips. "God, you're sweet emerald fire."

Cat forced her lashes open, and became hotly aware of the naked desire in Slade's face. His eyes held her captive with a look that went straight to her heart. This man was supremely confident of his masculinity.

"Did I turn into a frog or something while I slept?" she asked huskily, smiling.

Slade caressed her hair. "Hardly. You're more like Sleeping Beauty!"

It was too much for her and Cat could barely think. Suddenly aware they were on the ground, she glanced around. "Where are we?"

Slade slowly moved out of his crouched position, knowing that if he didn't, he'd be sorely tempted to kiss Cat again. "We're in Del Rio, Texas. We've landed at Mourning Dove Ranch in time to see the sun set in a couple of hours."

"We're at the ranch? Already?"

"Sure." Could she be as shaken as he was by that kiss? he speculated. Or was it simply that her bearings were off?

"How long did I sleep?" Cat looked at him shyly. Slade had his answer.

"A long time." He reached out, brushing her flushed cheek. "But you needed it. Come on, I'll help you up."

Cat took his hand, biting back a cry of pain when Slade carefully levered her into a sitting position. Her face ashen, Cat thanked him and gripped the edges of the cot. Slade went to the hatch and opened it. The early evening sun and a slice of blue sky showed through the door. Dry Texas heat flowed through the cabin. Cat took a deep breath, then released it, feeling the tension pour out of her.

Slade grinned and lifted his hand in welcome as Carlos, his manager, came down the long, narrow dirt strip in a beat-up Jeep. "Our chariot has arrived, my lady," Slade announced to Cat. "Are you ready to go to your castle?"

"Lead on, my prince," she said with a flourish, moving to the door. "I'm rather curious to see this castle you've hidden in the desert."

And desert it was. The earth was the color of bone, and was strewn with twisted, jade-green sagebrush. A few long-eared, black-tipped jackrabbits were in evidence, and the sun was strong and bright.

Cat gripped Slade's hand as he led her down the stairs. She stood back and watched as Carlos climbed out of the olive-colored Jeep. He greeted them in Spanish, waving his straw cowboy hat exuberantly. As the men heartily embraced each other, Cat smiled. Carlos and Slade acted more like family than employer and employee.

With one arm around Carlos, Slade turned and introduced her to his number-one man. Carlos bowed grandly, then took her hand and kissed it.

"Señorita Kincaid, welcome to Mourning Dove. We've been expecting you for some time now." Carlos's coffee-colored face beamed with genuine sincerity as he released her hand.

Cat slid Slade a glance. "You've been expecting me for some time?"

Slade shifted awkwardly.

"*Si, señorita,*" Carlos confirmed, seemingly unaware of his friend's discomfort. "Come! My wife, Pilar, has your room ready. Señor Slade told us of your injuries and Pilar can hardly wait to mother you as she has our other six children. She even has chicken soup waiting."

Cat smiled and walked with Slade toward the Jeep. "Six kids?"

"*Si.* Señor Slade has sent two of them to college already. He's practically their uncle. The other four are helping with the ranch when they're not in school."

Cat's luggage, which had once been destined for Australia, was carefully placed in the Jeep. Slade sat in back, perched precariously between all the bags, while Cat sat in front. She was grateful that Carlos carefully negotiated the dirt road leading from the airstrip to a rambling adobe brick ranch house surrounded by sturdy cottonwood trees. Cat tried to ignore the aggravating rib pain that seemed to be settling in for good, and concentrated on the ranch instead. The house was a testimonial to Texas's tradition of spaciousness. She noticed solar reflectors on the roof, and the number of windows made her gape. She turned her head slightly to Slade, who sat behind her.

"You wouldn't have had something to do with the design of this house, would you?" she asked sweetly.

His teeth were white against his tanned skin. "Why? Does it show?"

"Yes. How much reconstruction did you do after you moved in?"

"After I made my fortune from the El Camino, I was able to afford the walls of windows facing east and west. There's more, but you'll see it all when we get inside."

Cat guessed that there were at least fifteen rooms in the house. Four chimney stacks rose from the roof. It would be fun to tour this house, she thought. What would it reveal of Slade?

Carlos parked the Jeep beneath a cedar-topped garage with no sides. Next to it stood a woman who looked to be in her forties, and whom Cat assumed to be Pilar. Her black hair was tightly wound into a crown of braids and she wore a simple white peasant blouse and a scarlet skirt. Her welcoming smile reminded Cat of Slade's, and she smiled in return, feeling lighter and happier than she had in a long while.

Pilar gripped Cat's left hand and squeezed it gently, introducing herself in halting English. Her warm brown eyes sparkled as she motioned for Cat to follow her.

If Cat could have taken a deep breath, she would have. The ranch reminded her of a geode: plain, gray and undistinguished on the outside, but once opened, a crystalline palace of shimmering beauty. Cat walked from the foyer and into the expansive living room. A slanting cathedral ceiling rose skyward with windows facing west to catch the late-afternoon and setting sun's light. In one corner a floor-to-ceiling granite chimney, glinting with feldspar and mica, rose like a speckled black-and-white giant.

Trees and jungle foliage grew along a waterfall and stream winding through the living room. The wall opposite the windows held ten long shelves with a gem collection that took her breath away. Cat automatically held her ribs as she walked to the wall. Strategically placed lights brought out the rough, unpolished gems that ranged in size from as small as her fist to as large as a watermelon.

"Oh, Slade . . ." she whispered, entranced as she stood staring at them. She felt him come to her side.

"Like the collection?"

"Like it? This would rival some of the better museums I've been in."

"Each specimen is from one of my trips."

Cat couldn't resist stroking a cantaloupe-size blue topaz crystal growing out of brown colored lepidolite rock. "And I'll bet each one is a story," she said, grinning, and returned the gem to its niche.

Slade tried to look serious. "I told you, I'm a master spinner of tales. True tales, I might add."

"I intend to take you up on some of them, believe me," Cat said, while inwardly estimating that this gem collection was easily worth at least a quarter of a million dollars.

"Not today, however." He led her across handwoven Navaho and Hopi rugs and out of the living room. "Pilar's already giving me dirty looks because I haven't taken you to your room and gotten you into bed to rest."

"Slade, I'm not an invalid. As a matter of fact, I hate being sick and I can't stand being bed bound. Busted ribs might prevent me from riding one of those horses in the corral, but they can't stop me from being mobile."

He motioned down a wide hall and opened the first door on the left. Sunlight spilled into the room and one wall was composed all of glass supported by weathered cedar spars. Palms, their fronds grazing the slanted ceiling, graced each corner. A handwoven multicolored quilt covered the cedar double bed. The dresser and drawers were also of cedar and, if Cat wasn't mistaken, hand carved. The room was spare, but homey.

"Over here is a desk, should you feel the urge to write a letter," Slade said, motioning toward it, "or make phone calls. There's also a stereo and a TV hidden in the cabinet over there, should you get bored with our company."

"Slade, what a thought!"

"Carlos will bring your luggage in a minute. In the meantime, the bathroom's over there and if you want to sweat out anything, the spa is directly outside the glass doors, across that brick patio and straight ahead. I'll see you later."

Cat turned as Slade quietly slipped out the door, leaving her to get adjusted to her new surroundings. She was grateful for this act of consideration. In fact, she felt better already. A knock on her door announced Carlos with her bags. Pilar arrived moments later to put all her clothes away for her, leaving Cat feeling extremely pampered and a little helpless. To remedy that feeling, she decided on a hot shower. Stepping to the dresser, she chose a pair of pale blue cotton pants and a dainty, short-sleeved turquoise blouse. Now that she was between jobs, she could allow herself to dress more femininely. On the job she always wore khaki pants, a T-shirt or a short-sleeved blouse.

Alone again, Cat stripped down, gently pulling apart the Velcro binding around her rib cage. The cloth bandage that had surrounded her torso fell away, leaving a weltlike imprint on her flesh. She reveled in the hot shower and wrapped herself with a white towel afterward. Relaxed, she padded into the bedroom to face the chore of getting dressed. No longer was she in the hospital where one of the nurses could help her get into her bra and then expertly wrap the elastic bandage around her ribs. Slade had discussed it with her earlier, saying that he was sure Pilar could do it for her instead.

Pilar was eager to help and understood Cat's instructions fully. She hooked Cat's lacy white bra and helped her into her slacks. Despite all her well-meaning attempts, however, Pilar could not rewrap the torso bandage properly. By the fourth try, Cat was sweating from the pain while Pilar tried futilely to maneuver and close it.

"I'm so sorry, *señorita*. Perhaps you can go without it?"

"I wish I could, Pilar. Would you go get Slade, please? He knows how to close it."

Pilar's eyes widened slightly as she set the wrap aside, but she said, "I'll get him right away, *señorita. Uno momento,* eh?"

"Si," Cat agreed. Already, she could feel a flush crawling up her neck and into her face. Slade would see her blushing. Well, what else could she do? Wear the bandage, not bathe and smell? No way. Slade was a paramedic: he would know how to rewrap her quickly and expertly.

There was a brief knock at the door and Slade entered. "Pilar said you're in trouble," he said, slipping through the door. He saw Cat's red cheeks, and knew at once that she was having problems.

"Pilar gave the bandage the old college try, but it didn't work. Would you mind wrapping it around me?"

Slade nodded, deliberately keeping his gaze above her neck as he approached her. "I'd ask Kai Travis to do this, but I just called their ranch and they won't be home for two more hours, according to their maid, Maria."

Cat watched him pick up the bandage and she stood, carefully raising her arms so that he could place it around her. "That's all right. Pilar did her best. I guess we both should have expected this. Wrapping ribs is an art."

Slade leaned down, perusing the large black-and-blue bruise that covered most of her right side. He gently touched the outer edges of the area. Cat inhaled slightly. "Hurt?"

"It's okay."

"Lie to anyone but me, Cat."

"It hurts like hell."

Slade grimaced. "And Pilar's handling of the situation hasn't helped, has it?"

"Hindsight. Don't be upset with her. Can you get it on?"

"I'm not upset with Pilar. Grip my shoulder with your left hand and hold on." He noticed a thin white scar that traversed the left side of her rib cage. "Looks like you've taken your share of rib injuries before,'' he commented. ''All right, exhale. I'll make this as fast as possible.''

Cat did as Slade requested, her fingers sinking into the folds of his blue chambray cotton shirt. She tried to steel herself against the coming pain. Slade was quick and efficient. She felt his other arm go around her shoulders the instant he closed the Velcro on the left side of her ribs, below her bra.

''You're a good patient, Cat Kincaid,'' he praised huskily, watching all the color drain from her face. Despite the pain, she hadn't moaned or complained. Slade guided her to the edge of the bed to sit down. Picking up her blouse, he helped her slip it on. Then he crouched down in front of her, buttoning it for her.

Cat forced a slight smile. ''Thanks...'' Each touch of his fingers on the pearl-shaped buttons sent a tremor through her, erasing the pain, fanning a liquid flame higher and brighter within her.

''We can do one of two things,'' he told her. ''I can try to teach Pilar the art of wrapping or do it myself.'' He glanced up at her. ''Frankly, I don't think your ribs need extra punishment while Pilar learns. You have any qualms about me doing this for you once a day?''

Cat shook her head. ''No. Anything's better than having someone learn to do this right now. It's just too painful for me.''

''It's my fault. I thought anyone could wrap ribs.''

Relaxing as the pain lessened, Cat managed a slight smile. ''It's nobody's fault, Slade. I'm not upset if you aren't.''

Slade captured the top button, just above the slight swell of her cleavage. ''We'll manage this together,'' he promised, noting that his voice had thickened. He couldn't react like this to Cat, or she'd choose to suffer through Pilar's attempts, no matter what the cost to herself. No, when he kissed her again, Slade wanted her to know it wouldn't be an occasion for pain. He wanted her to be totally willing and

if he had read the sultry look in her half-closed green eyes
correctly, they were both anticipating when it would happen again.

"You're done," he said briskly. "Now, I was making a
pitcher of 'welcome to Texas' margaritas out at the bar.
Care to join me?" Slade stood and held out his hand to her.
He saw disbelief in Cat's eyes, as if she'd expected him to
take advantage of the situation. His smile broadened.

Cat gripped his hand, watching as her fingers were swallowed up in his palm. Tiny shivers raced up her arm as she
rose.

"Do you make a mean margarita, Slade?"

"How mean do you want it?"

"Make mine a double."

"For the pain or for the embarrassment?"

Cat wondered when he was going to let go of her hand as
he led her to the door. He seemed reluctant to relinquish her
fingers. "You're less of a brigand than I first thought," she
confessed.

"Didn't you know? Texans are the epitome of discre-
tion. Not to mention being gallant gentlemen."

"Careful, or you'll start believing your own tales."

His laughter floated down the hall as they walked toward
the living room. "Caught. Again."

Cat followed him to a cedar bar that sat opposite the huge
fireplace. Sunlight lanced through the area, setting the
honey-colored cedar aglow. She took a seat on one of the
leather-upholstered black bar stools while Slade went behind the bar and finished making the promised pitcher of
margaritas. Pouring two, he placed them on a tray then
motioned her to follow him out to the screened-in porch.

The breeze was dry and lifted a few errant strands of her
damp hair. Slade pulled out a chair and she sat down, taking the proffered drink.

Slade sat opposite her, crossing one leg over the other. A
hundred feet from the porch, a slender ribbon of water

wound its way through a line of cottonwoods. He sighed happily. Everything he valued most was right here before him—including this slender young woman he had promised to nurse back to health.

"What did you use, 150-proof tequila?" Cat grinned, a sweet shiver rippling through her.

"You asked for a double," he reminded her innocently. "I took you at your word."

Cat eyed the cold, beaded glass. "This would neutralize a tank," she grumbled good-naturedly.

"Drink it slowly. Texas is like the Caribbean or South America; you're living at a different pace than most Americans."

She sipped the tart drink and nodded. "I've served my fair share of time on those kinds of jobs, too. I call it Bahama time."

Slade grinned. "Yeah. If you ask, 'How far is it?' they'll say, 'Not far, not far.' And if you ask, 'When?' they'll say, 'Soon, soon.'"

"Maybe those people have the right attitude, Slade. Maybe we westerners are too driven and don't know how to relax." She stretched luxuriously.

"Do you know how?" he asked, holding her amused gaze.

"No. I keep looking at this enforced eight-week convalescence and see myself going crazy. What will I do?"

Slade gave her an eloquent shrug. "I've got plenty of work waiting—assay reports, charting, core samples to check." Slade slid her a careful glance. "If you get bored, you might want to pitch in..." he baited.

Cat chuckled and raised her glass in toast. "Not a chance, Slade. Not a chance."

Cat couldn't get to sleep, no matter how hard she tried. Each time she closed her eyes, images of her entrapment in the mine loomed before her. Thank God, Slade had kept her

going, or she'd have given up all hopes of rescue. Slade.
Almost immediately, she felt relief from the terror gnawing
away at her. She drifted off to sleep, remembering how his
lips had felt....

Toward 4:00 a.m., Cat jerked awake. Shakily she got up
and pulled on her white cotton robe. Making her way
through the still house, Cat stood at the screen doors. Although she was cold, sweat bathed her brow. How long she
stood there, her forehead resting against the cool aluminum molding, she didn't know. Only when she heard a door
open and then quietly close did she straighten up, her attention drawn to the hallway.

Slade rubbed his face wearily as he padded into the living
room. Seeing Cat standing forlornly near the doors, he
halted abruptly.

"Cat?"

"I'm all right," she replied faintly.

He heard the strain in her voice and walked over. Even in
the dim light, he could see the tension etched in Cat's somber features. "Bad dreams?" he guessed, moving toward the
bar.

With a shaky laugh, Cat followed him. "Yes. In it, my
Australian contractor was calling me to find out where the
hell I was. What about that contract we signed, he kept
saying." That was one of her dreams. The one that had
awakened her involved the mine cave-in. Pride stopped her
from admitting as much to Slade. She sat down on the bar
stool and watched as he began making a small pot of coffee. Just having him nearby eased some of the fear ripping
through her.

Slade pushed the errant strands of his hair off his brow
and turned around to retrieve two earthenware mugs. Then
he leaned against the counter that stood between them.

"How can you fulfill your contract now?" he demanded. Concern was evident in his voice. "You're going
to be laid up for two months solid. Isn't there a clause

somewhere that refers to acts of God or some such thing to get you off the hook?''

Cat turned away. Right now, Slade looked endearingly mussed and she had a powerful desire to slip her arms around his broad, capable shoulders and seek the solace he was offering. Without a doubt, Slade would hold her if she wanted and give her the peace she sought. Torn by so many conflicting emotions and her fears of ever entering a mine again, Cat remained silent.

"Hey..." Slade gently touched her arm. "What is it, Cat? Come on, you can tell me..."

Cat hung her head, not wanting Slade to see the stinging tears blurring her vision. "I, uh..."

"Great start," he teased, "what else?"

With a loud sniff, Cat managed a half laugh and half sob. "You'll think it's stupid. Childish."

As much as Slade wanted to continue touching her soft, warm skin, he forced his hand to drop away. Leaning against the bar, his head bent forward almost touching hers, he said, "Okay, straight-arrow, shoot. I don't think a contract is the reason you're crying." His voice lowered to a velvet coaxing. "Fear of entering a mine is probably more like it. Right?"

Cat nodded slowly. "Oh, I feel so damn stupid, Slade." She raised her head, dabbed away at the evidence of the tears and stared at him. "Here I am, a grown woman—not a scared little child. So I was in a mine cave-in; big deal. I ought to be able to face my fear of going in again instead of shriveling up and dying inside whenever I think about it. Or dream about it."

With a slight smile, Slade shook his head. "As a kid, I was always afraid of thunderstorms. I still am to this day. Get a lightning strike too close and this guy cringes and ducks."

"I doubt you're afraid of anything, Slade."

"Think I'm fibbing?"

"I don't know. These days, I'm one knot of confusion."
Cat smiled slightly at him. "Maybe you'd say something like
that just to make me feel better. I don't know..."

Slade had to physically stop himself from pulling Cat
close to him. Right now, she was very, very fragile. "Look,"
he began softly, "you're going to go through all kinds of
daily and nightly hell with this fear. Get used to it. More
important, don't close up. Talk about those fears, Cat.
That's one of the reasons I wanted you with me: I've survived more than my fair share of cave-ins. I know what
you're going through and I can help you if you'll let me."
He reached out, capturing her tightly knotted hands on the
bar. Gently, he pried each of her fingers free until they were
relaxed between his own larger hands.

His warmth spread through her, enveloping her pounding heart. Cat met his tender expression. "Was anyone there
to help you through nights like...this?"

"Most of the time, no. And I'm not ashamed to admit
that after the first cave-in, I hit alcohol to escape from the
same type of hell you're going to experience." Slade grimaced. "After a few bad weeks, I got off the booze and
cleaned up my act. I crawled through it and survived, just
like you will."

Her heart wrenched at his admission. "I don't know how
you stood it, Slade. Right now I don't want to be alone.
That's a first for me; practically all my life I've been alone
or lived in remote places. I liked it. But now..."

He squeezed her hands. "We all have barriers we can't
overcome alone, sweetheart. And I promised you, you won't
have to go through this alone..."

She mustered a tender smile. "I told you I was a bad patient. Thanks for being here for me, Slade. The next step is
to stop having nightmares about Ian Connors trying to
pressure me into fulfilling that contract."

Chapter Five

A week later, Cat's worst fears came true when she received the dreaded call from Ian Connors, owner of the Australian mining company. She had been drinking her third cup of morning coffee, reading a book Slade had written on sedimentary gemstones, when the phone rang. Pilar answered it and pointed to the phone sitting near Cat's elbow.

"A Mr. Connors, *señorita*?"

Cat felt a sharp stab in her stomach as all her carefully hidden fears exploded within her. Pilar shot her a look of concern as Cat picked up the extension.

Closing her eyes, Cat took the call, too occupied to see Pilar quietly slip from the kitchen and hurry across the patio toward Slade's hobby shop. Mouth dry, heart pounding at the base of her throat, Cat barely got out a civil hello to Ian.

Pilar, alarmed by Cat's unexpected behavior, rushed out to Slade's shop to tell him that Cat had turned alarmingly pale. He followed her back without delay. Folding his arms against his chest, he grimly watched Cat as he eavesdropped on the heated conversation.

"Look, Mr. Connors," she was explaining, a hint of tremor in her voice. "I simply can't come. I'm under doctor's orders to rest for two months. There are a number of other highly qualified mining engineers who can take my place. You don't need me."

Slade's eyes narrowed as he saw Cat nervously wipe her perspiring brow. In the past week, she had tried so valiantly to fight her inner battle with fear. And yet, he had sensed her aching need to lean on him, to trust him to help her. His mouth flattened into a thin line as he pondered the situation.

"I know what my contract says, Mr. Connors. You don't need to remind me. Look, there's no use shouting! That's not going to get us anywhere. I'm no happier than you are that that mine caused me so much injury." She twisted around on the stool, uncomfortable. "And no, I'm not going to fulfill the terms of the contract. You what? Are you joking?" Cat rolled her eyes and stifled the urge to swear. "You're going to sue me?" She clenched her teeth momentarily. "Okay, you go right ahead and try. But before you do, let me give you the phone number of the surgeon who saved my life! He can fill you in on all the gory details."

She was breathing hard by the time the call was completed. Slamming down the phone, Cat regretted the action instantly. Holding her right side, she slipped off the chair and headed out of the house and onto the screen-enclosed patio.

A few minutes later, Slade ambled out with two glasses of cool, frosty lemonade. Cat's lower lip was compressed into a tight line, and her eyes flashed with emerald fire as she glared over at him.

"I suppose you heard?"

"He's just upset. Here, this is nice and cool. Come and sit down with me here and let's discuss it."

Unable to contain her anger, Cat put the lemonade down and began pacing the entire length of the porch. "Of all things, Slade. Ian Connors thinks he's going to sue me for breach of contract!"

Slade rose to his feet, holding out his hand to her. "Come on," he coaxed, "let's go for a walk down by the stream."

It seemed natural for Cat to slip her hand into Slade's. As they wandered down the stone path toward the stand of cottonwoods and the ribbon of water, she relaxed even more. She gave Slade a warm look.

"You're good for me."

"I try to be, Cat. You deserve it."

She shook her head. "I wish Greg had felt that way." Then she added, "We almost got married."

Slade slowed down as they neared the stream. Multicolored rocks peeked out from just below the water's surface and shimmered in the early-morning sun. He motioned for Cat to sit against the trunk of a cottonwood and then joined her. "Want to tell me about it?"

Cat chose two stalks of grass and plucked them. She handed one to Slade and then put the other into the corner of her mouth. Tipping her head back, she stared up through the dark green, sunlit foliage.

"It's the closest I ever came to marriage."

"You make it sound like a disease." Slade watched as the tension drained from Cat's features.

"I don't mean it to sound like that. I fell head over heels in love with Greg. Imagine, at twenty-seven taking the blind nosedive of an eighteen-year-old girl."

Slade smiled slightly. "There must have been some chemistry there to have done it."

With a painful nod, Cat said, "There was. Or I thought there was."

"What went wrong?" Slade resisted taking the small, graceful hand that lay so close to his. Was she even aware of her sensuality? He loved the feminine swing of her hips and the luscious mouth that begged to be kissed. And sometimes her breathless laughter sent a keen ache through him.

"Greg was a geologist, like you. He was thirty, single and had been knocking around in the industry since he was twenty-four. His whole life revolved around finding the mother lode."

Slade heard the disgust in her voice. "A treasure hunter?"

"Of the first order. Gold, platinum or any kind of precious gem mining. It didn't matter to him. He lived for that find of a lifetime."

Slade suddenly recalled their conversation when they had flown in from Maine, and remembered how Cat had reacted to the possibility that he might also be a treasure hunter. He certainly didn't want Cat to place him in Greg's category. Had she already? Clearing his throat, he asked, "Greg put money before people?"

Throwing the chewed stalk of grass away, Cat picked another. A frown creased her brow. "Yes. Only I didn't realize the depth of his treasure fever. The whole thing came to a head when he found gold on some land he had purchased near the Kalgoorlie mines."

With a whistle, Slade turned around, facing her. "The Kalgoorlie gold mines are among the best in Australia."

"Overnight, Greg became a very rich man," she recalled, bitterness staining her words.

Slade picked up her hand. "But?"

"What we had became second best," she admitted hoarsely. "Greg put gold above us. He really didn't need what I had to offer him. Gold fever became his wife, friend and lover."

Slade ran his thumb across her soft cheek. How he wanted to gather Cat into his arms and hold her! He could see tears glistening in her eyes and he gently placed his hands on her shoulders.

"Listen to me, Cat," Slade said in a low voice charged with emotion. "Greg didn't deserve you. Anyone who puts money ahead of the most priceless gift in the world hasn't got his head screwed on straight."

Cat fought back the tears and met Slade's level look. "Do you, Slade?"

He shook his head. "I may have green-fire fever, but it has never come between me and the woman in my life." His hands tightened momentarily on her shoulders. It was important that Cat believe him. "I do know what money can and cannot buy. Do you understand that?" *Please, say you do,* he begged silently.

Impulsively, Cat leaned forward, placing a kiss on his cheek. Slade smelled male, of sunshine and perspiration. "I believe you," she said huskily, smiling up at his surprised expression. Running her fingers down his left arm, she sat back.

Shaken by her spontaneity, Slade felt a molten heat spread through his hardening body because of her touch. He gave her a shy smile, the words coming haltingly. "I hope, Cat, that you always know you're more important to me than any business concern." Gathering his courage, he added, "I like what you and I have. Money can't buy that."

Without a word, Cat rested her hand in his. "I like what we have, too, Slade. But I don't know where it's going."

"Is that important right now?" He tried to brace himself for an answer he did not want to hear.

"No," Cat said softly. "My entire life's in a tailspin professionally. The only good thing to come out of all this is what we share. And for that, I'm grateful. You're steady and you've offered me someone to lean on. And right now, I need that." She smiled tenderly. "Maybe this restless, globe-trotting mining engineer needed that all along and was too blind to realize it."

"Well," Slade said huskily, "a crisis has a funny way of putting things into proper perspective. Having you here is like sunlight to me, Cat. I don't know where we're going, either, but I like it. I like what you bring out in me, and the talks we have. You're important to me . . ."

Leaning toward him, Cat placed her arms around Slade's shoulders. She wasn't able to give very much of a hug because of her healing ribs. "You have a funny way of making yourself a part of my life, Slade," she whispered near her ear.

Gently, Slade placed his hands on her waist. "You're more valuable than any gold mine, sweetheart. Believe that with all your heart and soul." As he got to his feet and helped Cat to stand, a sweet euphoria swept through him.

Three days later, Slade was still remembering their conversation as he doodled absently on a note pad. There was plenty of work clamoring for his attention, but he had a hard time concentrating on anything except Cat. Slade turned around in his leather chair, staring out of the window toward the patio below. Suddenly Cat appeared, dressed in a pair of kelly-green shorts and a white tank top. She was slowly taking her afternoon stroll across the brick-topped patio. She looked lonely—just as lonely as he felt. Slade, restless, tossed the pencil onto the desk. Getting to see Cat for a few minutes each morning to help her with the rib wrap, and then for an hour at lunch, wasn't enough. Not anymore. The eight hours a day demanded of him to coordinate the opening of the Verde mine held less and less interest for him.

With a snort, Slade got up, moving to the window to watch Cat as she wandered aimlessly on her way. Questions raced through his mind. When should he broach the fact that he wanted Cat to work for him? Right now, she wasn't even sure she wanted to continue being a mining engineer. Cave-ins had a way of forcing one to look at fear. How each individual handled it was another question. The past weeks had effectively erased Slade's original reason for wanting Cat to recover at Mourning Dove. No, more and more, Slade wanted *her*. Each morning he awoke he was happy as never before because of Cat's quiet presence.

Glancing down at his watch, he saw it was two-thirty. To hell with work; he wanted to spend the rest of the afternoon with Cat. It was too late for the picnic they had talked about earlier. But there was still time to take her to a fishing pond nearby. Whistling softly, pleased with the idea, Slade shut off the light and strolled out of his office.

"There you are," he greeted her cheerfully.

Cat lifted her head. She sat in a lounge chair beneath a trellis shelter of bougainvillea vines. Her pulse began to pound as she met Slade's blue gaze. She closed the magazine on her lap as he approached.

"Uh-oh, you look like you're on the prowl." She eyed him with wary appreciation.

Slade sat down at the end of the chair, staring admiringly at her long legs, now tanned gold from days in the sun. He longed to run his hands all the way up them and feel her response. Tucking his torrid thoughts away, he met her teasing look.

"I am," he warned her. "I was hunting for you." He gestured toward the Travis ranch in the distance. "Figured the day was too nice to waste working. How'd you like to catch our dinner tonight?"

Cat hesitated, wanting to contain her eagerness. "Fishing?"

"Sure. Matt and Kai have a nice little river that's filled with bass. I've got the fishing tackle. All I need is my favorite lady to come along. Game?"

Cat gave up trying to disguise her delight. "You bet. But I'm not a good fisherman. My brother Rafe's an ace at it. If I hook anything, it's by sheer dumb luck."

Slade grinned and stood, offering Cat his hand. She took it without hesitation. The sun had tanned Cat's once-pale face, and her green eyes sparkled with good health once again. He hoped part of her happiness was due to his presence. "I suspect you're a lot better than you let on," replied Slade, gently pulling her up. "Come on, you can help me get the tackle and we'll be on our way. Maybe if Kai's home, she can join us."

"Wonderful!"

As they drove to the Travis ranch, Cat confided, "I'm glad you can pull away from work every once in a while."

The wind was hot and dry against his face. "I'm not a workaholic like some people you might have known."

Cat recognized the reference to Greg, but made no comment.

"Gold fever has a way of demanding your body and soul," Slade continued. He caught her thoughtful expression. "So, you like your man to be spontaneous and not hooked into the work harness all the time. What else do you like?"

Caught up in his expansive mood, Cat relaxed as they drove slowly down the dirt road. "My dream man would cherish our relationship above anything else."

"Even if you were pauper poor?"

"Poor in one way, but rich in another," she agreed with a laugh. "But this is a fantasy, remember? There's no such thing as a dream man—or woman, for that matter. But I'd like him to take me on picnics out in the wilderness where we could share a bottle of cold white wine or join me in the kitchen to bake chocolate-chip cookies."

"Hey, let's do that when we get back. I love chocolate-chip cookies."

Cat went warm inside. She could barely tear her gaze from Slade's wonderfully shaped mouth. She longed to have him kiss her again, but he'd been treading so carefully. His touch was nearly impersonal when he helped her with the rib wrap. Only lately had he even held her hand and, once, embraced her briefly. She wanted more, Cat realized. Much more. "Are you serious?" she challenged.

Giving her a hurt look, Slade held up his hand, as if swearing to his statement. "No kidding, I'm a sucker for cookies. And ice cream. And one particular exotic woman..."

Heat flamed into her cheeks and Cat allowed it to sweep straight through her. "Thank you," she managed, unable to hold his penetrating look. Both of them were tautly aware of the tension that crackled between them. Never had a man made Cat feel more like a woman.

Slade, unable to resist, picked up her hand and placed a gentle kiss on her palm. "You're welcome..."

Unstrung by Slade's sudden shift in mood, Cat fished quietly beside him at the river. The tall, stately pecan trees hugged their side of the bank, providing welcome shade. Kai Travis had greeted them when they'd arrived, provided icy lemonade, but had declined joining them. If Cat had looked closer, she would have seen a merry look in Kai's wide eyes that spoke volumes. Why did she feel Kai was deliberately leaving them alone?

"Hey! There goes your bobber!"

Cat jerked upright. She had been lounging half asleep against a pecan tree, rod in hand, when the red-and-white bobber at the end of her line was pulled down beneath the jade depths of the river. Slade's excitement sizzled through her and Cat scrambled to her feet. He was at her side as she gave a firm jerk upward on the pole. Immediately, the rod tip bent nearly double as the fish on the other end was hooked.

"I got him, Slade!" She struggled to flip off the safety on the reel. It had been years since she had gone fishing and she was rusty and clumsy. Slade stood nearby, excitement in his voice.

"Looks big. Hold on, I'll get the net. Keep tension on that line or he'll flip out of the water and shake the hook loose."

Cat looked out of the corner of her eye as Slade swept the net into his hand and walked to the edge of the bank. "What a fighter," she gasped, slowly reeling the fish closer.

"You're doing fine, sweetheart. Hey...he's a grand-pappy. Why, that bass must weigh close to five pounds. Okay, bring him in nice and slow..."

With a triumphant laugh, Cat set the rod aside after Slade had captured the bass. He expertly slid the hook out of the paper-thin mouth of the fish. Proudly he held the fish up for her to examine.

"For someone who hasn't fished much, you've got some kind of luck," he congratulated her. Slade put the bass on the stringer, then placed it back into the water to keep it alive until they were ready to go home. He knelt down and washed his hands. Cat stood beside him, her cheeks flushed with victory. Her smile went straight to Slade's heart.

His sapphire eyes darkened with intent as he stood up. Sweeping Cat into his arms, he held her gently against his damp, hard body. "You," he whispered thickly, "are something else." Then he claimed her parted lips.

Instinctively, Cat slid her arms across his shoulders. Slade's mouth was strong, cherishing. He ran his tongue in an outlining motion, placing small kisses at each corner of her lips. A soft moan welled up within her and Cat trusted her full weight to Slade, lost in the growing fire of their mutual explorations.

"Sweet," he said in a rush, framing her face, lost in the tide of her returning kiss. The smoldering heat exploded violently within Slade as her mouth met and equaled the pressure of his own. Gripping her shoulders, Slade drowned in Cat, all thoughts taking flight. Feelings were what counted with him. He followed the inner yearnings of his heart, drinking deeply of Cat, losing himself in her womanliness.

Disappointed when Slade's mouth left hers, Cat looked up and was enveloped in the cobalt intensity of his gaze as he stared down at her. The world swayed and she gripped his arms.

"Cat? Are you all right?"

All right? She was delirious. Trying to smile, she nodded. "D-do you always catch a woman off guard like this, Slade?"

He groaned softly, cupping her chin, holding her dreamy expression. "There's just one woman I want to catch off guard, and that's you, sweetheart. No one else...just you..."

Waves of tidal strength rocked through her and Cat closed her eyes, pressing her cheek against his palm. "No one has ever made me dizzy, Slade Donovan. Ever."

Dizzy himself, Slade reveled in her openness and honesty with him. Here was the woman he had always known existed, and she was sharing herself with him. Light-headed and a little shaky, Slade gently drew Cat into his arms. The day was hot, their shirts damp from perspiration, but he didn't care. "It's your fault, you know."

"What is? The kiss?"

Slade rubbed his jaw against the softness of her sable-colored hair. "Definitely."

Cat pulled away, laughing at his teasing. "How could it be?"

Mirth danced in his features. "You promised me chocolate-chip cookies, remember? I go crazy when a woman offers to bake me cookies."

With a playful look, Cat stepped out of his arms. "You're so full of it, Slade Donovan."

He recaptured Cat's hand, pulling her to a halt before she could escape completely. "Now wait a minute, I was kidding about the cookies, not the kiss."

"Really?"

Slade gave her a measuring look, wondering if Cat was serious or if she was just giving him a good dose of his own medicine. "I can do without the cookies, but I can't do without you."

"That's nice to know, Donovan; I rate higher than a chocolate-chip cookie."

He wanted to throttle her. "You rate a hell of a lot higher than that and you know it."

Merrily, Cat slipped from his grasp and retrieved her rod. "Really? Well, we'll see." She gave him a look filled with challenge. "I'm going to put you to the test, Slade."

"Oh?"

Satisfaction wreathed Cat's smile as she baited the hook and then tossed the bobber back into the river. "Tonight, after dinner, I'm going to bake you three dozen chocolate-chip cookies. I'll use my mom's recipe, and they're better than any other kind you've ever eaten."

He brightened. "Great."

"There's only one catch to all this, Donovan."

He frowned. "What?"

Cat sat back down, her back against the pecan tree, grinning. "You have a choice: a kiss from me or those three dozen cookies tonight. Which will it be, I wonder?"

Slade gave in to her teasing. There was no question in his mind that he'd rather have the kiss. Still, he couldn't resist playing Cat's game. "Cat, how can you do this to me? Do you realize how rare it is that I get homemade chocolate-chip cookies?"

Choking back her laughter, Cat tried very hard to keep a straight face and appear to concentrate on fishing. "Didn't you just say I rated higher than a cookie?"

"This isn't fair! Of course you're more important than a cookie." Slade stood over her, hoping to intimidate her into thinking twice about the choice she offered him.

Cat looked up, giving him an innocent look. "If that's true, then you'll settle for a good-night kiss instead of those cookies I'm going to bake."

"What will happen to those cookies, then?"

"I'm sure Pilar's children would love them, aren't you?"

Groaning, Slade stalked over to his rod. "You don't fight fair, you know that?"

Barely able to keep the smile from pulling up the corners of her mouth, Cat nodded. "Neither do you. You're just getting a taste of your own medicine, Donovan. How does it feel?"

Slade sat down, balancing the rod on his knees, and gave her a devilish look. "You're going to pay for this, Ms. Kincaid."

"Uh-oh, threats! Threats!"

Joy swept through Slade as he watched Cat laugh like a delighted child. She was beautiful in so many ways. And grudgingly, he admitted he'd finally met his match. The little vixen. Well, he'd win the last round in this sparring between them. And what sweet, luscious revenge it would be.

That evening, after Pilar had left for the night, Cat went to the kitchen to bake. Slade hung around, watching closely as she made her mother's recipe for chocolate-chip cookies. Every now and again, Slade would lean over her shoulders and swipe a bite of the dough. And then he would steal a light kiss from Cat. Tinkering with the cappuccino maker, Slade worked nearby on the tile drain board. Cat looked soft and feminine in a pale pink sundress. The square neck on the dress showed off her recent tan to a decided advantage.

"Did I tell you how pretty you look in that dress?"

Cat began to drop the cookie dough onto the sheet. The corners of her mouth lifted slightly and she pinned Slade's longing gaze. "Is this your way of getting a cookie? Flattery?"

Slade placed the lid on the cappuccino machine, screwing it down tightly. He met her smile. "Cookies can't hold a flame to you."

Laughing lightly, she murmured, "Why, thank you. Can I help it if I think you have ulterior motives designed to weaken my resolve?"

"Sweetheart, if I want to weaken your resolve, I'll be a hell of a lot more straightforward about it."

"Uh-oh, Texans are rather brash, aren't they?" Cat walked around Slade and moved to the oven. He leaned petulantly against the drain board, watching her through half-closed eyes. She found it hard to fight the attraction he always generated in her. Eyeing the oven's temperature control, Cat straightened up. She brushed away strands of damp hair from her brow.

"Texans are honest," Slade defended, eagerly absorbing her every movement.

Placing the sheet of cookies in the oven, Cat closed the door. "Even if it kills them," she agreed. "There. In about ten minutes, the first dozen will be ready. How's our cappuccino coming?"

Slade roused himself from staring at her. Her flushed cheeks and the serenity surrounding her made her just that much more enticing. Everything was happening so quickly. He didn't want to rush Cat or make her feel as if he was stalking her.

"Here," Slade said, handing her a large mug of the steaming brew, frothy with hot milk. Then he joined her on the living-room couch. The last of the cookies had been baked and were set out to cool. The merriment in Cat's eyes as she took the cup made him smile. With a contented sigh, Slade sat back, his shoulders almost touching hers.

"How are you doing?" Cat asked, sipping contentedly at her cappuccino.

Slade rolled his head to the left, drinking in her smiling features. "Okay."

"You're holding up amazingly well for a Cookie Monster."

"Yeah, I know it."

"I've got them counted, Slade. So don't come sneaking out here in the middle of the night to steal one. Or two. Probably half a dozen."

Slade joined her laughter and picked up her hand. "I've got something even better than that, Cat."

"What?" She loved the feel of his big, firm hand.

"I was privileged to see you working in the kitchen."

"Being a mining engineer doesn't mean I can't do anything else."

"Now, don't go getting contrary. That was a compliment. You looked kind of pretty and at home in there. I liked the feeling." His voice lowered. "For the first time since I bought this place, it feels like a home." And then he met Cat's sober gaze. "Do you know what I mean?"

Her voice was barely above a whisper. "Yes, I know..."

Reluctantly, Slade released her hand. "What we... share...is so good, Cat."

Cat set her mug on the coffee table. Slade gave her a puzzled look as she rose and walked to the kitchen.

"Now what did I say?" he demanded, sitting up. "Cat?"

Cat returned with a saucer stacked with cookies. She handed them to Slade. "Nothing's wrong," she told him, sitting back down beside him. "Everything's right..."

Delighted with her change of heart, Slade picked up a cookie. He was about to take a bite out of it, then hesitated. "Does this mean I still get my kiss?"

"I hereby release you from having to make a choice," Cat said, her eyes sparkling.

"Here, this one's for the cook. She's one hell of a fine lady."

Cat took the proffered cookie, giving Slade a tender smile. Holding up her cookie in a toast, she murmured, "And here's to one hell of a fine man."

Happily, Slade touched her cookie with his. He consumed four of them without another word.

Laughing, Cat snuggled into the couch, her legs tucked beneath her. The beatific look of pleasure on Slade's face made her feel good. She reached out, resting her hand against his shoulder. "You're such an easy person to please, Slade Donovan. Does it always take so little to make you happy?"

He glanced over at Cat, matching her smile. "That's me in a nutshell, sweetheart. Small, simple things in life are the best. Like that kiss we shared this afternoon..."

"Or the cookies..."

"Yeah, them too. But the kiss was sweeter. Better." And then he brightened. "This is pretty good—not only do I get these great-tasting cookies, but I also get to give you a good-night kiss."

"Don't gloat, Slade."

"Was I gloating?"

"You know you are. You're as bad as Rafe when it comes to getting everything your way."

Rafe called her less than a week later. Joyfully, Cat picked up the phone when Pilar told her who it was. The early-afternoon sunlight spilled through the windows as Cat took the phone into the living room, making herself comfortable on the apricot-colored couch.

"How are you?" Cat asked, barely able to contain her happiness.

"Things could be going a hell of a lot better, Cat."

Her brows dipped. "Oh, no. What's wrong, Rafe?"

"You remember I told you about Jessica?"

"The lady investigator from the Bureau of Land Mines?"

"Same one," he said gruffly.

Gripping the phone, Cat felt her brother's unspoken anguish. "Oh, Rafe, what happened? I know how much you love her. Didn't you fly up to Wyoming to see her?"

"Yes...but...things just didn't work out for us, Cat. Not the way I wanted, at least. Listen, enough of my troubles. How are you? You sound better. Happier."

Her heart bled for Rafe. How many times had he talked of Jessie to her? Any fool could see that Rafe was head over heels in love with the woman. Shutting her eyes, Cat had no defense against her brother's pain. "Oh, I'm surviving."

"Isn't Slade Donovan treating you right?"

The threat in Rafe's voice made her laugh softly. "Now don't go getting growly like an old bear just waking up from hibernation. Slade is—well, he's wonderful, Rafe."

"Then what's the problem? You're worried. I can hear it in your voice."

"It's just the calls I'm getting from mining companies who want to hire me. Seems like everyone knows I can't fulfill the terms of the Australian contract and they're trying to entice me into other jobs. They're like Nar hunting down a rabbit."

Rafe's laughter was explosive. "That damned eagle. Speaking of hunting, did you know he grabbed Goodyear the other day?"

Buoyed by Rafe's sudden good humor, Cat was swept along by it. "Oh, no. What happened? Did Millie get on her broomstick and fly after him?"

Chuckling, Rafe recounted the latest escapade of the golden eagle and the nearly-thirty-pound, overfed cat, Goodyear. "Well, you know how Nar dive-bombs the chicken coop every once in a while to keep everyone on their toes?"

"Yes, the little turkey."

"Now, Nar would be insulted if you called him a turkey."

"Jim Tremain calls him a flying pig and he's right! Well, go on. What happened?"

"Pig is right. Anyway, Nar spotted the Goodyear blimp outside the horse-paddock area. I guess Goodyear had caught his first mouse ever."

"As fat as that cat is, I'm surprised he's caught one. Sure the mouse wasn't crippled, blind and already dead from old age?"

"Who knows?" Rafe laughed. "Anyway, I was saddling Flight up to help herd some cattle to the south range when I saw Nar land about ten feet away from Goodyear. The cat hadn't hurt the mouse. He was just holding it between his front paws gloating over it. Frankly, I don't think Goodyear knew what to do with it. Millie feeds him so many table scraps he's never had to hunt a day in his life."

"What did Nar do?"

"He flapped his wings and came clucking and chutting up to Goodyear. The cat flattened his ears and crouched over his mouse. He wasn't going to give up his feast to that brazen bird."

Cat could barely stifle her giggles, and held a protective arm across her stomach. "Did Nar take the mouse?"

"No. He made a lightning strike for Goodyear's tail and picked him right up off the ground. You should have heard the racket. The mouse squeaked and ran. Goodyear was shrieking like a scalded cat. Nar lumbered toward the meadow, trying to get airborne, dragging Goodyear in a wake of dust. Can you imagine a thirteen-pound eagle trying to lift off with a thirty-pound fatso? I was laughing so hard, tears were running down my face. Goodyear was digging into the grass and dirt trying to stop Nar from moving forward. Nar kept getting jerked around until finally he crashed. Both he and the cat hit the dirt at the same time. You should have seen it—dust, feathers and cat fur were flying everywhere."

Crying with laughter, Cat couldn't speak for almost a minute. "Oh, no! What happened? Did Millie ever get wind of it?"

"Nah, I ran out of the barn to stop Nar from dragging the damn idiot cat around by the tail. There was a huge cloud of dust and all these screams from Nar and snarls from Goodyear. Just as I got there, Goodyear shot out like a fired cannonball with a couple of feathers in his mouth. Nar limped out the other side with a real hurt look on his face. I stood there laughing. That cat finally got even for all the times Nar teased and chased him. Last I saw, Goodyear was rolling at high speed toward the safety of the chicken coop, Nar's tail feathers in his mouth."

Wiping the tears from her eyes, Cat said with a giggle, "Finally, after all these years, Goodyear evens the score! Did you tell Dal that her eagle got the worst end of the confrontation?"

"Yeah, I did. I don't know who laughed harder, Dal or me."

Cat smiled tenderly, cradling the phone. "You're so good for me, Rafe. All I have to do is remember Nar and Goodyear's latest battle and I'll die laughing."

Suddenly shifting gears, Rafe asked, "Have you heard anything about the Emerald Lady Mine or what they were going to do with the owner?"

Cat sobered slightly. "Lionel Graham has been handed a large fine by the government."

"Well deserved," Rafe applauded.

"I don't think he'll be able to build any more mines in the U.S. without the government watching him closely. He got what was coming to him."

"Slade had been right about him all the time," Rafe added.

Cat made a wry face. "Tell me about it. If I had listened to him in the first place, I wouldn't have gotten into my present bind."

"But then, you wouldn't have met Slade."

Rafe was right. Cat closed her eyes for a moment. "And I'm very glad we've had the time together."

"Good," Rafe rumbled, his voice warm and pleased, "you deserve some happiness."

"Between you, Slade and Kai Travis, I'm surrounded by people who make me smile and laugh."

"So, you like the Travis gal, eh?"

"Yes. She and her husband, Matt, are wonderful. Slade has had them over here for dinner once a week and we have a great time. You should see their one-year-old, Josh. I've never seen a cuter tyke." And then Cat cringed. Why did she have to bring up the subject of babies to Rafe? She knew how much he'd wanted kids before his wife had died in childbirth.

There were a few awkward moments of silence, then Rafe cleared his throat. "You sound better now, Cat. I'll give you a call in a week and see if you're still improving."

Trying to rally for his sake, Cat murmured, "Don't worry. Between Slade and Kai I have to get better."

Chapter Six

Kai loosened the blood-pressure cuff from around Cat's left arm. "Perfectly healthy and normal. Not bad after four weeks." She set the cuff aside and examined the nearly healed scar along Cat's scalp. "You're just as tough as Slade," she teased. "Are all you rock-hunting miners built out of the same genetic material?"

Cat met her smile. Kai had a genuine warmth emanating from her that made Cat feel good. "I'm not as tough as I look."

"Nonsense. Come on, let's go enjoy a late-morning margarita on Slade's back porch. It's almost noon and I can't stay long. Maria is watching Josh until I get back. Let's spend a few minutes catching up on what we've been doing the past few days." Kai reached for her hand, giving it a squeeze. "I'm really glad you're here, Cat. Out on this Texas desert, I get a little lonely for feminine company."

Cat followed Kai out into the living room and sat down at the bar. Kai made a mean margarita, almost as good as

Slade's. "I don't know what I'd have done without you, Kai," Cat admitted.

Kai dropped the ice cubes into the blender, shut the lid and turned it on. "Slade would have been utterly lost without your help."

"What do you mean?"

Kai poured the margaritas into two long-stemmed glasses, her eyes sparkling. "I'm sure he's told you why he flew up to Maine to find you. After all, he wanted only the best engineer to build that mine of his down in Colombia. He'd talked for months of a way to lure you away from your other commitments. Believe me when I tell you that when Slade wants something, he doesn't take no for an answer." Kai added a slice of lime to the drinks. "But then, you've experienced his persuasive sales abilities, so you know what I'm talking about. I don't think I've ever seen Slade as intense as he was about hiring you. He wanted the best." Her eyes twinkled and she leaned forward, her long auburn hair falling around her face. "Just between us, I think Slade's enjoying your company so much he's forgotten about the mine. When I talk to him, he always speaks of you, never about the Verde."

Cat nearly choked on Kai's statement. She barely tasted the tart drink, thrown as she was into a maelstrom of powerful emotions. Slade had wanted to hire her to build him a mine? He had hinted about a business deal, but she had forgotten all about it. Maybe his offer to have her recuperate at the ranch was just part of his business plan. Why hadn't she questioned Slade more closely? But then, how could she? As badly injured as she was, she had willingly accepted Slade's offer to recuperate here. What an idealistic fool she had been.

"It's good," Cat forced out in a tight voice, all her focus on the unannounced business deal.

Kai smiled and came around to join her. The white slacks and bright green blouse did nothing but bring out her natural beauty. "Great! Hey, you know we should go shopping soon. Slade could fly us into Houston for the day. He always has business with Alvin, his partner, there. I'm sure he wouldn't mind if we tagged along."

Slade had a partner. A business partner. Cat didn't like what she was hearing. Was Slade's care and seeming desire nothing more than a means to get her to work with him on his mine? A knifelike pain tore through her. Had Slade's kisses only been a disguise for what he really wanted? No wonder he'd downplayed her problems with Ian Connors. If Slade wanted her services, he'd gladly tell her to drop Connors.

Her fingers tightened around the frosty stem of the glass. Shaken, Cat took another gulp of the margarita. *One way or another, I have to find out why Slade really brought me here. Maybe it wasn't out of the kindness of his heart, as I thought.* Inwardly, Cat died. Until that moment, she had never really gotten in touch with the depth of her feelings for Slade. And now it was sheer, aching torture to admit just how much he had come to mean to her.

After Kai had gone, Cat sat in the silence of the living room. *I've just found out why I'm here at Mourning Dove Ranch,* Cat grimly told herself. She gingerly ran her hands over her healing ribs and went to the kitchen, where Pilar was starting preparation for lunch.

"Did you want coffee, Señorita Cat?" she greeted her, lifting one soapy hand.

Cat managed a smile and went over to a large pot, pouring herself a cup of coffee. "I can get it, Pilar. Thank you." She needed time to think. "Is Slade in his office?"

"Either his office or hobby shop," Pilar replied. "Would you like an early lunch?"

"No, thank you. I'll just go out to the porch for a while." She had no appetite.

Cat sat down at the table, staring beyond the screened-in porch. Absently, she smoothed the burgundy skirt that was imprinted with a profusion of white, pink and lavender orchid blooms. Kai had insisted over the weeks that she have something other than pants to wear and had given her a gift of the Mexican skirt and blouse. Cat fingered the lace of the boat-necked white blouse she wore, her mind spinning.

Cat's mind focused on Slade. Was he planning to send men and machinery down to Colombia to gear up for the mine he wanted to build? For eight hours each day he would disappear into his office. Was Slade playing a waiting game with her? Cat tried to search her memory for some betraying facts. Slade would join her, like clockwork, at noon, for an hour-long lunch. She could never quite get used to his devastating effect on her—that special warmth flowing up through her, the added beat to her heart when she first saw him crossing the living room and moving to the porch where Pilar served lunch. Merriment was usually lurking in his eyes when he approached her. Cat frowned, the coffee tasting bitter. Right or wrong, she was drawn powerfully to Slade, and it was more than physical. How she felt about him and what he wanted from her warred within her. She had to talk to Slade and clear the air.

Cat rose, her mouth set in a determined line. She wanted to do something—anything—to settle what lay between them. In another few weeks she would be fit and ready to work again. Cat set the coffee cup on the drain board, gathering her courage. Padding silently through the house, she walked across the garden and patio. The palms of her hands grew damp as she followed the left fork. Cat tried out a number of opening lines in her head as she walked along the path to Slade's shop. She slowed, coming to a sliding-glass door that was partially open.

Slade was bent over what she recognized to be a multi-wheel gem polisher. He had a gem in a brown, waxlike substance known as dop, and was grinding the shape of the gem against the spinning wheel. His long workbench, to the right, was strewn with a can of dop sticks that would hold a rough-cut cabachon-shaped gem. Faceting equipment, which would shape a gem to blinding brilliance, was nearby. Cat stood in the doorway, tense.

Sensing her presence, despite the level of noise, Slade turned around. "Come in . . . if you can find a place to sit down." Taking off his safety glasses, Slade leaned over, pulling a stool toward him, motioning for Cat to join him.

"I—thanks." Cat sat down.

"Looks like you're a little bored."

Somehow, he looked more pulse-poundingly handsome than usual to her. Slade wore a faded red T-shirt that emphasized the powerful breadth of his chest and tight muscles. His jeans were streaked with dust and soiled across the thighs, where he obviously wiped his fingers as he worked.

"I didn't know you were a jeweler," Cat began lamely, unsure how to begin her preamble.

Slade grinned, putting the glasses back on and returning to the work at hand, turning on the polisher again. He expertly positioned the cabachon he held on the stick between his hands. "Making jewelry is my hobby."

Cat leaned forward, fascinated. "An unusual hobby for a man."

"But not a geologist," Slade corrected, lightly pressuring the stone against the wheel. A whirring sound continued for several seconds before he lifted the stone away. Slade dipped it into some water, and rubbed away the accumulated material that resulted when the rock was polished. There was satisfaction mirrored in his face. He held the stick out to her. "Take a look. That's pink tourmaline from the El Camino mine. Beautiful specimen, isn't it?"

Cat held the stick, observing the gem. Slade was no amateur in his fashioning of the stone. The tourmaline was at least four carats in size, and Slade had used the oval cut to bring out the breathtaking pink fire from the depths of the stone. "It's lovely," she whispered.

Slade smiled. "There's no color on earth like this," he agreed, running his callused finger over the gem.

"You're hardly a novice," Cat accused, handing the stick back to him.

His smile broadened as he set it down on the table next to the lathe. "No, but my mother taught me to be modest about my talents. So what did you think I was doing back here?"

"Working on the latest geology reports, collecting data for a place where you might want to go next," she hinted, waiting to see if he would take the bait.

"I wanted to get this ring finished in time for my mother's birthday. It's only ten days away," he murmured, taking off his safety glasses.

"It's a lovely stone. I'm sure your mother will be thrilled with it."

"I sure hope you're right. So, you're itching to get back into the mining mode?"

Cat froze internally. "Not yet."

"Let's change our schedule, then. How would you like to go on a picnic with me today?"

Caught off guard, Cat repeated, "A picnic?" It sounded wonderful and she knew the sudden catch in her voice showed her surprise. She saw Slade smile as he got up and rinsed his hands off in a basin nearby.

"Well—I—there's something we have to discuss, Slade."

"Great. I'm cashing in on that rain check I promised you, Cat. We can talk over lunch. Why don't you tell Pilar we're going? She'll be happy to fix something for us."

Cat slid off the stool. Maybe a picnic would be the right place to broach the subject. "Oh? Does she want to get us out from underfoot?"

"She's been after me for the past two weeks to take you on one. I couldn't because it's hell traveling with taped ribs any more than necessary. Now, you're almost as good as new and I think it's just what we both need."

Cat turned away, feeling heat in her cheeks. "Have you had broken ribs before, Slade?"

He chuckled. "Yeah, when I was at the university I played football. One game I took three hits simultaneously and ended up under a pile of opposing players. I came out with four busted ribs. Needless to say, I didn't play the rest of the season." He lifted his head and turned toward her. "That's how I knew how much pain you were in this past month. You're a pretty brave lady, you know that?"

With a wan smile, Cat stepped out the sliding-glass doors. "Don't put me on a pedestal, Slade. I'll fall off before you can blink twice. I've got enough inclusions in me to match any emerald you find." Inclusions were the hairline fissures that could flaw the otherwise clear surface of a gem. In other words, they were mistakes, and she made her own fair share. And so did Slade.

"Inclusions make you interesting, sweetheart. Who wants a flawless gem? They're rather boring in comparison."

"You're a glutton for punishment, then. I'll tell Pilar of our lunch plans." Cat tried to stop the fear expanding within her. In the weeks they had lived together under the same roof, peace had reigned, not irritation or tension. No, Cat thought wryly to herself, the only tension her heart felt was a longing to draw closer to Slade. Toward the end of the picnic, Cat could talk to Slade about the mine.

Packing the wicker basket in the back of the Jeep, Slade guided Cat into the front seat. He wanted to tell her how beautiful she had become in the past month; her sable hair shone with gold highlights, and though it was a bit shaggy, it was more appealing as it grew longer. She was, by anyone's standards, a woman to be recognized. Pilar had given her a broad-brimmed straw hat to protect her face from the harsh sun overhead. Slade got into the driver's seat, and the Jeep started up with a cough and sputter.

"Where are we going?" Cat asked.

"A special place for a special lady," Slade answered. He pointed the Jeep down the flat expanse of dirt road, driving slowly and avoiding most of the holes in the road that might jar Cat. "It's on Kai and Matt's ranch. I only took you by one part of the river before. The part we're going to now has about four thousand pecan trees planted along it. And there's a beautiful spot near the water where they placed a picnic table. I thought you might enjoy a change of scenery."

The sun was warm and Cat held the hat on with one hand. "Kai wanted to know if I'd go into Houston with her to shop for a day."

Slade made a chortling sound. "Uh-oh. Women going shopping spells disaster. Houston will never be the same. Did you tell her you'd go?"

Cat shrugged. "I told her I'd think about it."

He heard the hesitancy in her voice, but didn't understand it. Usually, most women would give their right arm to go shopping in such a cosmopolitan and sophisticated city as Houston. But then, Cat wasn't the average female, Slade reminded himself. He almost sensed that Cat didn't want to leave the ranch, whatever her reasons. Had her nightmares dampened her otherwise keen traveling spirit? He decided to pursue that at an opportune time, later.

Slade spread the red cotton tablecloth across the green picnic table while Cat brought over the basket. Pilar had packed beef sandwiches, potato salad, some apples and a bottle of zinfandel, Slade's favorite white wine. The pecan trees rose straight and tall, already bearing a quantity of fruit. In the fall, they would be harvested during a five-day celebration. The noontime heat was well over ninety. Beneath the trees, with a cool breeze rippling off the small, quiet river that languidly flowed past them, it was an acceptable eighty degrees. Slade motioned for Cat to come and sit down. When she did, he sat next to her, something he rarely did at the ranch.

His move hadn't been missed by Cat, either. At first, she was going to say something, and then thought better of it. She wondered perversely if he had deliberately used reverse psychology on her so she would willingly welcome his advances. Cat shook her head, angry with herself. Slade had been the perfect host since she had come to his ranch. She decided to drop her wariness and simply enjoy him for the duration of the picnic.

"I didn't realize how skilled you were at jewelry making. Do you work on it every day?"

Slade handed Cat a plastic cup half-filled with the delicate white wine. "Yes. After I get caught up on paperwork, I head over to the shop. I use the samples I collect from my job assignments and play treasure hunter, stalking the gems I know are buried deep within the matrix."

"I'd like to see some of your finished work. Is that possible?"

"Sure. I keep all my fledgling attempts and mistakes in the back room."

"Knowing you as I do, I doubt if you've got any 'mistakes.'"

Slade set a plate loaded with food in front of her. "I've got plenty of mistakes. I just don't go around showing them to everyone."

"Why to me?" she asked, meeting and holding his gaze.

"What if I told you I wanted you to know me with and without mistakes?"

Cat's heart pumped hard to underscore the implications of his question. "Then I'd ask why you're according me that privilege." Was he going to tell her about his mine?

"Would you?" He looked at her closely.

She nodded, sipping the spicy, clear wine. "I think it signals a certain change in a relationship when both people let down their guard and allow the other to see all their qualities."

Slade took her statement seriously, biting into a sandwich. He was having trouble keeping the conversation light. The past week had been pure hell on him. He wanted to do something about the longing in Cat's eyes as she looked up at him. Food was the last thing on his mind right now. "That's another thing I like about you, Ms. Kincaid; you don't play the games men and women play so well with one another."

"But you play games, Slade."

He winced inwardly at the sudden sadness in her voice. He wiped his mouth and then his fingers on a paper napkin. He captured her hand, squeezing it gently. "Not with you, sweetheart." He saw the unsureness in her emerald eyes as she studied him in the intervening silence.

Cat swallowed a sudden lump in her throat. Tears pricked her eyes. Angrily she shoved these unexpected feelings back down inside, to be dealt with later, and shook her head. "I just don't know what to think, Slade. Ever since we met, I felt as though you wanted something from me. At first, I thought it was just because you were interested in me—as a woman. But later, once we developed a friendship, I changed my mind about that. Right now, I'm not sure what you want from me." She sat rigidly. "Kai mentioned you had a mine down in Colombia. By any chance does that explain why I'm here at your ranch?" She prayed it wasn't so.

Slade's brows dipped. He shoved the plate aside, concentrating on Cat, hearing the pain in her voice. "I'm sorry, Cat. I really screwed up, then. Yeah, I had flown to Maine to try and persuade you to come and work for me. But—" he managed a shy smile "—when I saw you all my logic went out the door. I hadn't expected you to affect me like you did." He picked up her hand, cradling it gently. "I wanted you to come here for personal motives, not professional ones. Please, believe me." Slade refused to relinquish her hand. He reached out with the other, lightly tracing her cheek and delicate jawline. "And when it comes to you on a personal level..." His voice turned harsh. "Do you know how damned hard it's been to keep my hands off you so you could heal? As much as I wanted to put my arms around you, hold you tight against me and kiss the hell out of you, I knew I couldn't." He saw hope suddenly spring like an emerald flame into her widening eyes.

"Look, let's untangle our communication with one another. Yes, I came hunting you down." He halted, struggling with words. "I'm lousy at talk, Cat. Let me show you how I feel about you." Slade leaned down, wanting, needing to feel her lips once again beneath his. "I've been wanting to do this for so damn long..." He molded his mouth to hers. An explosion of need reeled through Slade as her soft, pliant lips yielded to him. He felt her arm sliding around his neck and he groaned as she lightly swayed against his chest. He had to forcibly stop his hands from following her curves upward to the small, firm breasts resting against him. Instead, Slade framed her face, cherishing her wine-bathed lips, using his tongue to probe the corners of her mouth.

"You make a man thirsty for more," he groaned as he probed the inner, moist recesses of her mouth. A column of need roared through him, his body hardening with a fire of its own. Cat's breath was moist and ragged against him and Slade reveled in her ardor. He allowed his hands to trail down her slender neck and cup her shoulders. Reluctantly, he eased away, then stared down hungrily at Cat. She was his, all of her.

As Slade drew back, his hands captured hers. "Listen to me," he told her roughly, his voice heavy with desire. "I want you like I've never wanted another woman, Cat. And it's not because of what I need from you professionally." Slade caressed her cheek, reveling in her luminous eyes.

"Can you separate the issues? It's important to me that you can."

Cat was barely coherent after the branding kiss that had seared her lips. She hadn't been merely hungry for Slade's touch, she'd been starved, and her returning fervor had caught her totally off guard. Never had a man affected her so profoundly as did Slade. Touching Slade physically was merely an extension of everything else Cat already felt in her heart.

Her heart? Cat was careful not to place any emphasis on that unexpected and unknown quantity right now. If age had taught her nothing else, it had taught her that time would reveal what was real in their burgeoning relationship. Now, Slade was waiting for an answer from her. She stared into his eyes, seeing fear mingled with hope. Fear?

"I want to separate these things, Slade. Why don't you tell me what you want from me and then we can clear the air. I don't want to suspect your every move or intention. You can't blame me for reacting like this. Put yourself in my place."

Slade refused to allow Cat to reclaim her hands. He gave her all his attention. "Professionally, I want you to think about building a mine for me. That's all. The decision is up to you and I'm not going to pressure you about it." He gently squeezed her fingers. "But some of your reaction isn't warranted. At least, not with me and what we share."

She hung her head for an instant, wanting to believe Slade. "Maybe all the years of being in the field have made me more isolated than I wanted to be." She sighed. "Maybe I just need someplace I can go to when it all becomes too much to take."

"Don't you have a permanent address? An apartment on the coast? A condo?" Slade ran his thumb gently in small circles on the back of her hand.

Cat shook her head, relaxing beneath Slade's ministrations, wonderful tingling sensations fleeing up her arm as he lightly stroked her. "The Triple K is home."

"That's the family homestead. What about some place special for you?"

"No. The mine I'm building on my next assignment becomes my home. I live in a tent or trailer just like everyone else."

"Well, you apparently need more. I noticed you called the ranch your home today for the first time."

A shiver of longing moved through her and Cat acknowledged his statement. "I did, didn't I?"

"Yes."

Cat gave a rueful shake of her head. "I think I'm burned out and haven't even recognized my own symptoms."

Slade reluctantly let her go and brought their plates back over so that they could finish lunch. He wasn't hungry, but he recognized the need to step back and talk about their other problems. "I think this accident has helped open you up to some of your feelings," he said quietly, wanting to find a way to probe the content of her restless nights.

"I can't shake the nightmares, Slade."

He treaded lightly, sipping his wine. "Have you figured out why they're still with you?"

Cat picked up a ripe red apple, the surface slick and polished as she slowly turned it around between her hands. "As stupid as this sounds, I find myself standing at the opening to a mine. And then, I break out into a cold sweat."

"Afraid to enter it?"

Cat gnawed on her lower lip. "Yes. Of all things, Slade, I'm afraid to go down into an adit. I've spent the past ten years of my life in shafts, even those that miners were afraid to go into, and I never thought anything of it. Can you believe that? It's just blown me away." She looked down at her hands, closed tightly around the apple. "More important, it shouldn't affect me like it has. It's stupid."

"Ever fallen off a horse?"

"More times than I can count. Why?"

"Rafe said you can apply the same logic to a mine. There isn't a miner, an engineer or geologist who's been trapped who hasn't experienced that same strangling fear."

Relief was mirrored in Cat's features. "You're using the right word: strangling. Sometimes, when I think about it, I can barely breathe. I feel as if an invisible hand is choking off my breath and I'm slowly suffocating."

"Like you were in that cave-in."

Cold fear took away the heat within her. "Yes."

"Well," Slade said slowly, "there are two things you can do, Cat. One is to never enter another mine and give up a good portion of your work. Or you can go face that fear by entering a mine again. It's like getting thrown off a horse and then climbing right back on. The sooner you do it, the quicker the fear recedes."

"Does the fear ever go away?"

"It's different for everyone."

"You've been trapped. How does it affect you when you go into a shaft?"

"There's always a thread of fear deep down in me," Slade admitted. "But then, I swing my focus to why I'm down there, and the fever of finding a gem outweighs my fear."

"What have three cave-ins taught you?"

A slight smile pulled at his mouth. "To value each minute of each day like there will never be another. I used to live in the future; I don't anymore."

Cat closed her eyes, relief washing through her. "I'm so glad you understand." Her voice held a tremor. "Every day I find myself enjoying little things I overlooked before. I used to ignore so much, Slade."

"But you don't anymore," he said softly, giving her a tender smile that promised so much.

They finished lunch and Slade repacked the basket, placing it in the Jeep. Cat stood near the river, watching a bass leap out at a dragonfly that had flown too close to his lily-pad home beneath the water. As he turned back to her, Slade read the sad expression on her face. She was allowing him to sense her feelings, no longer hiding so much of herself from him. He found himself smiling. Each time they shared an encounter, it was as if another petal of their relationship had opened.

Slade's feelings were strong toward Cat and he didn't fight them. How many nights had he lain awake, thinking of her? She was like him in some respects, always traveling the world in search of a new adventure. Cat was also strong and independent, and he liked that about her. Yet, as he studied her profile, he was achingly aware of her vulnerability.

Cat was pleasantly surprised as Slade gently drew her back against him. Her lips parted as he brushed her hair with a kiss. "Slade..." She whispered his name.

"This is what I wanted to do," he told her in a low voice, his fingers gently massaging her shoulders. Her skin was soft and firm beneath his explorations. "The sunlight dances off your hair and I can see the gold in it."

Cat's smile softened. "Pyrite. Fool's gold."

"No way, lady. You're a rare vein of gold that few are ever privileged to see."

Her nostrils flared as she inhaled his salty, masculine scent. "I'm afraid, Slade."

He opened his eyes, holding her a little more firmly, disturbed by the tremulous quality in her tone. "Of what?"

"Of you."

"I won't hurt you."

"Not intentionally."

"Have you always run, Cat?"

She shook her head, glorying in his male strength, the tenderness he offered her. She needed it badly. "No, but you're different."

He rested his mouth against the silky strands of her hair. "Explain."

"You show how you feel. Most of the men I know are closed up like the mines we dig. I haven't had much experience with a man of your openness."

"Ah, I see." He pressed a kiss to her temple. "Never took on a Texan?" He deliberately teased her, feeling the tension in her shoulders. Then, almost as quickly, her tension dissolved beneath his cajoling tone.

"No. Never."

"What else bothers you about me?"

"Just that." Cat tilted her head, catching his teasing expression. "And what you wanted from me professionally."

Slade smiled, feeling the softness of her cheek against his sandpapery one. "I'm sorry I didn't discuss the matter sooner, Cat. The mine became secondary to your coming here to the ranch. You were what was important to me. I'm not lying, nor am I playing a game with you. If this has been on your mind, though, I wish you'd asked sooner."

"I was afraid of the answer, Slade," Cat admitted hoarsely. "No one likes to think they're manipulated or strung along."

Slade sighed deeply. "I guess I deserve that from you. My intentions were to discuss the mine when you were ready. Right now, you're still healing." He kissed her temple.

Cat leaned back against him. "What I want to know is, why aren't you married? A man with your attributes would turn any woman's head."

His smile disappeared and he gently folded his arms around her as they stood at the bank of the river. "Came close a couple of times," Slade admitted.

"But?"

"What woman was going to accept my traveling life-style and stay at home without me for months at a time?"

"She could go with you."

He shook his head. "Not the women I fell in love with. They wanted a home and a family. Until recently, I couldn't provide the kind of security they wanted. You know how geologists bum around the world. There aren't many women willing to make a home in the desert for a year, or live in a jungle in Thailand while you hunt for gems. Women get the worst end of the deal: loneliness. I can understand their position and that's the main reason I haven't married." Slade gazed down at her. "I told you before: I'm looking for a woman who's as footloose as I am."

Cat ignored the invitation in his voice. She was thinking along similar lines. Finding a man who would accept her vocation and allow her to travel had slimmed candidates to a bare minimum. "I don't find many men willing to let me roam, either."

"Just two old travel-weary vets of the rock industry, huh?"

Cat smiled. "With at least another couple of decades of bumming around left in them." If she could control her fear of mine entry.

"I think when I'm eighty, I'll still be a rock hound at heart."

"The earth is too alive to us to ever walk away from," Cat agreed. And knowing that, she suddenly vowed to overcome her fear. The earth had always been good to her.

"I like your attitude, lady. Come to think of it, I haven't seen much not to like about you."

"Wait." Cat laughed. "I get in a blue funk every once in awhile."

"And when you do, what happens?"

"I get crabby and crawl into my shell."

"Retreat is the better part of valor, maybe?"

"You understand."

"I try," Slade whispered, pressing one last kiss on her temple before he released her. *Soon,* he promised Cat softly, *soon you'll be in my arms like I've been dreaming for the past month.*

As they walked back toward the Jeep, Slade stole a look at her. "How'd you like me to tell you about my mine, sometime? When you're up to it, that is."

Cat stared nonplussed at him for a moment, digesting his question. "Let me think about it."

Slade held up both hands in a gesture of friendly surrender. "Great. I just don't want any more misunderstandings between us, Cat. You tell me when you're ready, and I'll spill out everything."

Cat nodded and slipped into the seat of the Jeep. "Fair enough."

Slade accepted her dictate and turned the key. The Jeep roared to life and they followed the dirt road beneath the thousands of pecan trees, heading back to Mourning Dove Ranch.

Cat mulled over his explanation about the mine and was relieved. He hadn't asked her to the ranch just to get her professional services. The intimacy Slade had established with her after lunch had sent such sharp longing through her, it was worse than the pain she had experienced with her broken ribs. Cat forced herself to think of other matters. Casting a glance over at Slade, she decided to find out more about his mysterious mining project.

Chapter Seven

As they got out of the Jeep and walked into the house, Cat gathered all that was left of her nerve and spoke up.

"Slade?"

"Yes?"

"I don't want to wait to hear the story of your mine." She came to a halt and rested her fingers lightly on his upper arm. "Do you have some time this afternoon?"

Pleasure shone in his eyes as he looked down at her. "That took a lot of courage, Cat. I was hoping you'd ask."

He guided Cat to the kitchen and gave Pilar the basket. Then Slade poured them some fragrant coffee and stole some date-nut bread that Pilar had just baked. He sat down next to Cat on the back porch, his long legs spread out in front of him.

She cast a glance over at him. "Why were you hoping I'd ask?"

"A long time ago, Cat, I found that people really didn't want something unless they asked for it. My mother used to shake her finger at me and tell me to hold my own counsel, opinions and advice unless someone asked for them.'' Slade gave her a little-boy grin as he polished off his chunk of warm bread. ''Over the years, I've found my mother to be right—as usual.''

''Wise words from your mother,'' Cat agreed solemnly. She wanted to rest against him and smiled to herself. ''Tell me about your mine, oh weaver of spells and fables.''

Slade nodded and settled back. ''A long time ago, back in 1531, the Spanish conquistador, Francisco Pizarro, landed on the coast of Peru. To his delight and greed, he found fabulous emeralds there, and in Chile and Ecuador. He became entranced with where these emeralds had come from and tortured countless Indians to get this information.

''Finally, in 1537, the conquistadors had the answer they sought: Chivor, Colombia. There they found emeralds in feldspar-rich veins of yellow-gray shale or limestone. Chivor's crystal-clear emeralds made the conquistadors bend the backs of every Indian they could find and put them into slavery to work the mine. Twelve hundred Indians were kept caged in Chivor's tunnels on a food ration that even a rat couldn't subsist on. Spain's monarchy couldn't tolerate the conditions the Indians were placed in, and ordered them freed of further enslavement. Eventually, production dropped off and the jungle reclaimed Chivor. The mine became 'lost.'

''Then, in 1896, Chivor was rediscovered by a Colombian mining engineer who used a three-hundred-year-old map he had found in an old manuscript. Chivor now operates as one of the largest privately owned emerald mines in the world.''

Cat smiled wistfully. ''You sound as if you wished you had been that Colombian mining engineer to have found Chivor again.''

Slade nodded, thinking how beautiful Cat looked when she was relaxed. "You'd better believe it. There's another well-known emerald site in Colombia. Chivor sits up where a breeze will stir and the temperature is cooler on the slopes of the jungle-capped mountains. The Muzo Valley, which sits in the Cordillera Oriental, an extension of the Andes Mountain chain, is hot, humid and insect-infested. The emeralds at Muzo are found in white calcite veins between beds of black shale.

"At Muzo, the emeralds are flawed heavily with inclusions, making them look cloudy. Chivor's emeralds are clear in comparison but lack the range of color that Muzo's hold. Muzo's emeralds are considered far more valuable because of this color range. Personally, I disagree. I'll take a less-inclusioned emerald over a cloudy one with color any day. Anyway, Muzo's reputation is that of greed, murder and thievery run amok. It got so bad that it was shut down in 1970 because of the number of murders and crimes. The mines of Muzo had been privately owned up until that time. The owners feared for their lives and the yield of their mines. They begged for government protection in the form of soldiers. The private companies agreed to lease their mines to the government in return for protection and guarding of their emerald treasure by the national police."

Slade glanced over at Cat. "The guaqueros, or treasure hunters, went on digging their rat tunnels into the emerald mines anyway. Cave-ins kill a lot of them. So does suffocation, because these rat holes aren't properly ventilated. The guaquero who manages to tunnel into one of the emerald mines then begins to steal. If he finds a stone, he must risk his own life trying to get it to an emerald dealer, known as an esmeraldero, who waits at the Rio Itoco, the river at the bottom of the Muzo Valley, to sell it."

"And have the police stopped some of the bloodshed, Slade?"

He grimaced. "To a degree, they have. But what has happened is that the police are either paid off by the guaqueros to look the other way while they steal from the mines or they just plain feel sorry for the tens of thousands of starving humans who have flocked from the squalor of Bogotá out into the field in search of their personal fortune."

"That's the history. How do you fit into this interesting puzzle?" Cat asked, watching his blue eyes grow warm with a smile. Slade made her feel good and she couldn't conceive of being away from his sunny presence.

"Let me tell you about my colorful partner who lives in Houston. Once upon a time, there was this grizzled old Texas diehard. His name was Alvin Moody and he made his fortune gambling on oil wells instead of dry holes. Pretty soon, his oil discoveries outweighed the dry holes he found, so he became one of the Texas elite money-wise. He's about six-foot-four and even taller in the stories told about him. Alvin's a meek name, and it doesn't fit him as far as I'm concerned. That aside, Alvin got restless with the gas-and-oil game. He wanted to stretch himself and had always had a fascination for gems. He'd heard of Chivor, Cosquez and Muzo in Colombia. And being the street-smart, junkyard dog that he was, he figured there were more emeralds than just in those three areas."

"How old is Alvin?" Cat asked, enjoying Slade's story.

Slade rubbed his jaw. "Let's see . . . somewhere around seventy-three. He's got snow-white hair, squinty blue eyes that'll drop you at thirty feet if you cross him the wrong way and a voice that booms like a bear."

"Sounds like a real character," she said with a chuckle.

"I think Texas glories in them," Slade agreed. "I was down in a sleazy bar at the bad end of Bogotá when I ran into Alvin."

"I won't ask what you were doing there," Cat said dryly.

"Same thing he was: looking for stories about the emerald-rich mountains of Colombia. I'd been there seven days and picked up quite a bit of bull. In between, I'd play rounds of poker with the emerald dealers, listen, learn and store it."

"You a good poker player, Slade?" Cat knew the answer to that without asking, but couldn't resist teasing him.

Slade grinned. "Wait and see. Alvin came into this dirty, smoky bar, twice as big as life, all decked out in a khaki safari suit, Texas cowboy hat and boots. He spotted our game and invited himself to sit down. There were four scruffy-looking esmeralderos who smelled of the Rio Itoco, plus me in my usual grubby geology gear and Alvin. Everyone in the bar stopped talking and gawked when he rolled on in and invited himself to our table. It was a hell of a sight."

"And so you all played poker?"

Slade hedged and held up his hand. "A fifth esmeraldero sat down. Juan Cortez was his name. He was a slimy-looking character; looked as if somebody was hunting him. He didn't have any money but we let him join the game because he said he owned three hundred and forty acres near Muzo and had a map where he knew emeralds were located. Whoever won, and believe me, he was planning on winning, would get the map. Cortez was hungry for some capital to start his venture into the area. That's why he wanted into the game."

"How did Cortez get this map?"

His eyes darkened. "Cat, you never ask an esmeraldero where he got anything or you're liable to be lookin' down the barrel of his pistol."

"Oh."

"The stakes got high. A lot higher than the cash I was carrying on me. I saw that glimmer in Alvin Moody's eyes. He, like I, believed that Cortez had the real thing by the way the guy was acting. I didn't want to fold my hand and Cortez wouldn't take my American Express credit card as a promise of cash."

Cat laughed. "Smart man! You might not be paid up or it could be stolen for all Cortez knew."

"Fortunately, Alvin came to my rescue. He didn't have to stake me but he said he'd loan me the money I wanted. If I won, he'd get half the mine." Slade's eyes twinkled. "Alvin had a busted card hand, so he was smart enough to sense that I was holding some pretty good ones or he wouldn't have made the offer."

"It wasn't out of the generosity of his heart, was it?"

"Hell, no. Alvin's a businessman. I'd have done the same thing."

"Cortez must have been holding some good cards, too."

"He was," Slade admitted, flashing a smile. "Alvin staked me. By this time, there was twenty thousand dollars on the table. Everyone in El Toro Posada was crowded around our table: farmers, miners and drifters. It was getting pretty tense, so I laid my pearl-handled Colt .45 revolver on the table close to my right hand where everyone could see it. The crowd stepped back a couple of paces. Alvin grinned. Cortez sweated. The other four esmeralderos all bowed out with a curse as the ante continued upward. In another ten minutes, there was forty thousand dollars lying on the table with just Cortez and myself still in the game. Alvin kept peeling off thousand-dollar bills from that wad of money he had pulled out of his pocket; cool as hell."

Cat sat up, rapt. "Well, what happened?"

Slade pushed an errant lock of hair off his brow. "I called Cortez's hand. He grinned that evil little smile of his. He had pointy teeth that reminded me of a weasel's. He said, '*Señores*, I'm happy to take your money,' and laid out a ten of clubs, jack of diamonds, queen of clubs, king of spades and an ace of clubs."

"A straight, ace high," Cat acknowledged, breath lodged in her throat. "And then what happened, Slade?"

"Cortez grinned wider and threw his hands over the pile of money and raw emeralds sitting in the middle of the table. Alvin said, 'Hold it, snake breath.' And he gripped both of Cortez's hands and then looked straight at me. 'Your turn,' he told me. So, I began laying out my cards one at a time. I started with a ten of hearts, jack of hearts, queen of hearts, king of hearts and finally, the ace of hearts.''

"My God," Cat whispered, "a royal flush. What a time to get one." And then she gave him a hard look. "You didn't cheat, did you?"

Slade looked momentarily wounded. "Me?" A devastating smile pulled at his mouth. Slade held up both his hands. "Sweetheart, I'm the luckiest damn bastard you've ever seen. Even luckier than Alvin, and he's not too shabby, either."

Cat laughed with him. "So what did Cortez do? Cry?"

Slade snorted. "I can tell you've got a lot to learn about these snake pits in Colombia. No, he lunged for my revolver. Alvin jerked him up like a rat out of a lab jar, holding him while he screamed all kinds of curses at us. I put all our hard-earned money into every pocket I had. I even stuffed it into Alvin's safari jacket and into that ten-gallon hat he was wearing. I knew we were in a hell of a lot of trouble. Any moment, any one of those men could jump us. I grabbed my revolver, firing it three times into the air. Everyone stepped back, eyeing us like a pack of wolves.

"Alvin held Cortez by his ragged clothes at each shoulder while I searched the little guy for his map. I found it, opened it up to make sure it wasn't a blank piece of paper. It wasn't. As far as I could tell, it was genuine. Cortez grudgingly signed the land deed over to us. We really didn't have the time to stop and check it out. We had to get out of there or we'd be dead meat. Alvin dropped Cortez and then unpacked that big, evil-looking .360 Magnum, Dirty Harry type of revolver he carries, and pointed it at the crowd while we backed out of the bar.

"Outside, we hightailed it for my Jeep and dug holes getting out of there. Alvin was staying at the Tequendama

Hotel, so we went over there to rest up, have a tall, cool one and see if the deed had been worth all our efforts.''

Cat stood, suddenly excited and unable to sit still any longer. ''This is all true, Slade?''

''Yes. It gets better. Want a drink?''

''I could use one.''

Slade slowly uncoiled from his relaxed position and guided her back into the house. Cat sat on the stool while he went behind the bar to mix up a pitcher of margaritas. She put both elbows on the polished cedar.

''How could you verify if the map was genuine?''

''We went to the deeds office in Bogotá and checked it out. Cortez had been as good as his word. As to the possibility of emeralds on it, we had to go to the location and find out. For all we knew, Cortez could have sold us a bunch of jungle with nothing but mosquitoes and anacondas crawling all over it. We packed up the Jeep the next day and took off for the Silla de Montar Valley.''

''Where was it located?'' Cat wanted to know, thanking him as he handed her a margarita.

Slade rested easily against the bar, sipping his drink. ''How about two valleys over from the Muzo mines?''

Cat's eyes widened. ''That close to another emerald field?'' she gasped.

''Yes, ma'am. When we located Cortez's landholding, it was in the saddle between Caballo and Lazo Mountain. That's how the valley got its name. Alvin and I spent a month out there.''

''What kind of rock base, Slade?''

He had her, he thought, seeing the sudden interest in Cat's eyes. Now she was starting to ask a mining engineer's questions.

''Calcite limestone. Prime sedimentary rock for emeralds. But then, you know that.''

''Not the black shale of Muzo?''

"No. From the core samples I took, there is a thick base of limestone just beneath the topsoil and subsoil strata." He took a pencil from his pocket and reached for a small notepad, drawing her a quick illustration. "Perfect limestone for emeralds here," he said. "Beneath it, black shale. My guess is that it's the same stratum that has been pushed to the surface at Muzo." He tapped the limestone stratum with the pencil. "Here, at our location, it's still buried pretty deeply."

"Why are you saying calcite limestone when all evidence points to the shale bearing the emeralds instead, Slade?"

He straightened up. "Wait here," was all he said, and he disappeared out the door through the kitchen.

Cat sat there for what seemed a long time. By her watch, it was only five minutes, but it felt like hours. Slade came back, an enigmatic look on his face and a kidskin leather pouch in his left hand. He gently handed her the pouch.

"Open it."

She hadn't realized that she was holding her breath as she loosened the drawstrings. Then she drew out five uncut emeralds still embedded in the white rock known as calcite. They completely took her breath away. The perfect, six-sided green crystals were buried in the surrounding matrix, glinting with staggering color beneath the light at the bar.

"Incredible, Slade..."

"Green fire," he whispered, leaning close to her, their heads nearly touching as they both stared down at the matrix. "Gem of the gods, something mere mortals would murder their best friend for and sell their soul to the devil to possess. Green fire..."

"I—it's simply beautiful." She held it up to the light. "From what I know of Colombian emeralds, these uncut emeralds have far fewer inclusions than most." Cat leveled a look at him. "Emeralds of this quality are worth a fortune, Slade."

"They came from the land we won from Cortez, Cat. Take a good look at this, hold it and let it burn into your memory."

She didn't have to be told to hold it. Automatically, Cat could swear she felt a shimmering vibrancy that only a true gem possessed. What she held in her hands was priceless, the dark green vivid against the pure white calcite. "They're too beautiful for words," she whispered, turning them slowly, watching the light refract through the clear, near-perfect depths of each crystal.

Slade cupped his hands around hers, holding her gaze. "Your eyes are even more beautiful than they are, did you know that? Now, maybe you can appreciate what I see when I look at you."

Shaken by the intimacy of his voice, Cat's lips parted. She felt the roughness of his hands holding hers, sending flames of longing through her. "W-what are you going to do with this?"

Slade released her and straightened up. "Put it on the shelf over there. Another story to tell my next guest or visitor," he said. "What would you do with it?"

Cat carefully placed the matrix back in the pouch and sat it on the bar between them. "Most men would have sold it."

"I always save the first gems I find at a new site." He gave her an intense look. "Remember what I said before: money isn't everything. This may be worth two hundred thousand on the open market, but that doesn't matter."

Slade watched Cat nod in understanding. An odd smile tugged at his mouth. "I told Alvin I wanted the best for this project. The limestone deposit is almost a flaky kind of black shale. The chances of cave-in are great. I wanted someone who was used to dealing with unusual mine situations. You were the only one I wanted for the job, Cat." He picked up the bag that contained the matrix of emeralds and set it aside. "Your reputation far preceded you, and I told Alvin that we're dealing with a mine in a country that's used to volcanic and earthquake potential. I didn't want just any mining engineer. There are special stresses and environmental items to be considered in how the mine will be constructed. That's where your special talents come in."

The idea was initially exciting to Cat. Seconds later, the pit of her stomach became a knot of cold, drenching fear. Yes, from what she knew of the rock strata of Colombia, earthquakes were always a hazard to a mine shaft sunk into the unstable earth. She broke into a sweat, focused on the fear that was now gobbling her up whole.

Slade frowned, noticing the sheen on Cat's forehead. The color had drained from her cheeks and the excitement he had seen in her eyes had flickered and died. Automatically, he reached across to close his hand over hers. "What is it?" he coaxed.

A lump grew in her throat. "I'm scared, Slade."

His fingers tightened. "Look at me, Cat. Come on now, listen carefully; the only way to conquer that fear is to face it. I know it's not easy. And it won't be pleasant. But I'll be there, if that makes any difference to you."

Oh, yes, that would make a difference, Cat wanted to blurt out. But the words were frozen in her aching throat.

Slade's low-timbred voice moved through her.

"Cat, if I didn't think this was best for you, I wouldn't even suggest it. Aside from my wanting you to sink that shaft, you have to enter a mine somewhere in the world. I'd rather it be ours. I can be with you. I can help you cope with that fear."

"I'll think about it," she whispered, taking her cold hands from his warm ones.

Slade measured Cat's hesitancy, trying to ferret out the reason for her behavior. He had seen the glow of adventure in her face minutes before, the promise of another challenge to be reckoned with and tamed. And he had also seen the fear swallow up that glow like dark thunderclouds rolling threateningly across the horizon. He placed both elbows on the bar and hunkered down.

"Cat, I don't have much time. While you've been recovering here the past six weeks, I've been in my office coordinating the leasing of heavy earth-moving equipment. Alvin's down in Bogotá right now directing the effort." Slade released a breath of air, his gaze moving over her pensive features. "You know as well as anyone what kind of effort it takes to get equipment, construction supplies and a host of other essential items into a jungle area."

Cat nodded, biting her lower lip. As much as she wanted to ignore Slade's persuasive words, she couldn't. She could no longer tell herself she was immune to Slade on a personal level, either. "It's tough any way you want to cut it," she agreed.

Slade absently moved the pouch around on the polished surface of the bar. "We're trying to be discreet about the movement of the equipment. If word gets out in Bogotá about our possible find, we'll have hundreds of treasure-hungry guaqueros following us." He snorted softly. "And that's just the tip of the iceberg. Once they know we've got something, all hell will break loose. We're trying to keep a lid on it, but time's short."

Raising her chin, Cat met Slade's sober blue gaze. "As much as I would like to help you, Slade, I don't know if I can walk back into a mine. And I couldn't stand outside a shaft that's being built by laborers and not go inside to check their work." She bowed her head. "I feel so humiliated. I've never admitted I was scared to anyone."

"You've never been brought to your knees before, Cat," he began quietly. "Most of us get the hell knocked out of us long before you took your turn. It's not the end of the world, even though I know it looks like it to you. And as for having no guts or backbone, you've got more than most. The cave-in is going to show you how to reach down inside yourself and find a new wellspring of strength, Cat."

She sniffed, tears rolling down her cheeks. "I'm empty, Slade. How can you draw on nothing?" she whispered painfully.

His smile was gentle as he leaned forward, kissing her closed eyes, tasting the saltiness of her tears. "Trust me, it's there. And you can draw on it when you have to face walking into a shaft again."

A sob broke from deep inside her, and Cat felt Slade's hands slide from her face. She sat there all alone on the stool, hurting and feeling more alone than she ever had in all her life. She had thought she knew what loneliness was, but she hadn't—not like this. When she felt Slade's arms go around her, drawing her against the warm hardness of his body, Cat abandoned herself to his strength. She had none of her own left; she took what he offered her of his, instead.

Slade pressed a kiss to her hair, aware of the subtle fragrance of jasmine around her. He held Cat while she wept, rocking her as he would rock a hurt child, allowing her to release the pent-up anguish she had tried to ignore. He felt his own eyes mist, and shut them, resting his jaw lightly against Cat's hair, murmuring words of comfort to her. The power of his emotions stunned even him; the protectiveness he felt toward Cat took him by surprise. He wanted to ease her hurt, absorb it so she could be cleansed of all the horror he knew stalked her twenty-four hours a day. Finally, her sobs lessened and Slade dug a handkerchief from his back pocket, lifted her chin and dried her face of tears.

Slade nudged stray wisps of damp hair from Cat's cheek and temple, easing them behind her delicate ears. His mouth worked to hold back a barrage of feelings. "When I first met you, something happened. And I know you feel it, too. There's a chemistry between us and I want a chance to explore that with you. Hell, we're not kids anymore, Cat. The rose-colored glasses were taken away from us a long time ago. I'm putting you between a rock and a hard place and I know it. I won't let you go, no matter how frightened you are of entering a mine. You can learn to trust me and lean on me. I won't let you down."

Cat let him hold her, unable to respond, yet desperate to believe him.

"I'll help you get back on your feet in two ways," Slade went on. "I'll provide a mine to work in and I'll be there to help you fight your fear." Slade caressed her flaming red cheeks. "Together, we're strong, Cat, and we both know that. Don't run and hide from this." Slade's heart fell when he saw that Cat remained numb in his arms. What else could he do or say?

Cat's eyes reflected the confusion she felt. Could her feelings for Slade heal this overwhelming fear of another cave-in?

Slade, feeling her slip away, groped to find something that would force her to stay. "If you can't agree to do it for the reasons I've just laid out for you, then do it because you owe me. I saved your life and this is what I'm asking in return: I want you to build me a mine in Colombia. An even and fair trade for saving your life. What do you say?" Slade held his breath, watching the shock register on Cat's face. He groaned inwardly. God, what had he done by blurting out the first thing that came to mind? Was he wrong to use her own sense of duty to blackmail her into conquering her fear?

Miserably, Cat looked away, far too uncertain of herself to deal with Slade's overture. She had to escape that wall of pain, run and hide in the quiet confines of her room. "Let me go, Slade. I've got to rest . . ."

He took a step back, allowing his hands to slip from her shoulders. Slade felt Cat withdrawing her temporary trust from him. He had blown it by telling her she owed him. Suddenly, he was afraid. Would he be willing to lose her to make her whole again? As he stood there, Slade knew the answer: he cared enough to risk everything to make Cat whole.

"Go ahead," he coaxed in a strained voice. "You're tired and you've been through hell today. Just lie down and sleep on it, Cat."

Sleep? How? Cat had walked to the sanctuary of her peaceful room, but despite the dizzying brilliance of the sun slanting through the trellis overhead, she felt as if she were again in the dark pit. Her conscience warred with her fear. Slade was right: she owed him. Then why had it hurt so much when he'd said it? Cat lay on her stomach, clutching the pillow between her arms, head buried in its goosedown folds. *I'm a mess inside. I can't think straight, I can't get a hold on my emotions. Why can't I just let my logic sort all this out?*

She lay there for almost an hour, an internal battle waging between her malfunctioning mental faculties and the tumult of emotions that refused to be ignored any longer. Cat cried some more, terrible animal sounds torn from her soul. They were sounds she'd heard others make, but never her. Finally, her eyes red-rimmed and the pillow soaked, Cat fell into an exhausted, dreamless sleep, an empty vessel floating aimlessly on a sea of dark, turbulent emotions.

Slade was frowning heavily, holding a tumbler of whiskey between his hands, when Pilar padded into the living room. She hovered near the bar where he sat.

"Señor Slade?"

He barely looked up. "Yes?"

"The *señorita*, she weeps like a woman who has lost everything." Pilar shrugged her delicate shoulders, then gave him a beseeching look. "I just passed her room on the way to the linen closet."

Slade's hands tightened around the heavy glass. "Thank you, Pilar."

She hesitated, tilting her head. "You are not going to see if she needs help?"

His mouth worked into a thin line, holding back the emotions that threatened to overtake him. "No," he said harshly, and then gave Pilar an apologetic look. He hadn't meant to take his anger out on Pilar because of his own stupidity. "No," he repeated more gently.

Pilar frowned, her huge brown eyes searching his for a long moment. *"Si, señor,"* she said, then turned away, going back to the kitchen.

Slade swore under his breath, scraping the stool loudly against the cedar floor as he moved. He stalked through the room, going out to the porch. Continuing outdoors, he opened the screen, striding down the slight incline toward the small stream winding lazily through the cottonwoods. Slade finally came to a halt at the edge of the clear green water, staring angrily down at the sun-dappled surface. Throwing down the last of the whiskey, his knuckles whitened as he gripped the tumbler. The whiskey was hot, searing, like the pain he felt for Cat.

I should go to her; she needs me. No, that's not true. If she needed me, she'd have stayed. She wouldn't have run to her bedroom. Slade snorted violently, his blue eyes icy with anger aimed at himself. *You blew it, Donovan. You dumb son of a bitch, why did you have to tell her she owed you?* He raked his fingers through his hair, unable to contain his inner fury over his desperate action.

Miserably, Slade allowed the full weight of what he'd just done to Cat overtake him. *I did it for her,* he told himself. But his cartwheeling mind wasn't sure. Confused and upset, he knew he needed some counsel. Kai Travis had always been his sounding board when he got into a bind. He needed her common sense, because he didn't know how to untie the knot he'd just created between Cat and himself.

* * *

Kai met him at the sliding screen door as he walked up the steps.

"Slade? You look awful. What's wrong?"

Self-consciously, Slade thrust his hands into the pockets of his jeans, looking down at Kai. "I'm sorry to ride over unannounced, Kai."

She took him by the arm, leading him into the living room and to the couch. "Since when did you need an invitation? What's going on? Is something wrong with Cat?"

He shrugged and sat down. "I really screwed up this afternoon with her, Kai." He rubbed his face tiredly.

Kai sat on the small hassock in front of him. "Tell me what happened."

The quiet tenor of Kai's voice shook loose all his suppressed anxiety and worry. Slowly, Slade unwound the sordid chain of events. When he finished, Kai grimaced.

"I'm sorry, Slade. I didn't mean to mention your mine to Cat. I had just assumed that you had already discussed the possibility of her working with you." She reached over, apologetically squeezing his arm.

"It's not your fault, Kai. Cat thought I had brought her to the ranch just to use her professional talents."

"Does she still?"

"I took her on a picnic earlier today and we got that issue straightened out." Slade shook his head. "And then I really blew it. I tried playing amateur psychologist by making her think she could repay me for saving her life by building the mine. How could I have been so stupid? Words were just pouring out of me. I was in such a panic, afraid that I was going to lose her. I didn't want to, Kai, I spoke without thinking. It had a devastating effect on Cat. She's probably still crying..."

With a sigh, Kai got up and went to the cabinet, pouring each of them a bit of brandy. She handed one snifter to Slade and sat back down. "Drink up, you need it."

Sorrowfully, Slade downed the stinging brandy. He sucked air between his clenched teeth, holding the delicate crystal in his hands. Slowly, the knots began to dissolve in his gut as he sat with her in the intervening silence.

"She's probably going to run," he muttered.

"You mean, leave Mourning Dove?"

"Sure, wouldn't you? Put yourself in Cat's place. I'm barely able to get her to believe that I didn't bring her to the ranch under false pretenses. And then I tell her she owes me." Slade suddenly stood up, unable to stand the anger he was aiming at himself.

Kai watched him pace for several minutes. "What will you lose, Slade?"

He halted. "Cat."

"You love her?"

"I didn't realize that I did until a half hour ago. I had all these feelings about her, Kai. I never thought there was a woman who could tolerate my life-style, but I know she can. Cat's just like me in many ways."

"And does she love you, Slade?"

He ran his fingers through his hair in aggravation. "Who the hell knows?"

"I think she does," Kai provided softly. "Slade, stop pacing for a minute and come and sit down."

Slade sat, staring at Kai. "Sometimes, I see longing in her eyes and I hear the emotion in her voice, Kai. Every time we're together, it's so damned special."

With a smile, Kai said, "I've been privileged to share a great deal with Cat since she's been here, Slade. I know you're very special to her, too."

"Well, I just destroyed whatever was there."

"Maybe, maybe not. Why don't you go home and talk with her? Iron this out and tell her how you feel. Let her know that you really didn't mean to make her feel guilty or hold her to building your mine. Tell her you were trying to make her address her fear."

"I just thought that she'd want to face up to it. I saw it as a perfect solution to all of Cat's problems."

Gently, Kai reached over and patted his sloping shoulder. "That's how you would have done it, Slade, if you'd been in her shoes. Let Cat tell you how she wants to handle her own healing process. Go on . . . go home and talk with her. I know it will do some good."

Slade caught Kai's hand, giving it a grateful squeeze. "We'll have that talk," he promised. "I've been wanting to make Cat a gift, anyway. Maybe, if I can persuade her to stay, I can get it done for her."

Kai's eyes twinkled. "Knowing how talented you are at making jewelry, I'm sure she'll be pleased."

"Better yet," Slade said, hope in his voice as he rose, "let's the four of us go to Houston in a couple of weeks. I can give it to Cat then. A sort of peace token for the way I've behaved."

Walking with Slade to the porch, Kai waved to him as he left. "Houston sounds like a good idea. And don't worry, your heart was in the right place, Slade. The words just came out wrong. Cat will forgive you."

Throwing his leg over his horse, Slade managed a thin smile. "I hope you're right, Kai. I'll let you know. Think good thoughts for us, will you?"

"Always."

Chapter Eight

Cat tried to repair the damage that her crying jag had done to her face. Slade had knocked at her door earlier, but she had refused to answer. She had to get a hold on herself before she faced him. She put color into her pale cheeks with a brush, and a rose-colored lipstick actually made her look almost normal. She winced, avoiding the look in her eyes as she combed her hair. She had taken a warm, cleansing shower and changed into some of her more practical clothes: a peach shell and a pair of no-nonsense khaki pants. Now, she looked more like her old self, before the trauma of the cave-in. The only thing different was that her hair was longer, making her look more feminine. Cat didn't want to cut her hair even though she knew she was going into the jungle again.

No, I want it to grow. I don't care. And she didn't question why she violently fought the idea of a haircut. Wasn't that what Slade wanted? A mining engineer, not a feminine-looking woman? He'd made that very clear earlier. A life for a life. Okay, she owed him, and she'd pay up. Kincaids recognized that some things in life were sacred; you save a man's life, he owes you. It was that simple. She shut her eyes, allowing the brush to lie on the vanity for long moments.

Cat tried to ignore the ache in her heart. Was she so mixed up after the trauma of the cave-in that she hadn't read Slade accurately? She had thought she had seen and felt something special with him, but it had all been an act to maneuver her into going to Colombia with him. When she opened her eyes and warily stared at herself in the mirror, Cat could barely stand to look at the image that stood before her. There was hurt and pain in the depths of her emerald eyes, and anger. Yes, anger at being betrayed by Slade. He had deftly used her to get what he wanted—and he wanted a tough-minded mining engineer. Okay, he'd get it his way. She firmly placed the brush on the vanity, girding herself for the coming confrontation.

Cat allowed all the anger and hurt Slade had caused to rise and protect her. It gave her strength when she had none of her own to call on. Opening the door to her bedroom, Cat walked purposefully down the cedar hall to find Slade.

Slade heard a knock at his office door and he made a half turn in his chair. Cat was standing outside the sliding-glass door, and immediately he was on his feet.

"Come in," he said, opening the door for her.

The coolness of air-conditioning hit Cat as she stepped through the entrance. She saw hope in Slade's eyes, and his exhaustion, and tried to steel herself against feeling anything remotely human toward him. As he slid the door closed and turned toward her, she said, "I'll pay off the debt between us, Slade. I've got another two weeks before I'm freed by the doctor to resume my normal activities. In the meantime, I want all the core-sampling reports, maps and any other geological items you can supply me so I can begin studying the mining situation in Silla de Montar Valley."

Slade's face softened and he took a step toward her. "Cat—"

She stepped away, arms rigid at her sides, her chin raised, eyes defiant. "No."

Slade froze, all hope shattering like an emerald struck by a pickax. When he finally spoke, his voice was charged with feeling. "I have a spare office in the west wing of the house. I can have all those things brought to you."

"Fine."

"Look, you don't have to jump into this with both feet. Kai said you still needed rest. I don't want you working eight hours a day—"

"My life for your mine. That's the way you wanted it, wasn't it?" Cat's jaw tightened. "I'll work however long I want. Don't try and set how many hours a day I can work even if I'm still mending." Her chin quivered. "I'm surprised you waited this long. It was probably killing you to wait six weeks—six weeks that could have been spent down in Colombia instead."

Slade's eyes narrowed with barely contained fury. "That's unfair, Cat. We need to talk."

She smiled wearily, some of her anger dissipating. "Nothing's fair in life, is it? You were raised with rocks. Well, so was I. I'll be just as tough as the situation demands. If you've got all the core and mining information I need, you'll have a rough blueprint for a mine in two weeks."

Slade opened his hands. "Cat, I didn't mean to make it sound as if you owed me. What I said was a mistake."

Her smile was brittle, her eyes dangerously bright with unshed tears. "We all make mistakes, Donovan. My mistake was in trusting you and your intentions. You've made it clear what you want and I'm prepared to give it to you. Your mine for my life. Okay, you've got a deal."

"Damn it, will you give me a chance to explain, Cat?"
"No!"

Slade wanted to strangle her. He also wanted to take Cat into his arms and erase the anguish he saw so clearly in her haunted expression. Her act was all a bluff on her part, and he knew it. And so did she. She was like brittle glass ready to explode right in front of him. But he didn't dare call her hand, or she might run away. No, he'd have to play by her rules, allow her to retreat and hold him at arm's length and maybe, just maybe, she'd gradually lower that shield she had in place and allow him a second chance. "All right," he rasped, "you've got a deal."

Cat swayed slightly, feeling light-headed. She took a step away, covering up her reaction by walking to the door. "Fine. Get me what I need to figure out a construction blueprint for you."

He followed her out to the patio. "Come with me," he said, trying to keep his voice steady.

Cat nodded and walked a few paces behind him as they crossed to the western wing of the ranch house. She tried to contain her surprise when he opened the door to a spacious office replete with several personal computers, calculators and drafting board. Everything she might need to formulate the kind of mine required was present.

Slade made a slight motion toward the office. "This will be yours. The IBM PC is hooked up to the data bank at Texas A & M in Houston, by phone modem, should you need more mining information."

She wondered if Slade had built this with her in mind, but bit back the question, not wishing to fight any more than necessary with him. Her strength had to be focused on the project at hand, not wasted on him. There was a cot in the corner complete with blankets and a pillow. Fine, she'd live, eat and sleep there. In two weeks, she ought to be able to come up with a decent preliminary blueprint to begin digging a mine.

"Thank you." She stepped past him, deliberately avoiding touching him.

Slade went to the drafting board, pointing to a black buzzer on the phone beside it. "If you need anything, you can ring me in my other office." He turned, pointing to a wall of cabinets opposite them. "Every core and drilling-sample spec I took on the mine is here. There are topographical maps of the valley, overburden, ore and basement-complex sample reports. I don't think you'll need anything else, but if you do, call me."

Cat refused to look at Slade and went to the cabinet. Everything had been carefully labeled, numbered and categorized. Her assessment of Slade's abilities grudgingly rose. She pulled out a roll of specs from the first cubbyhole. "I think I've got enough to keep me busy," she murmured.

Slade nodded and retreated. "Dinner's in two hours."

She went to the drafting desk, unrolling the specs and studying them intently. "Have Pilar bring it in here, please."

Well, what did he expect—for Cat to forgive and forget? Slade shut the door quietly behind him, a bitter taste in his mouth. This was a new side of Cat Kincaid: the brilliant, tenacious mining engineer who had carved out a name for herself in one of the toughest businesses in the world. He'd have to keep reminding himself of her steel determination, because she was certainly wearing it like armor now. And he'd forced her into donning it. Damn it, anyway!

Night melded with day and day with night. Cat immersed herself in the exploration of details that would help her determine what kind of mine shaft would be best suited for the Verde Mine. Slade had named the mine at the top of all the specs. "Green Mine"—that fit, she thought. Verde to her meant growth, as did anything green. Rubbing her eyes tiredly, she pushed aside the computer keyboard and placed her pencil on the pad. What day was it? They all blended together when she attacked Verde's challenge. Looking at her Rolex, now scratched from the cave-in, she saw that ten days had passed. A slight smile cut across her lips as she slowly rose. Dawn was crawling onto the horizon as seen from the wall of windows that faced east.

Sleep.... She took snatches of three or four hours at a time. Lying down with a groan, Cat closed her eyes. When she awoke, she would go back to her room, shower and get a fresh change of clothes. As she sank deeper into the embrace of sleep, Slade crossed her mind. To her chagrin, Cat had found that if she wasn't actively pursuing her job, he would slip into her thoughts, catching her unawares. And every time that occurred, her pounding heart would underscore the wild, unnamed feelings that came on its heels. As much as Cat wanted to hate him, she could not. She was angry with him, and disappointed, and she would never trust him again ... not ever.

Slade tried to contain his surprise when Cat came up to the sliding-glass door of his office on the tenth day. She had successfully avoided seeing him for nearly two weeks. Only Pilar's insistence that Cat was in the other office and appeared well had kept him from seeing for himself. Slade knew he didn't dare push Cat too far by showing up on her doorstep. He rose to open the door, but she beat him to it.

"Come in," he invited, pulling up a stool.

Cat felt the heat rush to her face. Why did she have to blush? She stood just inside the office, holding his anxious stare. Slade looked as tired as she felt. There were shadows beneath his eyes, as if he'd slept little. His clothes were rumpled, which wasn't like him. He always wore a crisp cotton shirt and dark blue jeans that outlined his beautifully narrow hips and well-formed legs. He was beautiful, Cat admitted weakly, her pulse pounding unevenly. As much of a bastard as he was, Slade still affected her physically, and she couldn't ignore the sensations racing through her even now.

"I've finished the rough calculations. I need to sit down and discuss them with you. Do you have a couple of hours to spare?"

Slade heard the strain in Cat's voice. How he had missed her! Ten days without Cat had been a prison sentence for him. He had longed for her voice, her effusive laughter, her quiet, steady presence. Hungrily, he now drank her in as she stood like a wary doe ready to flee at the first sign of danger. She was pale, he realized with a pang, and she wore no makeup to hide it. She wore a light blue short-sleeved chambray shirt, jeans and sensible brown shoes. It looked almost as if she were dressed for field work, except for the mandatory hard hat and rough boots. Her outfit didn't diminish her femininity in his eyes, though. The fullness of her parted lips sent an ache throbbing through him. Slade had often remembered kissing those lips.

"Sure, I've got the time." He sounded like an eager schoolboy on shaky ground. Well, wasn't he?

Cat turned without preamble and began the walk back to her office. Her hands were damp and she longed to rub them on her thighs to dry them off, but Slade would notice, and she didn't want to broadcast her nervousness. She almost smiled in spite of herself, though. Slade's harsh face had softened the moment he saw her. Was that an act on his part? Was it real? Cat groaned inwardly; why did she even care? Hadn't he shown his real character already?

Slade entered her office and saw two chairs sitting side by side at the drafting desk. Cat sat down, waiting for him. He wiped his sweaty hands on his jeans and then sat beside her.

"What did you come up with?" he asked. *Great, Donovan, you sound like a twelve-year-old boy whose voice is changing.*

Cat drew the first sheaf of papers between them, keenly aware of Slade's closeness. She tried valiantly to cap her own escaping feelings and cleared her throat. "I've made a study of the Chivor and Muzo mine operations before deciding what ours would be. Muzo's emerald fields are found in a loose, black shale that quite literally is on the surface. All they've had to do is clear out the jungle and go to work to reclaim the gems." She scowled, placing a paper in front of him. "Their mining operations are antiquated and, to say the least, environmentally damaging. As you can see in this color photo, they're using strip-mining techniques. They blast with dynamite and then go in with huge bulldozers, shoveling the black shale into vast washing and screening areas. Water is used to wash away the debris and leave the emeralds. What can't be bulldozed after a blast is jackhammered by miners and then pushed into the gullies." Cat glanced at him and lost her train of thought. She loved his mouth despite herself. It had ravished hers until she had melted into an oblivion of wildly boiling heat and desire. His nearness was devastating to her, and her voice faltered as she tried to pick up the reins of her conversation. "The gangue, or waste rock, is pushed into the Rio Itoco below. There the guaqueros sift through the tailings during the day, hoping to find a stray emerald."

Slade nodded, resting his chin on one of his hands. He saw her hand tremble as she turned the page of her assessment. Automatically, he wanted to reach out, take her hand and tell her everything would be all right. Miserably, he knew that wasn't true. If only he could make things right between them. With a monumental effort, he addressed her comments. "The people pan the waters of the river during the day and become tunnel rats at night. They try to either break into the terraces, which are heavily guarded by the Colombian police, or dig into the shallow mines."

"Right." Cat brought out another paper, swallowing hard. She had seen the tenderness in Slade's eyes as he locked and held her gaze. Despite everything, he did lay claim to her heart, Cat realized in anguish. She wanted to reach out and caress his cheek, to take away some of the pain that lay at the downturned corners of his mouth. Yes, they were both suffering. "Muzo's methods are outdated. Not only that, but indiscriminate blasting with dynamite is going to certainly destroy some of the emeralds."

Slade snorted. "That's already happened. At Chivor they blast cautiously and with low charges and only when necessary." Why did she have to look waiflike? It devastated him to think that he had caused Cat to appear almost a ghost of her former self. No longer was her skin that golden color, her eyes that glorious velvet green sparkling with life. When she stared at him, all he saw was fear and . . . was it longing? Was that possible? He clung to that possibility, barely hearing her speak about the assessment. Each word she formed with her full lips created a widening ache through him. He loved her.

Cat couldn't relax beneath Slade's intense stare and she retreated deep into her mining-engineer mode. "Your mine, on the other hand, will be a mixture of open-pit mining methods involving the terracing of the surrounding hillside, plus sinking a shaft." She cleared her throat and traced one line of figures on a core-sample readout. "My educated guess, based upon your channel samplings, is that the calcite-limestone vein surfaces here on the hill and slowly moves back down into the earth over here." Cat drew him a quick picture, showing the stratum that might hold emeralds between its thinly wafered sheets.

"What's your opinion? Are we in business or not?" he asked.

Cat straightened up, running fingers through her hair. She expelled a breath of air, taking another paper and handing it to him. "If my calculations stand up and if your channel samples were spaced properly, the Verde should yield one emerald for every twenty million particles of surrounding overburden. You're in business, all right."

Slade stared down at Cat's figures. Her numbers, all in dark leaded pencil, were agonizingly neat and precise. A slight smile hovered around the corners of his mouth. "This is even better than I had roughly figured."

"You'll have everything you want, Slade." The words had come out flat and emotionless as Cat stared at him.

Slade ground his teeth together, bristling over her unspoken accusation. Her eyes were a cool green. He tried to tell himself he deserved that from Cat because of what he'd done to her. Damn it, it hurt! And he was angry at her for prodding that festering wound that now stood between them. "Why don't you give me your mine evaluation?" he asked.

Cat slipped back into her professional mode easily, like a horse into a familiar, comfortable harness. She went over the determination factors: an estimate of future operations, a suitable production schedule, the grade, market and selling price of the product and the production life of the mine. She went into the size, shape, attitude and quality of the emerald deposit, which was determined by geologic studies and maps. She missed nothing in her smooth, methodical presentation. At the end of the second hour, with a large flowchart concluding the final presentation, Cat wrapped it up.

"The mine itself will be tricky. Transportation of certain types of timber is going to be a problem. I'm going to need heavy equipment to get that lumber out of the jungle. And you'll need to build a good road that won't wash out in the tropical rains of winter." She shrugged and gestured toward the plans on the drafting board. "All of this is detailed and you can read it at your leisure."

Slade nodded thoughtfully, watching as Cat shoved her hands into the pockets of her jeans and walked over to the wall of windows. The sun was slanting through the glass, making her sable hair come alive with threads of gold. He had sponged in her presence in the past two hours, as if starved. God, how he had missed her.

"You've done a thorough job on this, Cat. A damn good job." His voice shook with gratitude and pride in her abilities. Slade managed a tight smile, holding her thawing emerald gaze, realizing he had reached inside those defensive walls and touched her, the woman. "Now I see why you've got one hell of a name for yourself in our industry. It would take most people a good month just to put a preliminary study like this together. You did it in two weeks."

"You had everything I needed here," Cat countered, feeling warm and good as his praise flowed through her. "Part of the time factor is based on how much an engineer has to run around collecting all the pieces of various data that are needed to put a show like this together. You're good at your job, too, Slade."

He arched like a cat beneath her flattery, and his mouth stretched into a smile. "What do you say we celebrate? Matt and Kai want me to fly us to Houston for dinner tonight. We'll go to a nice restaurant and relax. We both need that."

Cat stiffened. At first, she was going to say no. But Kai had been a godsend the first two weeks of her stay at the ranch, and she owed her thanks. More importantly, Kai had become her friend. But every minute spent with Slade weakened her resolve, her past hurt over his actions. Cat anguished over the decision.

"Come on, say yes," Slade coaxed. "Kai's called over here three times in the last ten days wanting to see you. She's been craving some female company. What do you say?"

Cat gnawed on her lower lip and stared down at her shoes. "Okay." There was a razor-honed edge to her voice.

"I'll keep my distance from you," Slade said, sensing she wanted to hear some sort of verbal promise from him.

"Fine." She lifted her head. "I think it's best if it's business all the way between us."

"I haven't forgotten."

Cat eyed him. At first, she had been angry with Slade for tricking her. Then, she felt childish after leveling a barrage at him—although she had gotten it cleaned out of her system once and for all. But ten days had modified her initial anger. The past week had made her aware of just how much she liked Slade, regardless of what had happened to damage their relationship. Cat was afraid of her own feelings toward Slade. The less she saw of him, the more she was able to control them. "Good. I'll see you later, then."

Slade rose. "They'll be here at six tonight."

"Is this formal?"

"Yes."

That meant a dress. And judging from the look of longing in Slade's eyes, Cat knew she was in trouble. She had tried her best for the past two weeks to dress for business, not pleasure. She didn't want any more of Slade's mesmerizing advances weakening her resolve. Wearing a dress would invite his advances, and she knew it. How did she get herself painted into corners like this? If she hadn't been angry with Slade, it would be funny. Normally, her sense of humor rescued her; this time it didn't.

"I'll be ready about five-thirty or so," she promised.

"What color dress will you be wearing?"

"Turquoise."

Slade smiled enigmatically. "Perfect," he murmured. "I'll come for you at five-thirty."

Why am I taking so many extra pains to look pretty? Cat gave herself a disgruntled look in the floor-length mirror. She wore a designer dress, a stunning turquoise creation made of rich georgette and luminous satin. Together, the materials created an elegant dress for any special occasion. The deep-draped neckline was graced with a satin camisole inset. The satin sash with a rosette emphasized her narrow waist, while the full-circle skirt flowed with breathtaking grace each time she moved. The sleeves were full and cuffed at her wrists, adding to the overall frothy look. This was a dress to dance in, no matter how poor a dancer she was. Cat sighed, running her fingers across the beautiful, wispy fabric. That was how she felt around Slade despite everything he had done—feminine and . . . loved.

Cat chose pearl earrings set in a circle of thin gold, but realized something was missing. She needed some kind of necklace to set off the dress. Oh, well, such was life, she admitted regretfully. Taking one more look at herself in the mirror, she decided she looked unusually attractive. Was it the soft sweep of her recently washed hair? The dress? Glumly, Cat knew that despite everything, she wanted to be beautiful for Slade. Damn his hold over her!

When the knock came at her door, Cat turned on her turquoise sandals and opened it. She was completely unprepared for what she saw. Slade was darkly handsome in a black tuxedo, white shirt and black tie. He had shaved, erasing the five o'clock shadow he grew daily, and his hair was still damp and neatly combed into place. Her lips parted as she stared helplessly up into the warmth of his blue eyes.

"You look beautiful," he said huskily, holding out his hand toward her. His heart started violently as he absorbed Cat's unparalleled beauty. The fragrance of her perfume drugged him and his nostrils eagerly drank in her scent. The design of the turquoise dress enhanced the delicious, exotic tilt of her green eyes. Never had he seen her look so desirable. She was all curves and softness and Slade fought the urge to take Cat into his arms, crushing her against him. Holding himself in check, he shared an unsure smile with her. Cat was just as nervous as he was, he discovered to his relief. Her fingers were damp as she lightly placed her hand in his.

"Thank you," Cat said a little breathlessly, walking slowly toward the living room with him.

"Kai and Matt are already here. We've got time for a drink before we go." Slade accompanied her into the living room, where Kai and her husband, Matt, were sitting on one sofa, drinks in hand. "About an hour from now I'm flying us all to Houston and we're going to have dinner at the Brownstone."

"The Brownstone?" Cat stared up at him in disbelief. That particular restaurant was the best in the city. Slade had made it sound as if the night's excursion was going to be less posh, less intimate. "But—I thought—"

Slade grinned rakishly, guiding her to the couch opposite the Travis's. "You need a break. We both do," he explained in his dark, honeyed voice, his mouth close to her ear. "Want your usual? A margarita?"

Cat stared up at him, nonplussed. She saw the glint of mischief in his eyes. If she read accurately between the lines, Slade had deliberately set up this plan and put it into motion. "No. Give me a double Scotch on the rocks," she said, at a loss to stay ahead of his surprises. It was supposed to be business only between them, not pleasure. She was frightened of her own emotional reactions to him. Ten days had not assuaged her feelings for Slade. How could she control them for an entire evening in one of the most romantic restaurants in Houston?

Slade stood there uncertainly. "A double?" he voiced.

"I'm not the one flying, Slade. You are. I want a double Scotch on the rocks."

"Twist of lemon?"

Cat gripped her clutch purse tightly, trying to look cool and collected in front of their guests. "Yes." *Donovan, I'm going to murder you when we get back. I swear I will . . .*

"This was a wonderful idea," Kai spoke up. She wore a white chemise that brought out the highlights of her shoulder-length auburn hair. The gold earrings and slender necklace at her throat matched the sparkle in her eyes. "Frankly, when Slade called over, we were ready to go to the city, but didn't plan on the Brownstone." She laughed delightedly. "I love the restaurant! It's so Victorian and so thoroughly romantic."

One confirmation, Cat thought. She shot Slade a withering look as he ambled back over with her drink.

"Yes, he's always cooking up something, isn't he?" Cat said, taking the drink. When Slade sat down and hooked his long arm around her, Cat fairly sizzled. No matter how black her look, Slade smiled, enjoying her predicament. He knew her well enough to know that she wouldn't embarrass herself or him in front of company.

Matt Travis was equally handsome in a white tuxedo trimmed in black. It brought out his dark attractiveness, Cat thought. And both Kai and Matt looked so happy together. She envied them their loving relationship.

"That's one of the many things this lady likes about me," Slade drawled, giving Cat a wide smile.

Cat clamped her mouth shut after she swallowed a healthy gulp of Scotch, silencing her urge to protest the game he was playing with her.

Kai leaned forward, her eyes fairly sparkling. "Slade was telling us he had a surprise for you, Cat. I can hardly wait for you to see what he's done."

"He's done enough already," Cat said, choking on the words that sounded almost sweet coming from her.

Kai shared a knowing glance with her husband. "Slade, why not give it to Cat now? We saw what he's made for you and I'm just dying to see the look on your face when you get it. Slade? Please?"

Slade groaned. "Kai, when you give me that pleading look of yours, how can I say no?" He got up, setting his drink on the coffee table.

Matt grinned, putting his arm around his wife, giving her a warm embrace. "See why I fell under her spell, Slade? I told you before, you can't resist those beautiful eyes of hers."

Slade tilted his head, meeting and holding Cat's gaze. "I don't want to take anything away from Kai, but this exotic beauty over here has the most beautiful emerald eyes I've ever seen."

Cat felt heat rise in her face as his compliment reached through her like a caress.

"Agreed!" Kai said, smiling.

"Exotic's the right word," Matt said thoughtfully, studying Cat.

"Well, wait here, gang. Since Kai can't stand the suspense, I guess I'll have to give Cat her present now, rather than after dinner."

Cat nervously cleared her throat as Slade left the room. She looked at them. "What's he talking about, Kai? What's going on?"

She smiled warmly. "Oh, Cat, don't you know?"

Cat wished she did. Trying to hide her desire to escape, she shook her head. "No, I don't."

Matt patted his wife's hand. "Slade's sort of like a brother to us, Cat. Ever since he brought you here, we've seen a tremendous change in him—a good, positive change. We've watched him settle down and relax, for once. He's pretty happy with you around, you know."

"And Slade is the type of man who loves to give people gifts," Kai said, a wistful look on her face. "He's given us so much over the years we've been here."

"And to our son, Josh," Matt added warmly.

"Sometimes, I think Slade collects all his strays and turns them into an extended family of sorts." Kai lowered her voice to a conspiratorial whisper. "I told Matt all along, Slade is made for marriage. Until you came he was restless, Cat. You could see it in his walk, his eyes and the way he ran his life. Now, this past month and a half, he's been so incredibly content, it's blown us away." Her voice grew husky. "I don't know what your relationship with Slade is, Cat, but he thinks an awful lot of you." And then Kai traded a merry look with Matt. "We're keeping our fingers crossed for the two of you!"

"Now what's all this whispering about?" Slade entered the room, carrying a dove-gray velvet jewelry case.

Cat nearly dropped her drink. "Uh, nothing, just girl talk," she stammered. "You know..."

Matt and Kai chuckled like indulgent parents as Slade came and sat down next to Cat.

"Girl talk, hmm?" Slade's blue eyes glimmered with mirth. "If I know Kai, she's up to no good again."

"That's not fair, Slade!" Kai protested laughingly. She got to her feet and so did Matt, coming to stand near Slade. "Go on, show her!"

Cat gripped the tumbler as if it were her last hold on life. Slade set the gray velvet box on the couch between them.

"I will. Patience, pretty lady." Slade devoted a hundred percent of his attention to Cat, his smile waning. He soberly held her nervous gaze. "Ten days ago I started a project in my hobby shop. I wanted to make you something that would somehow tell you how I felt about you. I wanted a gem that would show you what I saw in you, Cat." Slade reached over, gently unclipping her pearl earrings. "You won't be needing these tonight," he told her.

Cat swallowed hard, swayed by the huskiness in Slade's tone. She heard the unsureness in his voice and saw it in his cobalt eyes. And suddenly, Cat wanted to reassure him that she would not reject him or make him feel embarrassed. Ever. "Ten days ago?" she whispered, an ache in her voice.

Slade's mouth twisted into a grimace. "Yes." He glanced up at Kai and Matt. "We had a big fight then," he explained to them, leaving out the details. He pried open the spring-latched lid.

Cat gasped, her hand flying to her breast. There, nestled on a deep-blue velvet cushion, was a set of opal earrings, a pear-shaped necklace on a delicate gold chain and a cocktail ring. The silence was eloquent as Slade, whose fingers were scarred and huge in comparison, gently took the necklace from its placement on the velvet.

"People remind me of gems," Slade told Cat in a low voice fraught with emotion. "To me, the opal is the most complex of all gems, like you." He settled the stone around her neck, easing the clasp closed. The huge pear-shaped opal, almost the size of a nickel in diameter, nestled into the hollow of her throat. Then Slade dared to meet Cat's eyes for the first time, afraid of what he might see and praying for the opposite. The words died on his lips as he drowned in the shimmering emerald of Cat's eyes, now filled with huge, luminous tears. In their depths he saw her incredible fire and warmth toward him. He didn't deserve this kind of a reaction from Cat after all the blundering mistakes he'd made with her thus far.

Suddenly, Slade wished Kai and Matt weren't there. The open invitation in Cat's gestures made him want to lift her up into his arms and carry her off to his bedroom to seal their fate. He wanted to make her his own, to drink her into his thirsty, starving soul. Cat could give him the serenity he sought. She was peace, he realized, as he gently cradled her hands. There was so much he wanted to blurt out to her, to apologize for. He longed to ask forgiveness. But now was not the time. If the compassionate look in Cat's eyes was any kind of a promise, she would yield despite the pain he'd put her through, and allow him to explain…to forgive him and start over with a clean slate.

As Slade clipped each of the opals to her earlobes, the iridescent layers of the precious gems gleamed with the fires of emeralds, rubies, topaz, and sapphires. The colors brought out the natural beauty of her eyes and he silently thanked God and Cat for giving him a second chance he didn't deserve.

Slipping the ring on the fourth finger of her right hand, Slade said quietly, "There's a matchlessness to opal, Cat. The layers of color change as you turn your hand one way or another. You're like that—you have so many brilliant facets that change, depending on your mood. You keep me enthralled to the point where nothing else exists for me." He held her gaze, his hands tightening slightly on hers. "You've become my day, my night, sweetheart. Nothing else comes close to you in importance. You've got to believe that. Richness from the heart outstrips monetary concerns. The color of your eyes when you look at me gives me a wealth of feelings and emotions that no emerald mine or money could ever give me. Do you understand?"

Shyly, Cat touched the opal at her throat, all of her disappointment and hurt melting away beneath Slade's beautiful words. He meant them with every fiber of his being, she realized, completely dissolved by his admittance. Placing her fingers in his hand, she gravely met his anxious look. Her voice came out in a husky, quivering whisper. "Yes...I understand, Slade."

He squeezed her fingers gently, a powerful wave of relief smashing through him. And when he dared to look into her green eyes, bright with tenderness and awash with tears, he knew she did.

Chapter Nine

"Are you enjoying yourself, Cat?"

Slade's words, whispered lightly against her temple, caused Cat to tremble. He held her close as the quiet music fell over them on the dance floor. "I shouldn't be, but I am."

His chuckle was a deep, pleased sound. Slade held her a little more tightly, aware of how her soft pliant curves fitted against his harder, unyielding body. "I took a big risk," he admitted, pressing a kiss to her hair.

"I'm still upset with you, Slade."

One eyebrow cocked and he looked down at her. If that was true, he didn't see anger in Cat's eyes. Instead, he saw the molten gold desire in her dark green gaze. "For what? Arranging this weekend in Houston with Matt and Kai?" he asked innocently.

She laughed and shook her head. "You're such a rascal, do you know that? One minute you're Peck's Bad Boy. The next, you've made up for what you caused by giving me the most beautiful gift I've ever gotten. And then you have Pilar pack a suitcase for me and hide it on the plane. If Kai hadn't told me on the way to Houston that you were planning a weekend here and not just the evening, I'd probably have dropped my soupspoon when you blithely announced it at dinner.''

He grinned engagingly, whirling her around, the airy folds of her dress moving like the wind around her tall, graceful body. The night was turning into magic, Slade thought, unable to contain his joy. "You'd never drop a soupspoon in front of anyone," he drawled. "You're too cool to do that."

"Being around you is like running a big risk without insurance, Slade."

He smiled. "Thank you."

"That wasn't a compliment."

"Am I a risk?"

"You know you are, Slade Donovan. So quit giving me that engaging little-boy look. It won't work."

"It's worked so far..."

Admittedly, he was right, Cat thought, unable to resist his smile. "What else do you have planned?"

He looked above her head, noticing Kai and Matt dancing nearby on the crowded dance floor. "Actually, Kai begged me to fly her to Houston to shop. I got to thinking about it and called her back and asked her if she and Matt would like to make it a weekend with the four of us. She thought it was a great idea. I've made reservations at the Westin Hotel over at the Galleria. Saturday morning, if you want, you and Kai can go shopping. Matt and I are going to do a little golfing. That evening, we'll go to an excellent French restaurant." He looked down at Cat, devilry in his eyes. "Then, we'll go to an amusement park nearby. They have one of the best bumper-car rides around."

Cat gasped. "An amusement park?"

"Sure. Kai wanted to do something different. I figure it's been at least twenty years since any of us went on a merry-go-round or tried to win a stuffed toy. It ought to make for a fun night."

Cat laughed delightedly. "It sounds wonderful. What else?"

"Brunch on Sunday morning. I figure we'll get up late and then reward ourselves by crawling into the hot tub in my suite. We'll sip champagne, have eggs Benedict and generally pry our eyes open. Then, around oneish, we'll head back out to Del Rio. How does the game plan sound?"

Cat tried to hide her enjoyment and didn't succeed. "It sounds great and you know it."

"Remember, this was Kai's idea, originally."

"Slade, one of these days your cleverness is going to catch up with you."

He sobered. "Yeah, I know. Contrary to what you might think, I got two rooms at the Westin for us. They're both suites and are joined by a door."

Relief flooded Cat. "Thank you, Slade..."

"I didn't want to," he admitted softly, trailing a slow series of kisses along her hairline, "but I did."

"It probably killed you," she said wryly, her knees weakening as each of his kisses melted her a little more.

Slade had the good grace to chuckle. "Yeah, I really fence-sat on that one." He eased Cat away from him, staring darkly down at her. "Look, after dancing when we get over to the hotel, we need to sit down and talk."

"Yes, about a lot of things."

"I've been a real bastard, Cat. I'm sorry. I didn't mean to hurt you like I have." Slade drew in a breath and forced a slight smile. "Tonight, come to my suite when you're ready."

Cat lifted her chin, lost in the warming cobalt of his gaze, her pulse unsteady. "I will."

Pilar had packed with great care, Cat discovered as she opened her luggage. The peach silk nightgown and accom-

panying robe had been carefully folded on top of everything else. She held up the shimmering gown. Should she
wear that over to Slade's suite? Or should she go over
dressed as she was? Indecision warred with what her heart
desired. "Oh, to hell with it," Cat muttered, heading to the
shower.

Slade was standing by the window overlooking the scin-
tillating lights of Houston at one o'clock in the morning. He
had gotten rid of his tie and opened the throat of the shirt.
The jacket had been shed on a silk settee and he'd eased out
of his shoes. In a spasm of nervousness, he'd poured himself a snifter of brandy. He held the glass in his left hand as
he stared out at the sleeping city. He and Cat had sobered as
the evening wore on, realizing the coming confrontation
between them. Slade expected to be justly brought to task by
Cat. What he wanted was to make love with her, to apologize that way, instead. But that wasn't a reasonable solution to everything. No, this talk had been long overdue
between them, and he was willing to endure it if it would
give him hope of a future with Cat. Any future was better
than none.

A faint knock at the adjoining door made him turn.
Slade's eyes widened appreciatively as Cat silently walked
into the room. A flood of heat uncoiled deep within him as
he stared at the huge fuzzy white hotel robe she wore. Her
hair was damp at the ends, indicating she'd just taken a
shower.

"Come in," he said, motioning for her to sit on the pale
blue Oriental couch nearby. He saw the high color in Cat's
cheeks and her unsureness. She was just as scared as he was.
A load slid off his shoulders when he realized that, and
Slade poured her some brandy, handing her the crystal
snifter after she had sat down. Cat curled up, her long,
coltish legs tucked beneath her body. Her hair was newly
brushed and he could smell her showered freshness.

"Thank you," Cat murmured, lifting the snifter to her lips. The apricot scent flowed across her tongue, warming her mouth and going down smoothly, relaxing her in its wake. Cat watched as Slade sat down, his hip only inches from her knees. A hesitant smile touched her lips. "I think we both needed this."

"Yeah," Slade agreed. He noticed that Cat still wore the opal ring and that gave him hope. "You're wearing the ring."

Cat smiled gently, lifting her hand to study the iridescent colors of the oval gem. "How could I not wear it?" She held Slade's gaze. "You didn't have to make all this jewelry for me."

"Why do you think I did it?"

The silence wove between them as Cat considered his quietly asked question. She struggled to answer. "I honestly don't know, Slade."

"Guess."

She grimaced. "I'm not very good at guessing games. Why don't you just tell me why you did it?"

"Because I want to know what you thought my intentions were toward you."

Cat closed her eyes, pain in her voice. "Slade, you don't make this easy on me. The worst possible reason you might have done it was to buy my forgiveness for tricking me into doing something you wanted from me." She opened her eyes, meeting his opaque stare. "You know that, if nothing else, I try to be an honorable person. My word is my bond. You knew that by saving my life I would owe you. And you used that knowledge in a way that I'd never have expected."

He turned the snifter slowly around between his large hands. "All right, that's the worst scenario. Any others?"

"That the gift was a way of apologizing to me?"

"Possibly. What else?"

Cat heard the strain in his voice. "No. None that I can see. Is there another, Slade?"

He nodded. "Yeah. All my life I'd been bitten by green fire, the dream of finding an emerald mine. There's just something about the gem that fascinates me. I'd set up my entire life-style and reason for being a geologist to make the big find." Slade pinned her with his gaze. "It wasn't for the money, but just for the sheer challenge of finding such a rare gemstone. I got close in Brazil when I discovered the tourmaline deposits at El Camino. That just made me that much more determined and thirsty to find green fire. I knew it was close; I could feel it in my bones like a gold prospector can feel when he's approaching a vein. I could taste it. And then, it happened: that poker game in Bogotá changed my life. Or I thought it had," he added wryly.

Slade held her unwavering gaze. "I then went in search of the very best mining engineer I could find. I sought you out. When I first saw you in that shack, Cat, I didn't know what to expect. I never realized how beautiful you were, besides being accomplished and an expert in your field. The magazine photos didn't do you justice. Anyway, when that cave-in occurred, I was worried for you. And those next three days of staying in contact with you on the radio slowly began to change me. It was subtle at first, and I can't exactly find words to tell you how you began to affect me and my objectives. And then I found myself wanting you to myself for more than just professional reasons."

Slade placed the snifter on the coffee table in front of them and stood up, thrusting his hands deep into the pockets of his trousers. His face was etched harshly with conflicting emotions as he turned and continued in a low timbre. "For eight weeks, you lived with me. Until the day of our argument and my blunder trying to play amateur psychologist with you, I never realized just how much you had come to mean to me." He ran his fingers through his hair. "I guess I had given up finding a woman to share my world. It took something like this to make me discover it, Cat.

"When I came back to the ranch, I went to my office and searched through every gemstone I'd collected over the years. I wanted to find something that would reflect to you just what you had become to me in this past month." The tension in Slade's face dissolved. "I didn't make the opals as an apology or to buy anything from you, Cat. I was hoping they would show you what I hadn't been able to do with any success, to tell you that you mean far more to me than green fire . . ."

Cat touched the warm, fiery-colored opal, tears blurring her vision. "I'm sorry I thought the worst, Slade. I didn't know . . ."

He shrugged almost painfully and sat down next to her. "I haven't exactly been good at expressing myself, either, Cat. And for that, I also apologize." He reached out, capturing her right hand, holding her luminous gaze. "You were hurting so much inside from the trauma and the mine accident that I wanted to help you, and I blurted out the first half-baked idea that came to mind. I figured that if I could set you up under a condition where you'd be forced to face your fear, it would work out fine. I could see my idea wasn't having a positive effect on you. I got panicky." His words came out low and tortured. "The last thing I wanted from you was a payment of your life for the mine. My good intentions to get you to conquer your fear backfired. Sometimes, my mouth gets ahead of my thoughts. Or, at least, dealing with you it does."

Cat murmured his name softly, sliding her hand along his sandpapery cheek. "I shouldn't believe you, Slade, but I do. There's something that keeps drawing us back to each other no matter how much we've hurt each other. What is it about you that makes me believe you? What?"

Slade closed his eyes, feeling the warm caress of her hand across his flesh. He brought Cat into his arms and she sank against him, trusting him once again. Nuzzling her neck and shoulders with a flurry of moist kisses, he inhaled her fem-

inine fragrance. "I don't know, sweetheart, I don't know."
He felt Cat stiffen as he pressed a kiss between the cleavage
of her taut, firm breasts before he raised his head. Reading
her tender expression, he saw her eyes were lustrous and
warm, with invitation in their green, sultry depths.

"The past ten days have been hell on both of us," Slade
told her thickly. "You're under no obligation to me for
saving your life, Cat. I would do it a hundred times over.
This mine down in Colombia has no strings attached to you
or me. I don't want you captive to me out of guilt. If you
choose to become involved with it, it's because you want to.
I'm going to fly to Colombia Monday morning. If you want
to fly down with me, fine. If you don't, I'll understand."
Slade stared down at her widening eyes. "No more pressure on you, Cat. Kai made me realize that no one has the
right to tell you how to live your life. If you're afraid to go
back down in a mine, that's something you have to deal with
in your own way and time. I can't force you back into a
shaft before you're ready. As much as I wish your life was
in my hands, it's not." He feathered a kiss across her parting lips, tasting the apricot brandy on them.

"Wait..." she pleaded breathlessly, palms flat against his
powerful chest. "Slade...who would you get to put that
mine shaft in for you, then?"

"I don't know yet. It doesn't matter."

"But it does matter!"

Slade's mouth curved upward and he slid his hands up the
sleeves of her arms. "Not right now, it doesn't."

Cat licked her lips, trying to pull from the heated cocoon
spinning around both of them. "Slade, listen to me. We're
not done talking."

He released her, sensing her concern. "All right, go
ahead."

"You're really serious about this, getting another engineer?"

"Yes."

Cat muttered something under her breath, searching Slade's features. "Look, that mine is going to be tricky to build. You've got very movable layers of shale and limestone that can quiver like a dog's back if there's even a slight earthquake tremor. Not every mining engineer has the experience that I have in building one to withstand that kind of unexpected stress."

Slade wanted to embrace her, realizing she was putting his safety above her own fear. "I'm aware of that. And I'll find someone who can do it."

Getting up, Cat paced the suite for several minutes. Finally, she turned to him, her face set. "Slade, I care what happens to you. I've just spent ten days preparing blueprints for the Verde. And frankly, there isn't anyone who can build that mine more safely than I can."

"I believe you, Cat. But you don't have to go. I don't want you down there unless you're sure you're ready to tackle mine entry."

She gave him a frustrated look. "Damn it, Slade, if I didn't know any better, I'd say you were using reverse psychology on me to get me to go down there with you!" She stamped her bare foot to underscore the depth of her feeling. "Not only that, you make me feel like a child! And no one has ever brought out those feelings in me like you have." She knotted her fists. "I can't live with you. I can't live without you. On the other hand, I'm so damned scared of having to go into a mine that I turn icy cold all over."

He rose, barely aware of most of what she'd said. "You can't live without me?" Slade asked, coming up and placing his hands on her shoulders.

Petulantly, Cat shot him a withering look. "I said it, didn't I?"

"Really? You kinda like being around me despite everything that's happened?"

"I can't live with you either, Slade. You drive me nuts. I used to be a stable, steady, sane person until you dropped into my life. I don't know which way is up anymore. Or down. Or sideways. When I get around you, everything else just kind of fades and there's only you..."

His smile increased like the radiance of the sun rising as he brought her to him. "There's you and me, Cat. Just you and me," he whispered, molding his mouth against those provocative lips that were just begging to be tamed. "That's all that matters..."

A soft moan slid up her throat as Cat melted a little more beneath Slade's caressing kiss. So much was happening at once. She could barely think coherently beneath his fiery, coaxing touch. A shiver of need jolted through her as his tongue stroked each corner of her mouth, a tantalizing promise of more to come if she wanted him. An ache grew deep within her and Cat realized that only Slade had the magic to bring her to surrender. He was barely caressing her and she could feel him controlling himself for her sake.

Breathlessly, Cat eased away, seeing how his hooded eyes smoldered with a vibrant blue fire of their own. A delicious warmth flowed down through her as Slade lifted her into his arms. Cat sighed, resting her head against his, closing her eyes. "You're not an easy man to understand," she murmured.

Slade looked down at Cat as he carried her into the darkness of his bedroom. "I know that, sweetheart. Let's heal some of the wounds that still stand between us. When the sun rises tomorrow, we'll both be the better for it."

Cat smiled as he gently laid her down on the quilted satin surface of the huge king-size bed. As she awaited him, he slowly undressed. Like the mountains carved out of the enduring earth, he was beautiful to behold. Every angle of his darkly bronzed body slipped like a well-fitted plane into the next. Slade's chest was covered with a mat of dark, fine hair. His shoulders were broad, thrown back naturally, shouting of his rugged heritage. A sleek torso flowed smoothly into narrowed hips and long, muscular thighs to lean but finely sculpted calves. As Slade moved to her side, Cat whispered, "You're beautiful..."

She ran her fingers lightly across his shoulders, feeling his silent, coiled strength. Slade's hands settled around her, moving slowly and sending a sheet of prickling fire outward toward her tightening belly.

A growl reverberated in Slade's throat as she slid her hand across his chest, following the wiry carpet of hair down across the slab hardness of his stomach to—

"Cat," Slade growled savagely, pulling her tight against him. He gasped, unprepared for the caress of her warm fingers around him. As he crushed her hard against him, he branded her lips with a fiery kiss, stealing the breath from her. The pebbled hardness of her nipples pleasantly chafed the wall of his chest, taunting him. In one motion, he slid his hand beneath the terry-cloth robe revealing first one breast and then the other. Slade gave her no chance to protest, smothering her full, glistening lips with another kiss. His long, teasing kiss demanded that she submit fully beneath his onslaught. Tonight, he wanted to please Cat as he had no other woman. Tonight was for her; tonight was for healing...

Dizziness sang through Cat as she lay helplessly in the path of Slade's ravishment. His lips created a trail of blazing fire from her earlobe, down her neck, across her collarbones and then... A gasp tore from her as his mouth settled over the first nipple. Reflexively, Cat's fingers dug into his bunched shoulder muscles, and she arched her entire body against him. Fire rippled outward, as if a stone had been tossed into the quiet surface of a deep pond, until a powerful, aching sensation gripped her loins. Each sucking motion drove her farther and farther from rational thought. She was flung into a universe where only emotion ruled.

Slade felt Cat's surrender to him, the discovery filling him with potency. She trusted him entirely. He lay on his back and pulled her gently on top of him. The instant her hip brushed his aching body, a hiss of air came from between his clenched teeth. Her eyes were barely open, her lips wet with further invitation as he settled her above him. Slade saw vague confusion register in her desire-clouded emerald eyes. He kept his hands on each of her arms to prevent her from falling.

"Your ribs," he explained thickly. "If I lie on you, I could hurt you. And I don't want to do that. For now, this is best." Slade smiled up into the shadowy planes of her radiant face and placed his hands on her hips, helping to guide her. "Come to me, sweet Cat, woman of the earth, my woman..."

A cry of pleasure tore from her as she settled down on him, her fingers digging into his arms. The fire that had simmered so long within her finally burst into brilliant life. One twist of his hips sent such a powerful tidal wave of pleasure that Cat sobbed. Together they were fused like molten, volcanic lava, each stroke, each movement a little deeper, more giving, taking and melding than the last. He whispered her name like a prayer given those who hold the earth in reverence. She felt him return all she meant to him in those shattering moments that tore a cry from within her. Cat went spinning off in a directionless universe of splintered sunlight. And then, precious moments later, Slade stiffened, groaned and clung to her as if to life itself. As she leaned down on him, her cheek against his warm, damp chest, she knew they had given each other the most precious gift of all.

Slade absently ran his fingers over her drying back, marveling at her natural beauty. Cat lay beside him, one hand across his chest, one leg across his. He smiled into the darkness. "Has anyone ever told you how giving and loving you are?"

A quiver of pleasure spun through Cat as she languished in the timbre of his voice. "Not like you have," she whispered, incredibly satiated and fulfilled.

"Every time I hold a handful of warm earth in my hands, I can feel the life in it." Slade splayed his hand across her shoulder, pressing Cat gently to him, kissing her damp temple. "I like you; you're the earth. You're warm, yielding, fertile and incredibly alive."

A soft smile played on her lips as she weakly ran her hand across the drying hair of his chest. "Then you're the ocean: quixotic, mysterious and powerfully emotional."

Slade turned thoughtful as he eased to his side so that he could see her. He cupped Cat's cheek, watching as her eyes barely opened and focused on him. "Believe me when I tell you that I've never made such incredible love with a woman as I have with you."

Cat felt euphoric. "Do you always have the right words?" she asked in a wispy voice, content to close her eyes and simply drink in his touch, his honeyed tone and male essence.

Slade's chuckle was derisive. "No. You know that better than anyone. I've blundered and tripped all over myself with you. And like the earth, you've forgiven me." He reached down, pulling up a sheet to cover them. He drew Cat into his arms, holding her gently for fear of putting too much pressure on her recently healed ribs. "My beautiful earth mother," he teased her huskily. "Let me hold you close to my heart."

Cat nuzzled beneath Slade's jaw, content as never before. For once, she was washed free of all her anxieties and fears. Slade had cleansed her; he had filled her with himself and given back to her. The last words she spoke before everything receded were, "You're healing me, Slade..."

The sun had barely edged along the horizon when Cat slowly awoke around six o'clock, unsure why she had left the cradling embrace of her euphoric dreams. She lay quietly in Slade's arms, a soft smile touching her mouth as he occasionally snored. One lock of dark hair had dropped across his smooth brow and she gently coaxed it back into place. For no reason, Cat was glad she was awake and Slade was still asleep. It gave her a chance to study him in the morning light.

Where are we going with one another? she wondered as she lay in his arms. *We have such a roller-coaster relationship. You lift me up higher than I've ever been and yet, like the restless ocean you are, you have the capacity to hurl me deeper into a morass than anyone ever has.* Cat studied Slade intently, trying to find the answers she sought. Last night, when he'd told her she didn't have to build that mine, she had felt a deep sense of relief. Slade had no ulterior motives where she was concerned, and he had proved it by releasing her from any obligation to him. She didn't want anything to happen to Slade. And yet, until that moment, Cat hadn't realized just how much he meant to her.

What was that saying? You must love someone enough to let them go, and if they come back to you it's from love. But if they leave and don't return, perhaps love was never there, anyway. Cat's eyes darkened as she focused on Slade's features. *Do I love you? I don't know. I'm not sure.* And then she almost laughed aloud because Slade had admitted as much to her last night: that she had somehow become more important to him than anything else in his life. Did he love her? He hadn't said so. And she was old enough to know that if Slade did, he'd tell her in time. Yes, time...time would yield what was and was not between them.

Cat found herself wanting a chance to find out where life would lead them. They'd had a rocky start with one another, and she knew it would become rockier because they had another equally powerful test before them: entering a mine. Now, however, Cat no longer struggled with the fear because she knew that when the time came, Slade would be there to help her.

Suddenly shaky at the thought, Cat grew uncomfortable. Slade would receive nothing from her, while she would be taking from him. Well, she must trust Slade on this point, let him guide and help her. All she had to do was communicate when she was in trouble. Somehow, Slade made her feel relaxed, almost eager to work with him, no matter what dangers the mine posed to either of them.

"Are you ready?"

Slade's tone was filled with amusement as he held Cat with one arm, his other hand wrapped around the pole of the carousel horse they sat upon.

A peal of laughter burst from Cat as she felt the merry-go-round gently start to move. She cast a look over at Kai and Matt, sitting haphazardly on another horse ahead of them. "Ready," she promised. Rich, warm feelings flowed through Cat as the memory of their night and day together came back to her.

Slade grinned happily. "After this, how about a round of bumper cars?" He kept a firm grip on Cat so she wouldn't fall as the horse moved up and down in time with the music. "Where's that sense of challenge you always like to grab by the horns, Kincaid?"

"Challenges, not death-defying feats, Donovan! Agh!" She nearly lost her balance when Slade moved around on the rear of the horse. Cat clung to the pole, but the carousel horse simply wasn't big enough for both of them. Still, she enjoyed Slade's closeness. She leaned back, catching his dancing sapphire gaze. "No bumper cars. Do you want me to crack my ribs again?"

Slade looked crestfallen. "Oh, sorry. I forgot." He brightened. "The Ferris wheel, then?"

With a moan, Cat said, "I'll think about it."

"I'll buy you cotton candy as a bribe. No Ferris wheel, no cotton candy," he teased, nibbling gently on her exposed earlobe.

With a laugh, Cat dodged his moist, tantalizing tongue. "You're such a rogue, Slade Donovan! You and Matt go on the Ferris wheel. Kai and I will find something tamer to ride.

"Come on, Kai," Cat said, as they walked out the exit. She pointed toward the merry-go-round again. "I think we girls ought to stick together. Men can take all the wild rides they want, just like how they drove cars when they were eighteen: without us."

Kai giggled and followed Cat after the men were safely aboard the huge Ferris wheel. "I think we ought to have liability insurance around Slade and Matt," Kai said good-naturedly.

Cat couldn't stop laughing as they made their way back up to the brightly painted horses. The men had bought them each cotton candy and they sat aboard their chargers waiting for the music and movement to begin.

Kai's eyes gleamed with humor. "It feels strange to be at an amusement park again. I haven't done this since I was a kid of fourteen."

"I suspect Slade never grew up," Cat pointed out dryly, watching the Ferris wheel slowly start rotating in the distance.

"Ever since Slade bought the ranch, things haven't been the same out in Del Rio, either." Kai chortled. Slowly, the horses began to rise and fall beneath them, the music lilting and infectious.

"I can imagine. Slade constantly catches me by surprise," Cat agreed.

"Welcome to the club!" Kai's smile was warm. "Matt and I have been hoping for such a long time that Slade would find someone like you, Cat." She reached out, squeezing her hand for a moment. "We can tell Slade loves you."

Shock almost made her fall off her horse. Cat stared at Kai. "Slade loves me?"

"You know that misunderstanding you two had two weeks ago?"

"Yes?"

"Slade came over that day, Cat. He wanted to talk so I dragged him into the living room to tell me why he was so moon-eyed."

"Moon-eyed?"

Kai grinned. "A Texas expression. It means sad."

"I see."

"I pulled everything out of Slade, piece by piece," Kai went on. She flashed Cat an understanding look. "He felt terrible about what he said to you. I don't want to seem like a nosy neighbor or anything, and I know it's none of our business, but Slade sometimes, in his haste to make something right that's going wrong, digs himself a deeper hole."

Cat nodded. "He did, Kai. But he apologized, too."

"Then things are better between you?"

Better? Cat thought, a rush of heat suffusing her. "Yes, much better," she reassured Kai.

"Oh, wonderful!"

Fifteen minutes later, Slade and Matt swooped up from behind them, each grabbing his respective woman.

"Gotcha!" Slade growled, whisking Cat off the horse and into his arms.

Her eyes widened considerably as they wobbled off balance for a second before righting themselves. "You're going to kill me, Slade Donovan!"

He chuckled and gently lowered her to the ground. "Have I yet?" he demanded archly.

"It's just a matter of where and when," Cat muttered as his large hands spanned her waist and he slipped behind her.

"Trust me," he coaxed near her ear, kissing her quickly.

Cat smiled, melting all over again at his nearness. "I do and you know it."

"Mmm, do you ever."

For the next three hours, Cat felt like a teenager again. The fact that they were one of the few older couples at the amusement park that Saturday night didn't bother them. She and Kai watched the men ride the bumper cars, Slade trying to show off for her by outmaneuvering Matt on the slick steel surface of the arena. The safety of the rail was comforting as Slade missed Matt and collided with two ten-year-olds because he couldn't control the direction of his car. Cat howled with laughter until her ribs started to hurt. But it was worth it just to laugh freely again. The ten-year-olds quickly disengaged themselves from Slade's plodding car and he waved to her. Only his pride had been impaired in the melee. Matt hustled his bumper car through an opening and smashed Slade's car from the other side of the enclosure. Slade spent the remainder of the ride backing out of the corner, only to be hit and driven back into it by every gleeful kid around. The entire rink broke into cheers as Slade drew a white handkerchief from his back pocket and waved it above his head in surrender, bowing to his ill-begotten fate.

Afterward, they drove to a nearby A & W. Cat had to laugh. Somehow a silver Mercedes-Benz just didn't look at home among all the souped-up pickups and gussied-up vans that jammed the place. But Slade was oblivious; he was having too much fun ordering from the machine. Soon a waitress on roller skates came out with a tray loaded with hamburgers, icy glasses of root beer and hot french fries for their late-evening snack. The car rang with nonstop laughter, and most of the time, Cat was laughing so hard that tears came to her eyes.

"Honestly," Cat told everyone, "I can't ever remember having had a better time."

Slade was pleased and fed Cat some more french fries.

"My stomach aches from laughing so much," Kai confided.

"My rear is bruised," Matt added dolefully, giving Slade an accusing look.

"My ribs hurt," Cat said, smiling at Slade, "but it was worth it."

Kai prodded Slade. "Come on, big guy, something has to hurt on you, too. After all, you were the one who thought he was a kamikaze pilot dive-bombing all those poor, defenseless kids out there in the bumper-car ring."

Slade's laughter was deep and rolling. He threw up both his hands in a gesture of peace. "Hey, what can I say? I'm just a kid trapped in a thirty-five-year-old body." He showed them a scraped elbow. "See? Do I get a Purple Heart for all my efforts?"

The car rocked with more laughter. An intense feeling of warmth encircled Cat as she met Slade's cobalt eyes and his roguish smile. So much was happening so quickly. One night in his arms had deeply changed her, for Slade made her feel good about herself, despite everything.

"Happy?" Slade asked later, pulling her into his arms.

Cat contentedly fitted herself beside him, the satin of her apricot silk gown molding against his heated, hard body. She sighed, glad to be in his arms, his breath moist across her cheek.

"Happy?" she murmured throatily, sliding her arms around his neck. "I'm floating."

He chuckled, kissing her cheek, eyes and nose, and then rested his mouth against her smiling, lush lips that parted to his advance. "Even with that bruise I found on your pretty derriere? What did you do, fall off the carousel horse?"

Cat leaned up, molding her lips to his strong, male mouth, lost in the heat of their tender exchange. His jaw was rough against her cheek, his skin smelled of soap and his hair was damp beneath her gentle fingers. "You know I got it when you dragged me off the horse," she teased. Slade's lips caught hers in a devouring kiss, and she melted as his knowing touch set her on fire again. "Oh, Slade, somehow you take the hurt away from me..." Cat rested against him, staring up into his smoldering blue eyes as he lay above her.

"Don't sound so surprised, sweetheart. Occasionally, people can do good things for one another."

"You make me feel magical," Cat said, cupping his stubborn jaw. Then with a tremulous sigh, she whispered, "I don't know when I've ever felt happier, or laughed so much. You're good for me."

"We're good for each other; it's not a one-way street, Cat." Slade tunneled his fingers through her silky hair, his voice deep with emotion. "We've had a rough and, if you'll pardon the pun, rocky start." He grimaced. "And it can get rockier."

She frowned, hearing the worry in his voice. "What do you mean?"

"Are you planning on going down to Bogotá with me on Monday?"

"Yes."

Slade rested his hand against her back and hip. "Look, I meant what I said about your not going. You could stay at the ranch, if you want or—go to another job assignment." It hurt to say the last of that sentence. "I think too much of you, Cat, and what might be, to have you go down to Bogotá unless you're very clear as to why you're going. I don't want you to go out of guilt. The slate is clean between us."

The troubled look in Slade's eyes made her heart wrench, and Cat offered him a slight smile. "I'm very clear about why I'm going down there with you, Slade. It's not out of guilt."

He accepted her explanation. Cat and their relationship were more important to him than the mine. The softness of her skin as he stroked her cheek sent another wave of exquisite longing through him. "It's going to be dangerous, Cat."

"What mine isn't?"

"I mean outside the mine. You'll have to wear a pistol at all times, and we'll be followed and watched. You'll have to have eyes in the back of your head."

"I've been in some pretty tense situations before, Slade. I'm no stranger to carrying a pistol when I have to. My dad taught me how to hit what I aimed at."

"Those guaqueros are tough and dangerous. They've been bred and raised in the back alleys of Bogotá's slums. If they think you're carrying an emerald on you, they'll slit your throat to get it."

Cat gave an exasperated sigh. "Slade, why, all of a sudden, are you trying to scare me out of going?"

"Because," he said thickly, leaning down to capture her lips, "your life means more to me than green fire."

Chapter Ten

Pools of sweat had darkened the color of Slade's khaki short-sleeved shirt, and Cat wiped her brow with the back of her hand, grimacing. For seventy-five miles, they had bumped along in a ten-year-old Jeep on the only rutted dirt road leading from Bogotá to the emerald fields of the Muzo Valley. They passed several motley-looking groups of men, all stripped to the waist, their coffee-colored skin glistening from the harsh sun overhead and the humidity of the surrounding tropical forest. When they were near the guaqueros, Cat placed her hand over the handle of her revolver. The guaqueros glared, their dark, narrowed eyes quickly appraising Cat and Slade, trying to determine whether they were carrying emeralds.

Cat glanced over at Slade. All his attention was focused on keeping the Jeep on the miserable excuse for a road they were on. It had been washed out due to an unexpected thunderstorm the day before. Mud was everywhere. The guaqueros were covered with mud; only the whites of their wary eyes were visible. Despite the hardships, however, Cat was happy. She was back in the field once again, braving the inhospitable elements that seemed to come with sinking a shaft in some remote part of the world. Only when she thought about having to go in and inspect the mine shaft soon to be under construction did the black fear envelop her.

They crossed the brackish Rio Itoco on their way past Muzo Valley. The river's once-clear waters had turned black with gritty shale washed down into it by the heartless bulldozers. Cat saw hundreds of guaqueros in the river at the V of the valley, backs bent as they sluiced through the river's lifeblood. They sought the one precious pebble that would bring them a better life. Slade had told her that if a guaquero found one emerald a year he was lucky. In the same breath, he'd said: "The instant the emerald is found, the smart guaquero will hide it. If others have seen him discover it, they'll ambush him on the only road to Bogotá. If he's smart, he'll sell it to one of the esmeralderos who wait on the banks of the Rio Itoco."

Her heart went out to the treasure seekers. Cat saw not only men, but women and children amongst those who crowded in the Rio Itoco's shallow waters.

"You never said there were women and children out here, Slade."

It was his turn to grimace. He took off the baseball cap he wore to protect himself from the overhead sun. Blinding shafts stole in between the straight *pao d'arco* trees swathed in reptilian-looking vines. "Didn't want to depress you, Cat. It's a sad state of affairs down here. The women and even the children dig tunnels into Muzo's shale mountains at night. Sometimes they suffocate because of lack of oxygen in the longer tunnels. Sometimes they die in cave-ins." He glanced at her, seeing the anguish register on her features. That was one more thing he liked about Cat: she was incapable of hiding her reactions. He gripped her hand momentarily, giving it a squeeze. "It's a perilous life at best, looking for green fire," he said.

The jungle closed around them once again and the frequent foot traffic of guaqueros in the Rio Itoco area shrank as the miles fell away. Humic acids of decayed vegetation surrounded them and Cat spotted a white monkey above them on one of the cable-strong vines before he went into hiding. The macaws' brilliant reds, blues and yellows made the dark, almost forbidding jungle come alive. Ferns, some as high as a man, cluttered the jungle floor, as did ringworm cassia and angel's trumpet shrubs. Perhaps most beautiful of all were the multicolored orchids, peeking out in breathtaking splendor to relieve the green walls on either side of the thin ribbon of a dirt road.

The odors of life and death clung to Cat's nostrils as Slade swung the Jeep up and out of the Muzo valley. The air was fresher and less humid as they traversed a shrinking road across the ridge, heading for Gato Valley. Compared to Muzo, Gato was spared man's plundering. No human beings were in sight. Gato, named after the jaguars that ruled the valley, seethed with wildlife and birds. Cat began to relax and let go of her pistol. Slade had given her stern warning that if a guaquero made any kind of move toward them, she was to draw the gun and ask questions later.

By the time they reached the third and final valley, Silla de Montar, the sun was a red orb hanging low on the horizon. Cat was bruised and banged from the tortuous ride. From the rim of the valley, she saw the two peaks that created the saddle for which the valley had been named. On the left was Caballo Mountain, where Slade and Alvin owned the Verde mine land. Clothed in the green raiment of jungle, Caballo gave no hint of what lay beneath its verdant mantle. Cat smiled, thinking how skillfully the earth hid her treasure from passersby. Only Slade's patient, methodical channel samplings had hinted of the wealth that lay on Caballo and down into the mountain's heart of lime-stone and shale.

"It's beautiful here," she told him, meaning it.

"The air's a little less humid over here than at Muzo," Slade commented, aiming the nose of the sturdy Jeep down a steep incline toward the valley floor. "I think it's because of the higher elevation." He flashed her a tired smile. "We'll be working up on Caballo and not down in the valley. That's a plus, believe me."

"More like Chivor's mines," Cat agreed. Her short-sleeved cotton shirt gave her some relief from the static heat and sweltering humidity. She took the red neckerchief she always wore out in the field and wiped the latest layer of grit and sweat off her face. In the distance, she could see the faint outline of two tented camps. Halfway up Caballo sat a smaller camp with three olive-drab tents and one fire. About a quarter of a mile below that was a small city of tents, bustling with men and activity. Construction machinery sat behind the main camp, steel chargers that looked dark and forbidding in the jungle twilight. In the valley, Cat could barely make out huge, neat piles of posts and stulls to be used in the creation of the mine shaft. Electricity was provided by a number of diesel generators, now heard faintly in the distance. All the comforts of home, Cat decided with satisfaction. Suddenly excited, she looked forward to meeting Alvin Moody, Slade's partner.

Cat couldn't resist a smile when she saw Alvin. He was stooped over a fire, stirring the contents of a black kettle, when he saw them. Slade hadn't exaggerated the facts, she saw as Alvin rose to his full height. He looked like an honest-to-God Texas legend come to life: a ten-gallon straw hat was angled low on his silver hair and a caterpillar mustache sat above his lean mouth. A long, brown, chewed-up cigar was clamped between his teeth. Cat turned to Slade as he braked the Jeep to a halt.

"Alvin looks like a page torn out of the 1860s," she said.

Slade grinned, shutting the Jeep off. "That's Alvin, all right."

"He's dressed like a marshall from Dodge City—leather vest and two six-shooters low on his hips," she pointed out gleefully.

"This is Dodge City and he is the sheriff, for all intents and purposes of this camp," Slade growled. "Those two pearl-handled Colts he carries are the real thing. He's used them a time or two, believe me."

Cat gratefully slid out of the Jeep, her muscles protesting as she stretched to unknot all the kinks in her back and rear. "Where's his badge?"

"Those Colts are his badge and they do all the necessary talking for him." Slade came around the Jeep, sliding his hand beneath her left elbow. "Come on, he's been waiting to meet you."

She laughed. "The big question is, am I ready to meet him! My God, he's a giant of a man!"

"Texas born and bred, sweetheart. In that state, they don't do anything on a small scale."

Cat agreed. As they drew up to Alvin, who stood with his large hands resting comfortably on the handles of his low-slung Colts, he grinned.

"Say," he crowed, sweeping off his hat in a courtly gesture, "you ugly-lookin' rock hound, you never said how purty this little filly was."

"Hi, Alvin. The name's Cat, Cat Kincaid." She extended her hand, grinning broadly.

Alvin gripped her hand, refusing to relinquish it as Slade stood nearby.

"If I'd told you how pretty she was, Alvin, you'd have left this pit and come back to Texas," Slade said, slapping him on the back.

"That's for sure, Slade. Miss Cat, welcome to the Verde mine," he told her, sweeping his arm toward Caballo

Mountain just above them. His pale blue eyes twinkled. "We're right glad you're here to help us."

"Thanks, Alvin." Cat cast a glance over at Slade. "Your partner had to do a lot of talking to get me out here."

Alvin chortled and finally released her hand. He settled the huge hat back on his head. "This Texan's got more ways to twist a cat's tail than even I do. I figured if anyone could talk you into consulting for us instead of that kangaroo outfit in Australia, Slade could do it. By Gawd, I was right. You're here and that's all that matters."

Slade looked around, taking off his cap and stuffing it in the back pocket of his jeans. "What's cooking, Alvin?"

Alvin gave him a hint of a smile from beneath his mustache. "In my kettle or around Caballo?"

Hunkering down over the kettle, Slade stirred it briefly. "Both."

Alvin motioned for Cat to sit down on a log near the fire. "We got us some sidewinders prowlin' around, Slade." He patted his Colts affectionately. "Nothing I can't take care of."

"How many?"

"About half a dozen guaqueros have been hoverin' around since the mining equipment and workers was brought in." He pointed to the left, toward the shadowy mountain. "Everything you ordered is here—bulldozers, backhoes, shaft equipment. The whole kit and caboodle. That pack of guaqueros came with it." He squinted to the east of them. "As far as I can tell, they're makin' camp up there on Lazo Mountain and waitin'."

Cat glanced at Slade, watching the frown on his face deepen. "Waiting for what, Alvin?" she asked quietly, almost afraid to hear the answer.

The Texan joined them, pulling three tin plates from a nearby wooden trunk that had seen better days. "They smell green fire, Miss Cat. This bunch has a nose for emeralds like a starvin' coyote does for meat on the hoof. Right now, they're being real patient and checkin' us out." Alvin cocked his head in Slade's direction. "El Tigre is headin' up that bunch of no goods."

Slade scowled. "Him?"

"Who's El Tigre?" Cat asked, suddenly interested.

Alvin heaped a tin plate with the vittles. "One of the meanest two-eyed snakes in the business of being a gua-quero. He's a puny little bastard. Lean as a whippet, with eyes like a viper. He got his nickname over at Muzo be-cause of his reputation of jumpin' other guaqueros after they've found green fire."

With a muttered curse, Slade stood and came over to where Alvin was doling out the food. "He's been accused of kidnapping, raping and thievery. Not necessarily in that or-der."

Her eyes widened. "Raping?"

"Sure," Alvin snorted, handing her a plate. "Men ain't the only ones to hunt for green fire. We got some tough women who pan right alongside the other guaqueros. El Tigre doesn't care if it's a male or female who has the em-erald on them. He treats both sexes equally. If they don't give 'em the green fire, he'll do whatever's necessary to get it. That can be anything from torture to murder. If the gua-quero's smart, he or she will hand over the loot and thank God for getting away alive. Sometimes, just for the hell of it, El Tigre will butcher his victim anyway as a warning to other guaqueros. There's a hundred-thousand-peso war-rant out for his arrest by the owners of the Muzo mines." Alvin snorted. "El Tigre was born and raised in these mountains. Ain't no one gonna catch that oily weasel alive." He patted one Colt. "That's why you wear these at all times, Miss Cat. You eat, live and sleep with 'em."

Cat took the tin plate, now covered with beans and something with a red sauce on it. She sniffed it cautiously.

"That's rum beans for a main course," Alvin explained, "and sourdough bread and the tomatoes with biscuits is called pooch. It'll stick to your ribs."

Cat grinned. "As long as it doesn't grow hair on my chest, Alvin."

Alvin slapped his thigh, his laughter sounding like the rumble of thunder in his large chest. "Spunky little filly, ain't she? I like her, Slade. She's got a down-home sense of humor."

With a grin, Alvin served up a heaping plate for Slade and himself. The Texan sat across from them at the fire, wolfing down his portion of the food. "All I cook is cowboy food served on the open ranges of Texas. Rum beans has some bacon, molasses, mustard and a half a cup of good hundred-and-eighty-proof rum in it. Pooch is an old cowboy dessert."

The beans were tasty, maybe because she was starved. Alvin was a fine cook, Cat admitted. She smiled at him. "Well, I know you aren't going to try and poison me with your cooking, Alvin. This stuff is pretty good."

Alvin gave her an effusive grin, pleased by her praise. "I'll make you a real 'welcome to the Verde mine meal' tomorrow night, Miss Cat. I'll even throw in the horse-thief special for dessert. Hell, there ain't a cowboy alive who wouldn't ride hard like a horse thief to get a bowl of it." He winked conspiratorially at Slade. "We'll have her puttin' a few pounds on that skinny frame of hers in no time."

"Alvin, I'm not a heifer to be fattened up," Cat warned. "I like being thin."

"I like her that way, too," Slade agreed, laughing.

Alvin looked at them and said nothing, a knowing gleam in his eyes. "I'll only make half the amount of horse-thief special, then."

"No, make all you want," Slade countered quickly. "I'll eat the leftovers."

"See what I mean, Miss Cat? Men will do anything to get that dessert."

"I can hardly wait until tomorrow night," she promised him.

Conversation gradually drifted to the equipment, the work timetable and a long business discussion. The sun dropped behind the saddle formed by the two mountains, and the surrounding jungle suddenly came alive with the songs of insects. The mosquitoes had been pesky earlier; now they were vicious. The trio saturated themselves with insect repellent so they could sit around the fire without being attacked by the bloodthirsty insects.

By eleven o'clock, Cat was barely able to keep her eyes open, despite the interesting conversation. She got up, brushing off the seat of her pants.

"Which way is my cot, Alvin?"

Both men stood. "You and Slade share that larger tent on the left. The smaller one on the right is mine. Slade says you know how to live in jungles."

She smiled. "As long as you've got a mosquito net over the cot, that's all I'll need."

"You got it, Miss Cat."

"Are the guards set?" Slade asked.

"Yeah."

"Can they be trusted?"

Alvin grinned tightly beneath his silvery mustache. "Didn't I tell you? I brought some of my boys down from one of my Texas ranches."

"How'd you get them to come?" Slade asked admiringly.

"I'm payin' them double what they'd get to sit on a cow pony back home. They don't mind totin' around a rifle and standin' watches to make sure we don't get our throats slit."

Cat shivered as unpleasant reality settled over her. Seeing her shiver and rub her arms, Slade came over, placing an arm around her waist.

"We'll see you in the morning, Alvin."

"G'night, you two."

"Good night," Cat responded, casting a worried look up at Slade. Even so, she felt safe with him near. He guided her over to their tent, which was illuminated by a lantern hung inside.

"I told you this was going to be a rough place," Slade warned her in a low voice. "You can still back out, Cat."

She shook her head. "A Kincaid never backs out. We only know one direction, Slade: forward."

He opened the flap for her and ducked in after she entered. The floor was made of plywood in an effort to keep most of the insects, snakes and rodents out. A cot sat on either side and Cat tested the sturdiness of one of them, then sat down, unlacing her boots. A porcelain basin filled with warm water sat between the cots.

"I hadn't counted on El Tigre being here," Slade muttered, stripping off his damp, sweaty shirt. His chest gleamed with perspiration as he quickly washed up.

"Can't you call in the Colombian police to capture him?"

Cat sat there watching Slade, realizing once again how beautiful a man he was. Then she smiled, because Slade didn't like that term applied to him. Nudging off her boots, she peeled off the heavy white cotton socks, waiting until Slade had finished with his spit bath.

Slade scrubbed his face vigorously, the cooling water a blessing against the humid heat. "Alvin and I are going to try and operate Verde like Chivor: a private mine with no state influence." Drying his face and arms, Slade threw the water out the door and refilled the basin from a five-gallon plastic jug that sat beneath the rickety table. He motioned that it was her turn to wash up.

"We haven't even begun mining operations, so what is El Tigre going to do?" she wondered, sending a worried look to Slade.

But Slade's mind was on other things. Taking off his khaki trousers, he dropped them at the end of his cot. Cat had shed her blouse, revealing her golden tan now deepened by the kerosene lamp above them. His body hardened for her all over again. Their living quarters might be spare, but that wasn't going to stop him from loving her. He'd like to time a trip to Bogotá after the mine was under construction, taking Cat back to civilization every once in a while. That way they could spend a night in a real bed with sheets, a hot shower and air-conditioning. Now, all that seemed like real luxury. Slade smiled, watching as she washed her arms and shoulders. His gaze moved slowly up and then down her tall, graceful body, and the stirring heat in his lower body became an aching reality. Slade was amused at himself. Cat made him hungry no matter what she was or wasn't wearing.

"El Tigre will watch, catalog and send his spies down to talk with our newly hired miners," Slade said, sitting down on his cot. "He's going to see who's the boss and who might know where the emeralds are located."

Cat toweled off, standing on the wooden floor in only her lingerie. She saw the cobalt flare in Slade's eyes and swallowed hard. How was it possible that only one smoldering look from him set her on fire? No man had ever made her feel her feminine power as he did. No man had ever made her feel so cherished. Shakily, Cat placed the folded cotton towel near the basin. Before she could turn, Slade had captured her hand, pulling her over to him. He guided Cat to his lap and she smiled languidly, placing her arms around his neck.

"Let's forget about the bandits, sweetheart," he told her thickly. "This is more important..."

As his hand slid lightly up her rib cage to cup her breast, Cat gasped, dissolving into his arms. Desire coursed through her as his thumb caressed her nipple, and she was lost to his warm, knowing mouth. Cat hungrily matched Slade's mounting desire with her own.

With a groan, Slade eased his lips from hers. Cat's languorous smile went straight to his heart as she rested weakly in his arms. "I want you," he growled.

"I know..." With a sigh, Cat sat up, running her fingers through his unruly hair.

Slade patted her nicely rounded rear, the silk of her panties driving him closer to total loss of control. He saw the exhaustion in her eyes and admitted he was equally fatigued by the long trip. As much as his heart and mind were willing to carry Cat over that delicious edge and love her, Slade put a check on his desires. He didn't want to take her to his bed when he was this groggy. No, he wanted both of them awake and eager. Right now, they were both ready to keel over. He contented himself with holding and sharing this precious time with Cat instead. Moments later, he whispered, "Come tomorrow morning, we're going to be putting in twelve- to sixteen-hour days. I may not be able to hold or kiss you out there, but remember how I feel about you. We'll make up for it here in the tent every night. Deal?"

With a small laugh, Cat embraced him. "Deal. But by the time we drag ourselves into the tent to sleep, we might be too tired to do anything."

"No, we won't," Slade promised, trailing a series of moist kisses from her throat to the provocative swell of her firm breasts. "Even when I'm eighty, you'll still turn me on. Come on, let's get some sleep. We're going to need it."

Reluctantly, Cat knew he was right. Slade's words filled her heart with unexpected joy. "I'll see you in the morning, Slade," she said, rising from his cot to return to hers.

After getting the mosquito netting in position, Cat settled down to sleep. Slade turned off the lantern, and a consuming blackness quickly descended on them. The sounds of insects mingling with the howl of monkeys provided a

strange symphony. Cat barely heard them, since her head
and heart centered on Slade's last comment. They were
growing closer to one another, and Slade was becoming her
friend as well as her lover. As her eyes closed, Cat recognized that theirs was an ideal combination. She had known
men in the past who only wanted her as a lover. Others she
had liked well enough to call friend, but they hadn't stirred
the embers of her heart or body to vibrant life. Slade did
both. She felt a never-ending thirst to satiate herself with
him in every way possible. As Cat sank into the oblivion of
sleep, she found herself glad, despite her own personal fears
about entering a mine, that she had come to Colombia.

Cat silently asked the earth to forgive their invasion as the
first bulldozers roared to life. They would clear away the
jungle over the site of the open pit location for the Verde
mine. She stood on a small rise, white hard hat in place,
watching as the powerful, growling noise of the huge machines reverberated through the surrounding jungle. Slade
was down there with the dozer operators, making sure each
man knew what he was doing. Alvin was coordinating other
activities with the hired miners. As soon as the earth had her
green mantle scraped free, the miners would carefully go
over the newly shorn earth and walk it, an inch at a time.
They would be looking for emeralds before another foot of
overburden was scraped away.

Cat turned and went back to the newly erected shack,
which would serve as her headquarters during the entire
venture. The Indians had built her a small building composed of *pao d'arco*, or trumpet tree. The wood from the
sometimes-two-hundred-foot giant would be the prime
source for shoring beams in the mine. As Cat spread out her
next blueprint on the roughened drafting-board surface, she
smiled. Some of her fear left as she focused on the
complexities of starting up such a project. With the throaty
sound of bulldozers in the background, Cat took off her

hard hat and sat down on the stool. Her final calculations would prepare for the excavation that would eventually become the mouth of the Verde mine shaft.

Night did not fall until after nine o'clock. Cat was still in her office on the hill, struggling with figures on her calculator, when the door opened. Thinking it was Slade, she turned, squinting from the light of the lantern that hung on the wall in front of her. She froze, her hand automatically moving to the Colt she carried on her hip.

"Do you want to die, *señorita*?"

Cat's mouth went dry as she stared at a dark-skinned man barely her height. He was dressed in black-and-gray military fatigues. Two bandoliers of ammunition crisscrossed his thin chest and an array of knives, grenades and other military hardware were held in web belts. Two more men, less well equipped, slipped inside, shutting the door quietly behind them. Her gaze moved back to the leader.

"What's going on?" she forced out. Her pulse was racing, her throat growing dry. The look on the leader's oblong face was anything but friendly.

He smiled, showing his crooked yellow teeth. Motioning to the maps, he said in halting English, "These are the maps where the emeralds are?"

Cat's fingers closed over the handle of the Colt, but she knew she would be foolish to try anything. All three soldiers carried weapons.

"No," she lied, "I'm an engineer. I build mines. These are construction blueprints."

His smile remained fixed as he slowly approached her. "I'm El Tigre, *señorita*. You have heard of me, no?" He twisted one drooping end of his greasy mustache, which hung down over his mouth.

Cat nodded carefully. "Yeah, I've heard of you."

"Then you know enough not to lie." He let his hand fall on an eight-inch sheathed blade in a black leather belt at his waist.

"I'm not lying."

El Tigre's brown, feral eyes glittered and he ruthlessly assessed her in the thick, mounting silence. "No? Then who knows where the emeralds are to be found?"

Cat slowly turned, letting her hand move away from her pistol. "Listen, the owners don't even know if there are emeralds here, Señor Tigre."

He laughed; it was a curt, harsh sound. "No one gathers this kind of equipment and men if there aren't emeralds, *señorita*. Don't think me stupid!"

There was no way to escape; only one door had been built into the shack. The portable radio was set on the drafting board, but she couldn't signal Slade or Alvin that she needed help. Cat had the feeling if she made even the slightest move to escape, the Colombian guaquero would turn violent, like a rabid dog.

"I've been hired to build, that's all. I'm not a geologist."

El Tigre stepped up to her. "Then who is?"

Cat winced, assailed by the sour, unwashed smell of his body. "The geologist is still up in the States."

"Maybe, maybe not..." He reached out to touch her cheek.

Cat reacted out of instinct. The sound of the slap she delivered to the man shot through the shack. She scrambled out of the chair, her back against the wall, braced for whatever retribution might come.

El Tigre cursed, holding his injured jaw, glaring at her. "You," he snarled softly, "will live to regret this. I'm not done with you, *señorita*." He grabbed several sets of blueprints, turned and snapped orders to his men. They opened the door, disappearing into the gathering night. Before he left, El Tigre lifted his finger, waving it at her threateningly. "No one touches me, especially a gringo woman. Sleep lightly, *señorita*, for I'll be back. And next time, have the information I want or your pretty face will look like this.'' He jerked the knife from its scabbard and stabbed it into the drafting board, tearing long, deep scars through the remaining maps and wood.

Slade had noticed three men go up to the construction shack on the hill. He had climbed down from the bulldozer he'd been manning to give the driver a break. By the time he had gotten to the Jeep and driven up the rutted excuse of a road, they were gone. He walked in the open door and immediately saw Cat slumped against the drawing board, her head resting in one hand. And then he saw the destroyed blueprints beneath her elbow and the damage made by the knife.

"Cat? What happened?"

She looked up, giving Slade a wobbly smile meant to neutralize the concern in his voice.

"El Tigre and two of his men dropped in for a chat—of sorts."

Slade was instantly at her side, anxiously turning her toward him. "Did he hurt you?"

"Scared the hell out of me, but no, he didn't hurt me." She leaned against Slade's powerful chest, sinking into his arms. Only then did Cat release a shaky sigh, showing just how scared she had been.

"Tell me everything," he ordered harshly.

Afterward, Slade gathered up the rest of the blueprints, rolled them and stored them in the Jeep. The scowl on his brow had deepened as Cat had relayed the sequence of events. As they bumped on down the road toward base camp, he muttered, "I didn't think he'd jump us this soon."

"We should probably thank him, Slade."

"Why?"

"If he's got that good a nose for green fire, then your mine is a success even before we get a chance to start looking for the calcite matrix."

With a snort, Slade agreed. He gripped the steering wheel hard, his knuckles whitening. "You think on your feet pretty good. Telling him the geologist was in the States was an excellent idea."

Cat traded a glance with him. "Only if he believes it." She tried to quell her own fear that if El Tigre knew Slade was the geologist, his life, too, was in very real danger. She tried to shove back the nightmare played out by her overactive imagination. El Tigre would torture the information out of Slade, and she knew it. After having met the bandit, there was no doubt in her mind that he'd kill Slade after he got the information. An icy shiver moved up her spine.

"There's no safe place, is there?" she asked hollowly.

Slade brought the Jeep to a halt near their tent. He reached over and covered her hand, now clenched against her thigh. "No, there isn't. Come on, let's tell Alvin what happened. We'll figure something out."

The next week went by without incident. Two of Alvin's cowboys guarded Cat at all times while she worked at the shack. The jungle was removed, leaving the black overburden of soil. Almost immediately, a thin white vein of exposed limestone was discovered by the miners. Cat had watched in fascination as Alvin and Slade went down with the miners, gently breaking up the soft limestone with crowbars, prying it apart to see if they could find the telltale white calcite. And all the time, her gaze moved restlessly across the wall of jungle surrounding them. Somewhere in there were El Tigre and his cutthroat band.

The five or six hours Cat slept, with Slade nearby, became important. She rarely saw him during the day, although he would drop in unexpectedly to see her. The stolen kisses, unseen by anyone in the privacy of the shack, became her sustenance. At night in the privacy of their tent Slade's hands would slide knowingly down her damp body, filling her with the fire of their longing and erasing her fears.

The mine became secondary to the threat El Tigre presented. Cat lived with the terror that the guaqueros would capture Slade.

Going back into the shack after dinner one night, Cat focused on her next project: getting the hardwood tree, *pao d'arco*, cut and brought down from the hillsides of Caballo so the beams could be cut and measured for use. The numbers before her blurred and Cat squeezed her eyes shut. You're tired, her mind screamed. Yes, she was tired. Sleep came grudgingly, if at all. She tossed and turned on her cot, El Tigre's viperlike eyes haunting her. *If nothing else,* Cat thought as she opened her eyes, pulling the hand calculator toward her, *it's made me own up to the fact that I'm in love with Slade.*

One week later, it happened.

"Pay dirt!" Slade breathed. The three of them crouched on the ground over a partially exposed limestone vein halfway up Caballo's western flank. A miner had discovered the white, flaky calcite matrix in the oppressive afternoon heat. Slade had called Alvin and Cat on their radios. They stood nearby while he patiently pried the matrix, as large as his hand, out of the embrace of the limestone. Pleasure wreathed Slade's features as he held the matrix up for them to see.

Cat gasped. Alvin gave a pleased chortle. Slade grinned rakishly, holding the white calcite in his palm. There, in its center, were four hexagonal green crystals varying in height from one inch to six inches. None of them was less than a quarter of an inch in diameter. Stunned, Cat watched as the rays of the sun glinted through the emerald crystals, showing their clarity.

"Green fire," Slade said hoarsely, holding the crystals up toward the sun. The molten emeralds gleamed like living beings, catching and refracting the light.

"My gawd," Alvin whispered, "look how clear they are."

Slade's face glistened with sweat, his teeth white against his darkly tanned flesh. "Muzo's deep color and Chivor's clarity. This is what I had been hoping for..."

Word of the find spread through the miners like a ripple of wind through a field of wheat. Cat stood back, watching the spectacle unfold. For a week, they had carefully poked and prodded through the limestone vein without success. A six-foot-high cyclone fence topped with barbed wire had been erected around the pit. As she stood watching the hope suddenly come alive in the Indians' faces, Cat felt frightened. El Tigre was out there, watching them—she could feel his eyes. She turned away, heading back to her shack on the hill. By four o'clock, the first of the dynamite that had been drilled into the limestone face would be triggered and an opening would be made. The mine—her mine—would begin taking shape, and soon she would have to go back inside the earth.

Despite the hundred-degree heat and ninety-percent humidity, Cat was cold. She took off her white construction hat, wiping the sweat from her brow with the back of her hand. The day she had been dreading had come. Part of her was happy about the emerald find, and Cat was sure there were more stones to be discovered. Taking a breath to support her deteriorating courage, she plunged ahead with her plans. A dynamite expert from the U.S., Tony Alvarez, was standing at the door to her shack when she arrived.

"We're ready when you are, Cat."

Cat forced a slight smile, then went inside to grab her portable radio and hook it on her web belt.

"What have we got?" she asked, getting into the Jeep.

Tony hopped in. "I prepped the area after I got rid of the overburden." He used his long, expressive hands. "The shot holes are drilled and loaded with dynamite. The blasting caps are in place and my crew has just collared each of the holes with clay."

Cat glanced at him as she drove the Jeep down the dusty road toward the valley. "Are you going to use millisecond delays between detonations to produce maximum fragmentation of the rock?"

"Sure am, boss. I'm using a four-hole, pyramid-cut pattern. It will give us a seven-by-seven-foot entrance and blow out rock seven feet behind it. We're using low charges so we won't destroy any emeralds that get in the way of our creating an opening into Mother Earth."

"Good," Cat said. She parked the Jeep a good distance from where the series of blasts would take place in the hill. All jungle growth and soil had been removed, exposing the pale green limestone. From her vantage point, using binoculars, Cat could see that Tony had set up the wall for detonation. She signaled Tony to set off the siren. The high-pitched wail shrieked over the area of the Verde, alerting everyone that blasting was going to take place. Tony raised his arm, alerting his two men who stood by the plunger.

Her mouth was dry as she lowered the binoculars. "All right, Tony, give them the signal."

The plunger was shoved down, making electrical contact with the pattern Tony had drilled into the limestone face. Ten explosions rocked Caballo, each seconds apart. Limestone spewed outward in fragments, and a huge, roiling white cloud of dust rose in the wake of the detonations. Cat's ears ached from the puncturing, thunderous roll that each one had caused. The air was pregnant with humidity and swallowed up the sound. Ears ringing, Cat lifted the glasses to her eyes. The dust slowly cleared and, as it did, she got the first look at the opening.

"Looks good, Tony," Cat praised. She had chosen a slope mine, using a slanting entry to follow the vein of limestone that carried the calcite and emerald. The dynamite had done its job, creating the entry, or adit, into the hillside. Now excavation of the debris would begin and the first of the *pao d'arco* beams would begin to be shored into place. The Verde mine had just been born.

Chapter Eleven

Come on, I'll go in with you." Slade rested his hand on Cat's shoulder, feeling her tension. He saw the distraught look in her eyes and smiled. "What's this? Did you think I wouldn't escort you into the Verde mine?"

Cat relaxed beneath the massaging power of Slade's fingers on her shoulder. She had stayed away from actually entering the new mine shaft as long as she could. The last time she had seen Slade, he had been far above them in the pit, working side by side with the miners, looking for another calcite nest. A good, warm feeling flowed through her as Slade matched her slow walk toward the maw.

"I thought you were busy elsewhere," she said, knowing her voice sounded strained.

"Remember?" Slade said, becoming serious, settling his hard hat on his head. "I told you that you were more important than green fire."

A tremulous smile fled across Cat's mouth. "Judging from the look on your face earlier when you held that calcite bearing the emerald, I wondered, Slade."

His smile was devastating. "Don't. I promised you I'd be here when you needed me."

The shadow of the hill enveloped them, and Cat slowed to a stop a few feet from the shaft entrance. Already, wooden forms were being erected to create a permanent opening to the Verde. Once the forms were in place, concrete would be poured into them. Thick, rectangular beams of *pao d'arco* lay in huge, neat piles nearby. Some were already being hauled over to the mouth of the shaft.

Cat felt her stomach shrink into a knot. Her lips felt dry. She didn't dare hesitate in front of the miners who covertly watched her. The limestone was jagged from the explosions and would have to be knocked off the walls to prevent injury. She stepped into the mouth, vaguely aware of a minimal temperature drop. Slade remained at her side as they walked back the first seven feet. They stood in the center of the footwall where the rubble had been removed, both looking overhead, studying the manging wall.

Slade glanced down at her. Even in the shadowy grayness of the mine, he could see how pale Cat had become. Small beads of sweat stood out on her wrinkled brow as she assessed the ceiling with a critical eye. A fierce wave of pride overwhelmed him. Despite Cat's fear, she was holding her ground.

"We're going to need rock bolts," she said, pointing to the spiderweb pattern on the ceiling where the rock had been fractured.

Slade nodded in agreement. Often, the systematic use of rock bolts reinforced roofs of mines that might cave in, or they strengthened existing walls in case of earthquake. "We've got an ample supply," he said.

Suddenly, Cat wanted to run. She wanted to scream. Swallowing hard, she forced herself to measure off the distance to where the first post and stulls would be set. The activity helped keep her fear contained, and as she talked with the Indian foreman in Spanish, a little more of the fear receded.

"I want those rock bolts under high tension, Pablo."

The foreman, a man close to fifty with graying hair beneath his red hard hat, nodded. *"Si, Patrona."*

"I'll be testing them," she warned him.

Slade smiled to himself. Cat would, too. That would mean she'd be spending a hell of a lot of time in the mine measuring them with a torque meter. Much later, Slade followed Cat out of the mine. He traded a knowing glance with her as she took off her hard hat, wiping her sweaty features.

"Congratulations," he told her in a low voice, "you did it. First time's always the toughest."

With a weary smile, Cat threw the hat back on her head. She watched the beams being hauled to the entrance. From here on, the building of the mine would continue for twenty-four hours a day with three crew shifts working. She would be up sixteen of those hours to keep pace with the rapid expansion of the mine until they hit a vein with calcite in it. Then, work would slow accordingly to open up the vein and hunt for the emeralds.

"I'm so shaky, my knees are knocking, Slade."

"How about if I hold you tonight?"

The gritty warmth of his lowered voice washed through her and Cat shared a soft smile with him. The words *I love you* were almost torn from her. "Sounds wonderful, fella."

"Hey, this evening, Alvin's celebrating the mine start-up by making a special dinner for us."

Alvin was a fine cook and Cat eagerly looked forward to most of his cowboy meals. "What's on the menu?"

Slade chuckled. "Texican beef, hunkydummy, potato dumplin's and apple pan dowdy. A meal fit for a king and queen, believe me. My mouth's watering already."

Cat's wasn't. "Hunkydummy? What's that?" Alvin had a couple of other cowboy recipes she'd just as soon forget about. Every night when they settled around their campfire where Alvin was fixing the vittles, Cat went over every item he was cooking before she ate it.

"It's a kind of bread with raisins and cinnamon sprinkled over the top of it."

"Oh, that sounds pretty good."

Slade laughed. "You're such a sissy," he chided.

"I'm from Colorado, Slade, not Texas. Some of the wild food Alvin whips up could only be consumed by a Texas cowhand. Give me a break!"

Back at the shack, Cat sat down at her drafting board. Her hand shook as she picked up a blue pencil. Closing her eyes, she dropped the pencil and sat there, allowing the cold wash of fear to drench her. After a few minutes, she lifted her head, a wry smile on her lips. How could she have lived so long and not known real fear?

Absently, she picked up the pencil, going through the motions of making notations on the blueprint. The fear wasn't all negative, she mused, nearly awed by that realization. No, it had shown her that another person could give her the necessary strength to press forward.

Had Slade's love given her that support? Cat hesitated over the blueprint as she centered on that question. He had never said he loved her, nor had she told him. Nevertheless, she felt whole as never before, regardless of the fear that stalked her about mine entry. With a soft laugh, Cat shook her head. So, was this real love, this feeling of completeness that Slade automatically gave to her? Cat couldn't imagine life without Slade's presence. He made each minute, each hour important. And they were, with him.

Eventually, Cat returned to the demanding work in front of her. But numbers, formulas and figures couldn't compete with the powerful sensations in her heart. Cat allowed the full gamut of her emotions to surface and be felt. She could barely breathe for the sheer joy of being alive in every sense of the word.

Near four o'clock, Slade knocked on the door and entered. He saw Cat bent over her drafting board, hard at work. A swell of pride and love overwhelmed him as he stood in the open doorway, watching her. As she turned, he saw the sudden happiness in her green eyes because he was there. Slade was deeply moved. With a smile, he held his hand out toward her.

"Come on, I'm taking you someplace special."

Cat stared at his large, powerful fingers; they were dirt-stained and his nails worn to nothing from prying calcite apart, looking for green fire. Without a word, she slipped her hand into his.

"Where?" Her voice was breathless with anticipation.

"While El Tigre is busy watching Alvin and his men digging for green fire, you and I are going to slip off to share some well-deserved time together. What do you think? Are you ready to be carried off by your knight on his white charger?"

Gladly, Cat put down her hard hat and followed Slade out the door. "More than ready, my lord. Lead the way."

Slade gave the Jeep an apologetic look as they climbed in. "Not exactly a white charger, but it'll have to do. Still game?"

"You bet. Is this a surprise or can you tell me where we're going?"

He wanted to ruffle her hair, run his fingers through it and feel the silk of her skin beneath his hands. His voice husky, he traded a tender look with Cat. "I want it to be a surprise. I've been planning this a long time before we came down here. Just sit back and enjoy the ride, my lady."

With a sigh, Cat nodded and leaned back. The movement of the Jeep as it took them up and out of the mining area cooled her sweaty skin. She felt Slade's hand cover her own and she squeezed it. "I love you," she almost whispered. Cat had trouble not saying it out loud to Slade. The adoration in his dark sapphire eyes made her tremble with need.

As they crossed the only road up and out of the valley, Slade turned off, heading down a little-used path. The foliage and low-hanging vines swatted at them and the Jeep cautiously crept forward. Brightly colored macaws ranging from blue and yellow to a garish crimson and purple cawed raucously, their late-afternoon siesta disturbed by the noise of the vehicle. Cat filled her senses with the heavy, intoxicating smell of orchids hanging in patches of brilliant color against the jade jungle.

"If I didn't know better," she confided to Slade, "I'd say this was a slice of heaven tucked away by Mother Earth."

"It is. All right, close your eyes before we go around this bend in the path. I'll tell you when to open them."

Heartbeat escalating, Cat heard a distinctly different sound ahead and to the right of them as they rounded the corner. The Jeep came to a halt and she felt Slade's arm around her shoulder, drawing her close. His voice was low and dark next to her ear.

"Now you can open them. Welcome to our heaven, Cat."

A gasp of pleasure escaped from her as she stared at a small waterfall sitting thirty feet above them. Slade had brought the Jeep to a halt at its base in a small grassy clearing, complete with brilliantly colored flowers of all varieties. A circular pool of an inviting aquamarine color held tiny white suds floating at the foot of the waterfall. Deep green moss hugged small gray boulders along the bank. At the quietest point were several pink-and-white water lilies floating like crown jewels on the surface.

"Slade...this is incredible!" Cat whispered, struck by the beauty surrounding them.

He got out, pleased. "It's all ours. And," he emphasized, helping Cat from the Jeep, "private." He halted near the lip of the bank and turned, placing his hands on her shoulders. As she lifted her chin, her emerald eyes lustrous, Slade groaned softly, capturing her. He claimed her pliant, welcoming lips beneath his, reveling in the scent of her hair and damp skin. Fire tore wildly through him as she melted willingly against him, her arms coming around his shoulders. Slade couldn't get enough of her, ever.

Tearing his mouth from her lips, he rasped, "Today...out there at the mine, Cat..."

Dizzy with the scent of his virility, Cat forced her eyes open. "Yes?" She clung to him, wanting nothing more.

Slade framed her darkly tanned face between his hands, absorbing Cat's sultry look. "I wanted to kiss you, to tell you how damned courageous you were. It's one thing to live through a cave-in. It's another to walk back inside again. You did it, and I'm so damned proud of you."

She managed a tremulous smile, sliding her fingertips across his shoulders. "Be proud of us. I was glad you were there, believe me."

"You were going in whether I was there or not. That's what counted." He leaned down, capturing her mouth again, drowning in the only taste and texture that could satisfy his yearning.

Gradually, Cat broke away, heart racing wildly, her breasts swollen and nipples taut. She wanted Slade's touch so badly, it had become a craving. Barely able to think after his exquisite assault upon her senses, Cat whispered, "I'm discovering I can't live without you, Slade."

He grinned, kissing her lashes, nose and mouth. "Nothing wrong with that, my proud beauty."

She smiled as his tongue lazily traced her lips, sweetly sipping from each corner until crazy tingling sensations shot through her, intensifying her ache for him. "I didn't realize how lonely I was until you came into my life," she admitted softly.

Raising his head, Slade melted beneath the tender flame deep within her eyes. His fingers trembled as he sifted strands of her hair through his hands. "I've been looking for you a whole lifetime, Cat. Come on, let's take a well-earned bath. I want to love you afterward . . ."

Everything else ceased to exist as Cat allowed Slade to unbutton and peel off her damp cotton shirt. Drowning in the love she saw in his blue gaze, she then helped Slade undress. No longer was she aware of the grit or dirt as he led her into the cool embrace of the waist-deep water. She watched as Slade took a handful of moss from the bank. It had a soft, slightly abrasive texture as he sluiced water over her shoulders and across her breasts and gently began to wash her. For the next ten minutes, he did not speak. Instead, each touch became his focus. Then Cat took the damp moss and washed him.

"I found this place a week after we came up here to the Verde the first time," Slade explained as he took the moss and allowed it to float away from them. His hands stilled on her glistening shoulders as he looked around them. "This is a place out of time, Cat. It's special. You can feel it."

Placing her palm against the matted hair on his broad chest, she murmured, "There are some places on the earth that have their own unique vibration." She leaned forward, slowly placing kiss after kiss along the hard, uncompromising line of his jaw. "Just like the vibration beneath my hand is special." She ran her tongue across his mouth, tasting the salt of his sweat and his male earthiness. "You are one of a kind, Slade," she whispered, claiming his mouth with all the fire she possessed.

A tremor shook him as her slick, warm breasts pressed against his chest. The sweet demand of her hips against his own powerful hardness sent a tumult of raw desire coursing through him. Cat was willing, pliant and so much woman that it brought tears to his eyes as he swept her against him, holding her forever. Hungrily, he claimed her mouth, lost in the primal senses that she stirred within him. As her thighs joined his beneath the water, his control was shattered.

Cat swam in the molten heat of their desire, barely aware that Slade had slipped his arm beneath her. Then he lifted her, carrying her from the pool to a carpet of grass. Cat relaxed into the verdant expanse and welcomed him back into her arms. Never had she wanted a man more. Never had Cat wanted to share the unleashed love that throbbed through her. She felt Slade's hand slide across her hip, gently parting her thighs. The mere touch of him against her damp, waiting core brought a gasp from her. Arching, she pulled Slade down upon her, welcoming him.

Patches of sunlight laced and danced through the heavy jungle canopy overhead. The ripeness of the grass aroused her, as did Slade's masculine scent. Nostrils flared, she met each of his powerful thrusts, responding wildly to his primal demands. Sunlight and darkness, day and night, loneliness and love. All those feelings, words and sensations spun through the hallways of Cat's emotions as Slade carried her beyond any pleasure she had ever experienced. White-hot fusion exploded violently within her and she cried out, sinking her fingers deeply into his taut shoulder muscles.

"Yes..." Slade cried hoarsely, gripping her tightly, twisting his hips to give her every bit of pleasure. "Feel me, Cat. Feel how much you mean to me..." Unable to stop his own need to claim her, he gripped her hard and buried his head next to hers. Explosion after explosion tore through him, ripping him apart and putting him back together again. The French called it *la petite mort*, "the little death." He called it love. With Cat, the meeting of their bodies was an overwhelming symbol of the love he felt for her. He didn't die that small death the French referred to. No, he never felt more alive, more joyous or more sure of his destiny as when he was buried within the yielding core of Cat's body.

With a sigh, Cat sank back into Slade's embrace, float-ing on a wave of sensations within her. A slight, tremulous smile pulled at her well-kissed lips. She ran her fingers through his dark hair, reveling in the cobalt fire banked in his eyes.

"You take my breath away..." she murmured.

Slade laid his head on her breast, holding her, listening to the ragged pound of her loving heart. "You make me feel so deeply that I can barely breathe...or think..." He laughed softly. "You make me feel whole, Cat."

She continued to smolder beneath his husky compli-ments, content to lie there with him forever. "I've never flown like this," she admitted, her voice throaty. "You free me, Slade. I didn't know how chained I was until you came and unlocked so many secret places within me..." Gently, Cat ran her hand across his drying flesh, reveling in both his power and his tenderness for her.

Barely opening his eyes, Slade moved his hand down her hip and across her finely curved thigh. "Love has a way of releasing the best in all of us," he murmured.

Cat turned, meeting his eyes as he raised his head to look down at her. "You've taught me so much in such a short amount of time, Slade. You made me aware of how alone I've been. You've made me hungry for you in a way I've never experienced." She cupped his sandpapery cheek. "You've got the keys to my heart. You know that, don't you?"

Gravely, he turned, kissing her palm as if she were fragile glass. "No one's more aware of that than me, sweetheart." He watched as a cloud marred the joy in her eyes. "What is it?" he coaxed. "Are you frightened?"

"Y-yes."

"Me, too. Let's be scared together, okay? Misery loves company and no one cares for you more than I do..."

With a muffled laugh, Cat embraced him. "You crazy Texan! What did I ever do before you crashed into my life?"

Matching her effusive laughter, Slade rolled over on his back, bringing Cat on top of him. She fitted against him perfectly and he absorbed the happiness that had returned to her face. God, how fiercely he loved her. *Soon,* he promised Cat silently, *you and I are going to show our hands; we're going to admit that we love one another.*

"I can say one thing," he stated out loud.

Cat leaned down, kissing the tip of his nose, euphoria making her feel giddy with joy. "What?"

"Life hasn't been dull since we met."

"That's an understatement, Slade Donovan!"

"Well," he said in a pleased tone, "when you consider we met at a cave-in, that's pretty symbolic."

She nipped playfully at the cords of his neck, inhaling his wonderful scent. "In what way?"

"I've always believed life speaks to us in symbolic terms. For instance, a bird can mean news."

"How do you interpret a cave-in?" Cat wondered, planting her hands on his chest and smiling into his warm blue eyes.

"What's a cave-in do?"

She wrinkled her nose in distaste. "Changed my life, that's for sure."

Slade grinned. "Exactly. It symbolized that each of us would have a devastating effect on each other. It was also an opportunity for a new beginning, together."

Cat grew thoughtful, then met his warming smile. "I like the way you see life, Slade. I've never thought of it in those terms, but it's provocative."

Running his hands suggestively up across her hips and back, he murmured, "And so are you."

Chapter Twelve

Cat walked down into the Verde mine. After three weeks of blasting and setting up posts and stulls, the tunnel now stretched almost a third of a mile into Caballo mountain. Rock bolts screwed into the limestone ceiling hung like silent baubles above her head every few feet. The chut-chut-chut of several portable generators hammered through the tunnel, providing electric light for the miners removing rubble and those shoring up the beams. The fear was still with her, but less a monster than before. The first week, Slade had miraculously appeared at her side every time she had to go in. Cat didn't know how he knew when she would go into the mine, but she was grateful for his unexplained presence.

As she walked along the adit, a coolness enveloped her. Her main concern was installing proper ventilation through the roof of the mine to the air outside. Exhaust from the generators fouled the air with colorless and odorless carbon monoxide. If it wasn't properly managed, it could eventually kill an unsuspecting miner. The footwall beneath her feet was swept free of all debris, something she had demanded. Dust in any form in a mine ate away at everyone's delicate lung tissue. At first, the workers begrudged the amount of cleanliness she wanted in the adit. Cat stood her ground with them and they finally did as they were ordered.

Gangue, or worthless material, was now being pried off the walls at the end of the tunnel. Cat had discovered a limestone vein bearing calcite yesterday and everyone's hopes had risen to almost a fever pitch. Every shift worker who entered the mine worked in silent tension as he walked the distance of the adit to where the vein was located. There was little talking as sweating men, stripped to their waists, worked. Crowbars in gloved hands, they carefully began to chip away at the vein, searching for green fire.

Cat felt excitement thrumming through the Verde as she checked the next set of posts, stulls and rock bolts. She slid her fingers across the limestone surface of the manging wall. From all appearances, as they went deeper, following the vein, the walls would strengthen, because the rock was more compact. That was good, since they needed all the help they could get from possible earth tremors.

It was nearly 1:00 a.m. when Cat left her shack and drove back down to base camp to call it a night. Everywhere she looked, the garish flood lamps lit up the blackness. Diesel-fueled generators ceaselessly supplied the necessary light so the graveyard shift could work throughout the night, hunting for emeralds in the open-pit area. Cat dropped off her two guards at their camp and swung the Jeep down the rutted road to their private camp that stood an eighth of a mile away.

Slade was standing by the fire beside Alvin while he stirred one of many kettles. He saw Cat's Jeep approaching when suddenly, out of the jungle, four shadowy shapes emerged behind the Jeep. Cold terror raced through him and he

raised his hand to warn Cat. Too late! He saw the guaqueros leap into the rear of the vehicle. The first held the
blade of a knife against her ribs. Slade took two steps forward, his hand moving to his pistol.

"Now," El Tigre breathed close to Cat's left ear, "you
will continue toward the encampment." He took her pistol
and handed it to one of his other men. With an icy smile, he
pressed the point of the blade a little more firmly against her
ribs. *"Comprende?"*

Cat kept her booted feet down on the brake and clutch.
"Si..."

"Bueno. Drive slowly, now."

Cat nearly gagged on the sour smell that assailed her
nostrils as El Tigre leaned over the seat, his body pressed
against her back and left shoulder. Her heart pounded
heavily and she wondered who he wanted. Slade? Alvin? All
of them? Cat saw several guards running down toward the
camp and Slade's tall figure silhouetted against the fire. As
they drove within twenty feet of the camp, El Tigre hissed,
"Halt!"

Slade saw the guaquero take the black-bladed knife and
press it to Cat's slender throat. The vicious blade looked
stark against the whiteness of her flesh. His fingers wrapped
around the pistol's handle.

"Whatever you want, you can have," Slade shouted to
them in Spanish, "just let her go."

"Señor! I am El Tigre. Your woman here has met me before. Come!"

Slade's eyes narrowed and he barely turned his head to
Alvin, who was standing there scowling.

"Follow us, if you can," Slade growled over his shoulder and then walked quickly toward the Jeep. He saw Cat's
eyes widen as she sat frozen in the Jeep. Anger coursed
through Slade as he saw El Tigre press the blade even more
against her flesh.

"Stop there, *señor*," El Tigre commanded. He grinned tightly. "You are the geologist, *si*?"

"*Si.*"

With a chuckle, El Tigre glanced down at Cat. "Your woman led us to believe you were in Texas. She is wily like a jaguar. But we wait and we watch. We see you out in the pit every day. If there is an emerald find, you are always called. Not her, not the gringo with the white hair. But you."

Slade held Cat's frightened gaze. "What do you want?" he ground out.

"Both of you. Come, sit here in the jeep." El Tigre's eyes glittered. "One wrong move and she is dead, *señor*. Watch."

Cat felt the razor-edged blade sink into her flesh. Her eyes bulged and her breath lodged in her throat as she felt the trickling warmth of blood running down her neck, soaking into her shirt. She closed her eyes, fighting off sudden faintness. Slade's savage curse startled her.

"That's enough!"

El Tigre smiled mirthlessly, easing the pressure on the knife. "Enough for now, *señor*. This blade has killed many. It doesn't care whether it's a man or woman. Nor do I. Now, drop your holster and pistol at your feet, then join us. And warn your men that if they try to shoot at us when we leave or try to follow, your woman will breathe her last gulp of air through her windpipe."

Slade slowly unbuckled the holster, letting it drop around his feet. He turned toward Alvin, telling him of El Tigre's orders. Immediately, all the guards lowered their rifles. Slade made his way to the Jeep and halted in front of it.

"Why don't you put that blade on me instead of her?"

"I think not, *señor*. No more talk! Get in!"

The moment Slade slid into the passenger seat, one of the guaqueros came forward. He immediately bound Slade's wrists with hemp rope. Satisfied, El Tigre eased the knife from Cat's throat.

"Drive, *señorita*. Turn around and take the road leading back toward Muzo."

Cat's mind spun with options and possibilities. She jammed the Jeep into gear and they headed out of the well-lit area, swallowed up by the shadowy jungle on both sides of the narrow, bumpy road. As soon as they were out of sight of the Verde, El Tigre relaxed, laughing.

"*Aiyeee, compadres!* I told you how easy it would be to capture them."

Thomas, his second-in-command, whose weapon was trained on Slade's back, nodded, a half smile on his mouth. The other two men cheered in unison, waving their weapons above their heads.

El Tigre rubbed Cat's right shoulder in a provocative motion, his dirty fingers trailing down her arm to the elbow. Cat jerked her arm away.

"Leave me alone!"

"This one has claws," the leader crowed.

Slade turned, his eyes a deadly black color, settling on the bandit. "You lay another hand on her, and you'll answer to me."

El Tigre smiled slowly. "You'll talk to me anyway, *señor*. You will tell us where you keep all those emeralds you're finding. If they are in a safe, you will give me the combination."

"Over my dead body."

With a chuckle, El Tigre pointed to Cat. "No, *señor*, over her dead body. She is how you say it, insurance? If you do not talk, she will die an inch at time."

Cat's skin crawled over the frigid tone in El Tigre's voice. He meant business. The twin beams of light from the Jeep stabbed through the darkness. There was no moon as they drove on, mile after mile, the blackness embracing them until Cat thought she was back in a caved-in mine once again. They had to escape! If El Tigre got them to his camp, they were as good as dead. She didn't dare look at Slade or the guaqueros might suspect something. Her mind raced to remember the road back to Muzo. Right now, they were climbing steadily out of the valley. Soon, they would be following the nose line of several ridges before dropping into the Gato Valley. Slade's hands were tied in front of him. Grimly, Cat wiped the sweat stinging her eyes.

Slade braced himself as Cat pressed down the accelerator once they had bridged the hill. The road was rocky and rutted. What the hell was she doing speeding up like this at this time of night? Didn't she know there was a series of sharp S-turns up ahead? The gravelly surface of the road would make the Jeep slide if she took them too fast. Slade glanced at Cat. Her face was grim and barely outlined by the dashboard lights. Then, realizing what she was going to do, he almost smiled. In those split seconds before they raced down on the first set of curves, Slade promised himself that if they escaped this with their lives, he'd tell Cat how much he loved her.

"Slow down!" El Tigre shrieked in her ear, pounding her right shoulder sharply with his fist.

Cat winced as his knotted fist struck her twice with hard, well-aimed blows. The lights from the vehicle outlined the first turn. She jammed her boot down on the accelerator. The Jeep lurched forward, careening toward the first curve. El Tigre cursed and was thrown backward. He fell into the two men who sat squeezed in the back, and Cat wrenched the nose of the Jeep toward the cliff. One man tumbled over the side, the gun flying out of his hand. Another fell off with a scream. For terrifying seconds, the Jeep slid sideways and then, as Cat wrenched the wheel back to the left, the heavily treaded tires screamed in protest.

"Jump, Slade!"

Everything was a blur as Slade threw himself out of the Jeep. He struck the road with his left shoulder, rolling instinctively into a ball to lessen the shocking impact. Flesh was torn from him, but he felt little pain. He heard the ve-

hicle roar off the road, sudden silence, and then a crash as
the Jeep smashed and tumbled down the steep cliff. Cat!
Where was Cat?

Drunkenly, Slade got to his feet, searching the choking
dust and darkness. He stumbled across unconscious guaqueros. Nearby was a rifle. He picked it up. Had everyone
else gone over with the Jeep? Where was she—

"Slade!"

He jerked to the left, crouching. Cat was running toward
him, her face smudged with dirt, her blouse ripped and
bloodied. Both had paid dearly for landing in the gravel.
Her fingers closed around his arm.

"Come on!" she gasped.

"Where are the—"

"Two went over the cliff with the Jeep," she sobbed.
"Come on, we've got to get away! Give me the rifle."

There was no time to stop and untie his wrists. Slade
nodded and they took off at a dead run down the road,
heading back for the Verde camp they had left at least ten
miles behind. Every once in a while, Cat would look back.
The rifle's safety was off and she held it close, ready to fire
if necessary. After running a mile they were both gasping
and gulping for air. Slade angled them off the road and into
the foliage of the jungle.

"Come here," he panted, holding out his hands toward
her. "Get these ropes off me."

Cat came and crouched at his side. She set the rifle nearby
and shakily began to untie the knots. "I—I think we're
safe."

"Don't count on it," Slade said grimly, sweat streaking
down his dirty, bloody face. "Those bastards have nine
lives."

She grinned tightly, the adrenaline high, keeping her mind
sharp as a steel trap. "So do we. There."

Slade rubbed his raw wrists tenderly. Then he turned his
attention to Cat. "How are you?"

"Cuts, bruises...nothing that won't heal. I'm just scared spitless."

His grin was wobbly. "Makes two of us. All right, come on. Those four guaqueros, or whoever is left, won't let us go easily. We've got to make it back to camp or—"

Cat stood, nervously watching the dark road, expecting to see shadowy shapes emerge from it at any moment. "I know. Here, you take the rifle. I'm not sure I could shoot straight if I had to. My hands are shaking like leaves."

With a nod, Slade guided her over the bank of the road. "You run in front of me. Keep your eyes peeled and ears open. If you hear anything, signal me. Don't talk. We can't afford to make any more noise than necessary."

The construction boots felt like lead on Cat's feet. She wasn't in the world's greatest shape, but not the worst, either. After jogging another two miles, she had to ask Slade to halt. Her throat was burning and her lungs felt ready to burst. They found sanctuary in a banana-tree grove, the huge, long fronds covering them so they couldn't be seen from the road. Slade knelt near her, his concentration aimed behind them. Cat felt safe, falling back against the trunk of a tree, taking huge gulps of air.

"You—never told me about this, Donovan."

Slade wiped his face, glancing over at Cat. "I told you it would be rough. This is the Dodge City of the eighties. It's wide open, and the only law is the gun you carry. You let it do the talking for you."

"I'm demanding hazardous-duty pay," she whispered, finally sitting up.

Slade reached out and gripped her hand, squeezing it gently. "If you've accidentally killed El Tigre, you've got a hundred-thousand-peso reward coming from the Muzo mine. Is that enough?"

Cat shivered, suddenly cold. The adrenaline that had given her the courage to deliberately wreck the Jeep and leap from it deserted her. Miserably, she shook her head. "I hope I didn't kill him..."

A flat snort came from Slade. "I do. That bastard was going to kill us."

She believed him, but it still didn't make her feel any better that she had possibly killed one or more men. Slade got up, bringing her to her feet. Cat felt dizzy and leaned against him.

"All right?" Slade asked huskily, pressing a kiss to her dusty hair.

"Yes... I'm whipped."

"Adrenaline letdown. We'll jog, walk, jog. We can't afford to dally."

The fifteen-minute rest hadn't been a good idea after all, Cat discovered. Every bone and socket in her body was beginning to ache in earnest. The scrapes on her arms and shoulder smarted. The boots she wore felt like twenty-pound weights on each foot. Lift them up, put them down, she instructed herself.

Five miles had fallen away under their jog-and-walk routine. Slade kept looking back, never dropping his guard. Cat kept angling toward the center of the road, where it was less rutted. He kept pulling her back, forcing her to walk on the side where it was hard to maintain a balance. If they had to dive for cover, Slade wanted to get into the jungle with one leap. He didn't try to explain to her, realizing Cat was close to exhaustion.

The bark of a rifle silenced the jungle sounds around them. Slade cursed, throwing his full weight forward, landing on top of Cat. They hit the ground hard and he rolled them into the foliage. More bullets spit up geysers where they had stood seconds before. Slade threw Cat off him, scrambled to his knees and hid behind a trumpet tree, both hands on the rifle. There! He saw the figures of two men weaving steadily toward them.

"Son of a bitch," he muttered. He jerked around to look at Cat. She was lying nearby, the breath knocked out of her. "Cat!" he hissed between clenched teeth. "Get up! Hurry!"

With a groan, Cat blindly scrambled to her knees and dove into the brush.

Slade aimed, drew a bead on the lead guaquero and fired twice. The second shot felled one bandit. Then, he had to duck as a spate of savage automatic-rifle fire spewed into his position. Bark exploded and splintered in all directions. Slade lunged for the earth, crawling away from the tree. He got to his knees, scuttling forward in the same direction Cat had gone.

The damp humid jungle floor smelled like so much rotted flesh to Cat. She fell and tripped numerous times over unseen tree roots or vines that snaked across her path. She had heard the gunfire, and adrenaline shot through her, giving her the second wind she needed to escape. Slade! Where was Slade? Had he been wounded? Cat turned, almost running into him. Slade gripped her tightly, his breath hot against her face.

"I got one of them. The other will trail us."

With a groan, Cat clung momentarily to him. "W-what can we do?"

He gripped Cat's shoulder firmly. "Listen to me, Cat. Aim yourself east, toward the camp."

She looked up at him, her face blank. "What about you?"

"I'm going to lie here in wait for him. That's the only way we're going to get out of this alive."

"But—"

"Go on and don't argue."

"No, damn it! I'm staying. I can't go into the jungle at night, Slade. I'll get lost!"

His face was glistening with sweat, eyes narrowed dangerously in the direction from which the guaquero would be sure to come. "At least you'll be alive in case that bastard gets me first. Now, go on. And stop arguing with me."

Cat stood her ground, her jaw set. "I'm staying, Slade."

With a curse, he jerked her to a trumpet tree, forcing her to sit down behind it. "You stay here and don't breathe. You understand me?"

She nodded, her eyes growing large. He started to turn away and she gripped his hand. "Slade?"

Impatiently, he twisted his head in her direction. "What?"

"I love you—"

The harshness on his face melted for a split second. "I know you do. Now just lie low and stay still."

Cat nodded and scrunched herself behind the girth of the tree. How long she sat there, frozen like a fawn while a predator stalked nearby, Cat did not know. She muffled her breathing, hand over her mouth, eyes and ears focused on the path they had made coming into the jungle. Cat quickly lost sight of Slade, who had moved out into the darkness. Time drew to an excruciating halt as the noises of insects covered all other sounds. Who was left? El Tigre? Thomas? Cat shivered. The guaqueros would be excellent trackers and hunters, having been raised in these jungles.

And then Cat's hunting instincts came back to her. She remembered her father teaching her and Rafe how to hunt and stalk food. Cat grew very still, breathed shallowly and listened carefully. There! She detected a faint, perceptible change in the number of insects singing. Cat gripped the tree trunk. Was it because Slade was still moving around, or was it a guaquero? In the minutes that followed, Cat had no doubt someone was coming in her direction.

Her heart beginning to pound in dread, Cat pressed one hand against her breast, wondering if everyone else could hear it pumping as loudly as she could. Could a heartbeat give her away? A soft crunching sound to her right made her jump. She froze, her nostrils flaring. A sour smell reached her. El Tigre! She'd recognize the odor anywhere. Oh, no! His shape melted out of the surrounding foliage, no more than ten feet from where she crouched. Where was Slade? Was he even aware of El Tigre's presence? The guaquero turned, the automatic weapon ready to fire in his hands, walking toward Cat.

A scream welled up from deep within her. Cat felt a trickle of sweat run down her temples. Her fingers dug convulsively into the tree trunk and she leaned down, face and body pressed against the rough bark, willing herself to become part of the tree. He was only five feet away. Did he see her? If he caught her, he would show no mercy. Cat's eyes grew huge as he took another careful step in her direction, the ugly muzzle of his military weapon pointed right at her.

Suddenly, the night exploded around her as Slade's dark shape lunged from the left. Both men fell heavily, grunting and groaning. Cat leaped to her feet the instant El Tigre's weapon flew out of his hands, and she scrambled for the weapon as the men wrestled on the jungle floor. The sickening sound of bone breaking beneath the power of a fist tore into her shock. Cat lurched to her feet, screaming at them. She shoved the muzzle of the gun down into El Tigre's heaving chest and Slade got off him.

"Don't move," she warned the guaquero harshly. "Slade?"

"I'm all right," he rasped, coming to her side. "Get up!" he ordered El Tigre.

The man glared at Cat, his eyes feral with hatred as he held his injured jaw. Cat slowly removed the muzzle from his chest and handed the gun to Slade. The roar of vehicles shattered the jungle. Cat looked toward the road.

"Alvin?" she asked.

"Yeah. Get up there and flag them down. I'll bring our friend here in tow."

Cat crashed through the thick barrier of leaves, vines and roots. She finally made it to the road as the first Jeep passed by her. Waving her arms, she managed to flag down the second one. It was loaded with armed guards from the Verde mine. Tony Alvarez was driving.

"Man, you're a sight for sore eyes!" he said, getting out. "Where's Slade?"

Cat gave him a weary smile. "Coming with El Tigre."

"You two gave that snake a run for his money, eh?"

"I guess we did. There's Slade."

The next hour became a blur for Cat. The guards were enthusiastic that El Tigre had been captured alive. Slade sat behind her on the way back to their camp, his hand resting protectively on her shoulder. Alvin was like a mother hen, insisting on scrubbing their cuts and bruises with soap and water plus a healthy dose of iodine. Tears had watered in Cat's eyes when he had plastered her injuries with the yellow tincture, and she wasn't sure if the tears came because of the pain or the fear of what might have happened if El Tigre had made good his escape with them.

Slade watched Cat out of the corner of his eye as she slowly began to undress in their tent. She sat wearily on her cot, her fingers trembling as she tried to unlace her boots.

"Here," he said, crouching down in front of her and removing her hands, "let me do that."

Cat straightened up. Her shirt was unbuttoned, revealing the lace and silk of her lingerie. "Thanks. I think I'm falling apart now that it's over."

"I know you are. Just sit and relax, the worst is over."

"Why aren't your hands shaking? Aren't you feeling torn up inside?"

Slade grimaced, gently removing the first boot and tackling the second. "This isn't the first time something like this has happened to me, Cat. Maybe I'm more used to violence than you are. It comes with the territory when you get into gem mining.''

"I've never seen it this bad, Slade.'' Cat swallowed a lump in her throat. "You can taste the violence in the air.'' She shivered as he pulled the second boot off.

Slade slid his hands up her curved thighs and looked at her in the flickering light shed by the lantern. Her left cheek had a cut on it and was slightly puffy. He knew she had landed on her left side, and luckily her shoulder, upper arm and elbow had received the brunt of the punishment.

He tenderly framed her face and said, "The next few days are going to be hectic. I'm going to take El Tigre over to Muzo. From there, I'm sure the Colombian police will be more than happy to take him into custody.''

A tremulous sigh broke from her lips. "But that doesn't promise an end to the violence, does it?''

Slade sadly shook his head. "No. As long as there's green fire, you've got men who will do anything to get it, legally or otherwise.'' He brushed away the first tear that rolled down her cheek. Cat was having a natural letdown after their narrow escape, and he leaned forward, molding his mouth lightly against her lips. He felt her tremble, her arms moving around his shoulders to draw him nearer.

"God,'' he groaned against her soft, yielding mouth, "you taste so good...''

"Hold me, Slade. Just hold me, please...''

In one motion, he got to his feet and joined her on the cot. Cat blindly found his arms as the first sob wrenched from her. Slade murmured her name brokenly, burying his head beside hers as she cried. He rocked her gently, whispering words of comfort.

"We're good for each other, sweetheart,'' he told her comfortingly. "Sometimes I'm weak and you're strong. Sometimes I'm strong and you're weak. Like tonight; you took one hell of a risk on that curve. You could have turned the wheels too sharply and that Jeep would have rolled over instead of sliding off the cliff. You knew what you were doing."

Cat sniffed, trying to wipe her nose. "It was pure luck, Slade," she said, hiccuping through her tears. "I'm not a racing-car driver." She looked up at him, taking the clean handkerchief he tucked into her hands. "I never even thought about the Jeep flipping over."

He grinned, running his fingers through her freshly washed hair. "What matters is the outcome, Cat. You made a perfect skid, giving both of us the time we needed to jump clear. In my eyes, you're the female equivalent of Parnelli Jones."

Cat laughed, but it came out as a hiccup instead. "I was scared to death, Slade. I-I didn't know if you'd caught on to what I was going to do. I didn't dare look at you..."

He held her lightly against him, allowing Cat to bury her head beneath his chin. "Must have been mental telepathy. One look at the set of your jaw and I knew you weren't going to go down without a fight." Slade pressed a kiss to her clean-smelling hair. "More important, this has taught me a lesson, Cat."

She closed her eyes, reveling in Slade's protective arms around her. Now she felt secure and safe. "What?" His heartbeat was slow and strong beneath her ear, soothing away the remnants of her emotional storm.

"You remember out in the jungle, when you told me you loved me?"

Cat was afraid to nod her head, but she did. Automatically she rested her hand against Slade's chest, as if to steel herself against what he might say. "I didn't know if we'd live or die, Slade," she began in a hoarse tone. "I know you may not feel the same, but that doesn't matter to me anymore."

"How long have you loved me?"

Cat closed her eyes. "I don't know. You just kind of grow on a person, Slade."

"Like mold?"

She laughed, her hand slowly unclenching. "You make loving another person sound like a virus."

"Isn't it?" And then he chuckled, pressing a kiss to her hair.

"No."

Slade closed his eyes, relief washing through him. "What I feel for you, Cat, I've never felt with another woman."

She pulled away from him and sat up, looking deep into his eyes. "Think we've got the same virus?"

A grin tugged at his mouth. "I don't know. Maybe we ought to compare symptoms. What do you think?"

Cat couldn't help but match his widening smile. The warmth and tenderness in Slade's eyes made her feel cherished. "This is a hell of a way to find out we love one another."

With a shrug, Slade picked up her bruised right hand, cradling it in his own. "People like us have to be hit over the head with a sixteen-pound sledgehammer, sweetheart."

"You made me aware of how lonely I'd been, Slade. And despite our shaky beginning, I really enjoyed your company those two months I spent at your ranch. I liked talking to you."

"And I liked just looking at you." Slade grazed her cheek with his. "Do you realize how beautiful you are to me? Every day, I'd count the hours between breakfast and lunch until I could see you again. And then I'd count them between lunch and dinner."

"You didn't have to hole up in that office of yours, Slade."

"At the time, Alvin and I were coordinating all equipment details being moved from the U.S. to Colombia. I was getting men from his ranch and working with the State Department on visas and passports. It was a couple of busy months for me."

She gave him an accusing look. "If you weren't in your office, then you were in your hobby shop grinding those gems."

He held up both hands, laughing. "Guilty as charged. I wanted to spend more time with you, but I felt if I did, you'd interpret it as me wanting something from you. Your health came first, not the project I had wanted to discuss with you."

"Touché," Cat murmured, realizing Slade was right.

"Still," Slade murmured, cupping her chin to make her look up at him, "I fell in love with you anyway."

"Because of my looks?"

"Other things, too," he said patiently. "I like the way your mind works. I was as starved as you were for those times when we could sit and simply share time and space with one another, Cat." Slade leaned over, his mouth caressing her parted lips. "And more than anything, I like you, Cat Kincaid. You make no apology for being yourself."

Cat quivered. "A lot of men are threatened by me."

"That's their problem, sweetheart. If they can't deal with an intelligent woman, let them turn and tuck their tails between their legs and run."

Laughter bubbled up in her throat and Cat rested her head tiredly on his broad shoulder. "I love you, Slade Donovan. For better or worse."

"It's gotten worse lately, hasn't it?"

She nodded, exhaustion flooding her as Slade held her. "I thought my fear of the mine was my worst enemy. Now I know there's something worse—guaqueros."

"Things will settle down now, Cat," he promised her. Slade gently positioned her on the cot and he lay down beside her. Pulling the protective mosquito netting over them, he murmured, "Just keep Bogotá in mind. If we're lucky, we'll get there in less than a week."

"What's in Bogotá?" Cat asked, her voice slurred with exhaustion.

"A surprise for you. It's something I've been planning all along..."

Chapter Thirteen

Cat stood out in the burning sun. It melted the knot of fear that insisted on staying inside her every time she had to step into the Verde. In her hand was the torque meter, ready to test rock bolts recently secured in the newest section of the mine. It was a crosscut sheering off to the left that would follow the vein. Yet something was nagging Cat and she tried to pinpoint the unsettling feeling. The sky was an unusual pale yellow, something she'd not seen before over the Colombian jungle. Then she smiled to herself: Colombia had taught her a lot of new things.

As she walked into the shadow of the busy mine, Cat centered on its positives. Slade had promised her a weekend in Bogotá more than a month ago. That hadn't materialized because he'd ended up having to take El Tigre to the capital and file charges against him. Slade had returned a week later, after they had finished dynamiting into the crosscut to follow the abrupt turn of the vein. They had dug almost three-quarters of a mile into Caballo when the vein suddenly plunged down and to the left. Up to that point, very little emerald-bearing calcite had been found. Verde was looking like a lost cause. The open pit, on the other hand, was rich with emeralds. The mine was not.

Cat nodded to a group of sweaty, dirty miners as they trudged out toward the entrance. It was noon, and time to eat. Her stomach growled, but she ignored the signal. Testing the rock-bolt tension was more important, and with the miners out of the way, she could do it more quickly. The darkness between the electric lights strung on each side of the adit always reminded her of the fear. At times claustrophobia nearly overwhelmed her, but she fought it. Her fingers tightened around the torque meter, and Cat moved her gaze up and down, automatically checking posts and stulls.

The crosscut came into view and she slowed. Standing at the Y, she was reminded of the mine in Maine that had nearly claimed her life. Lips compressed, she began to check each one of the newly placed rock bolts on the manging wall, concentrating on her job with one part of her mind, and thinking of Slade with another. He would be back today! He had been gone for three days, testifying once again in El Tigre's case in Bogotá. Cat smiled, remembering Slade's disgruntled comments that if he'd known about all the governmental red tape awaiting him, he'd have let the guaquero go. *Soon,* Cat promised herself, stretching up to place the torque meter on the next bolt, *soon we'll have that weekend together.*

Their relationship had subtly changed since the night they had admitted their love for one another, Cat thought. They had grown closer, establishing a friendship so powerful that she was sometimes awed by what they had created. It was a good feeling, Cat admitted, hearing the telling click, and checking the meter to read it. Making a note on the pad she always carried with her, she moved on to the next bolt. How she ached with love for Slade. Stolen kisses and passion shared late at night, bone-weary with exhaustion, was their only consolation. Soon...

"Cat?" Slade's voice echoed off the light green walls of the shadowy Verde.

Cat gasped and spun around. He was back! Before she could leave the crosscut, she saw him appear far above her at its lip. Despite the shadows, she saw his mouth turn up in a devastating smile of welcome. Her heart wrenched powerfully in her breast and she set the torque meter down as he approached.

Taking off his hard hat, Slade lifted Cat into his arms, crushing her against him.

"Mmm, sweetheart, you not only smell good, you feel good," he growled.

Her laughter was silvery as she threw her arms around him. "Slade! You're back early."

He sought and found her ripe mouth, then allowed Cat to slide down across his body. "I missed you," he said thickly, claiming her.

Slade's breath was moist against her cheek and she returned his hunger with hers. "I need you," Cat whispered huskily, holding him tightly.

With a groan, Slade held her. "No more than I need you, my beautiful lady."

Alone in the silence of the shaft, Cat languished in his arms, smothered with his volcanic desire, wildly aware of his hardened body against her own. Just the salty taste of his skin and the odor that was uniquely his overwhelmed her senses until she was dizzy with need.

Shuddering with a primal urge, Slade gently eased Cat from him. His eyes were burning with undisguised hunger as he stared down at her. "We're going to take off for Bogotá tomorrow morning. How does that sound?"

With a cry of elation, Cat hugged him. "Wonderful! Then this court business with El Tigre is wrapped up?"

Slade grinned. "Finally. He's getting twenty-five years at hard labor."

"Good."

"How's the crosscut looking?" Slade wanted to know, reluctantly releasing her.

"No better than the rest of the vein, so far," Cat admitted, motioning him to follow her to its end.

Slade scratched his head, then settled the white hard hat back on as he listened to her explanation of the recent dynamiting. The Verde itself was a major disappointment. Millions of dollars had already been sunk into securing the mine. He watched as Cat ran her fingers over the vein, which disappeared into the seven-foot-wide limestone wall that signaled an end to the crosscut until they could do more blasting.

"I'm having the miners on the second shift come down here with picks and crowbars to try and find some calcite." She motioned to the pile of tools and the five safety lamps placed there earlier that day.

Slade ran his hand over the vein, shaking his head. "I just don't understand this, Cat. I did extra channel sampling over this area to determine its feasibility." He glanced at her, his brows knitted. "Those small emeralds I showed you from the pouch were from this vein. It doesn't make sense that we haven't run into the calcite again."

"Listen," Cat explained reasonably, "you know gem mining isn't a very safe bet. Maybe your Texas luck held and you tapped into the only nest of calcite and emerald the vein carried when you made your channel sample. That's happened before."

He grimaced, his face glistening with sweat. "Ouch. Don't even say it."

"Well, if this crosscut doesn't yield something soon, I'm going to recommend shutting this portion of the mine down, Slade. You can't keep funneling money into a worthless operation. We both know that."

Slade stared at the limestone wall in front of them, his mouth twisted. "Yeah, I know it. Damn! I've just got a sixth sense about this vein. I know there's emeralds somewhere in this thing. I can almost taste it."

With a gentle smile, Cat reached over and touched his sun-darkened arm. "You've got green-fire fever, Slade. That's all."

"We're doing so well out in the pit. Matter of fact, what we're finding out there is keeping us from going into the red with the mine."

Cat gave him a sympathetic smile. "Count your blessings, Slade. At least the pit is yielding. One out of two isn't bad. You could have gone bust on both, you know."

He smiled and took Cat into his arms, kissing her long and tenderly. "You're my blessing, sweetheart," he told her thickly. "Green fire is one thing, but you're far more important to me—"

Slade's head snapped up, his arms tightening protectively around her. Cat felt the earth quiver once. A sound like a freight train started deep in the bowels of the earth, rolling toward them with frightening speed. Cat's eyes widened.

"Slade—"

"Son of a bitch!"

The earthquake struck with lightning fury. In seconds they were both knocked off their feet as the earth buckled and groaned. Cat struck her head on the footwall and was knocked semiconscious. Slade was hurled over her as the second wave of the quake shuddered through the mine. Rock began to fall from the manging wall as rock bolts snapped in half like guns being fired at close range. Dust spewed through the crosscut behind the avalanche of rock that fell to the footwall.

After the last of the tremors, Slade got to his knees, cursing and coughing violently. He reached out to find Cat, panic eating at him.

"Cat?"

"I-I'm okay," she said, and she struggled to her knees, wiping blood from her mouth. The dust was suffocating and Slade fumbled with the handkerchief she had around her neck.

"Lie down," he gasped.

Cat lay on the pebbled hardness of the footwall, the cotton handkerchief folded across her nostrils and mouth to act as a filter against the deadly dust. Slade joined her, his body against hers, to protect her from further injury. She hugged the wall, trying to stop hyperventilating. Trapped! They had been trapped by an unexpected earthquake! The grayish light on her hard hat was the only source of illumination in the chamber.

"I wonder how much rock fell?" Slade muttered, all the while listening for other sounds. It had been a sharp quake, and there were bound to be aftershocks.

"Not much, I hope. Are you okay?"

He heard the terror in Cat's voice, and kept his arm wrapped tightly around her. "Yeah. Hurt feelings more than anything else. You?"

"Bump on the head, nothing more."

"You've got a hard head."

"Yeah." She snorted. "Slade?"

"What?"

"How much rock do you think fell behind us?"

He tried to keep his voice cool and free of his own fear. "Probably not much. If we're lucky, most of those rock bolts held. Don't worry, Alvin will have us out of here pronto." He forced a laugh for her benefit. "He doesn't want to lose his chief geologist and the best mining engineer in the world."

"No, he'll come and dig us out because we appreciate his cowboy cooking so much," Cat rallied.

Slade chuckled. "Lady, I love the hell out of you."

Tears tracked through the dust on her face, but Cat didn't want Slade to know she was crying. When she spoke, the words came out staccato. "I love you too."

"We'll get out of this, Cat, I promise you." Slade slowly got into a kneeling position, keeping a hand on her shoulder. He located his hard hat, plugged the jack into the battery pack he carried around his waist and turned on the light. "Stay here by this post. We're bound to get aftershocks. I want to see just how far up the crosscut that cave-in occurred. Do you have a portable radio with you?"

Cat automatically patted her side. "Yes. I'll try and contact Alvin while you check out the wall." The gloomy darkness swallowed up Slade's tall figure. Cat licked her lips, realizing that this time there was no water to slake her thirst. She pulled the dusty radio out of its protective leather case at her side. Her heart sank as she switched it to the On position. The red light did not blink to indicate it was working properly. Then she remembered hitting the footwall first with her hip and then her head. The radio, when she held it directly up into the light from her hard hat, had a large crack running vertically through the tough plastic casing. Alvin wouldn't know if they were alive or dead . . .

She pushed trembling fingers through her dust-laden hair and returned the useless radio to its case. Cat rose to her feet. Oddly, she was calmer than she would have thought. As she turned to examine the damage to the end of the crosscut, a gasp tore from her.

"Slade! Slade, come here! Quick!"

He came on the run. "What?"

Cat grabbed him by the arm and dragged him over to the wall. "Look. My God, look at this, Slade." She pointed toward the vein.

Slade's breath jammed in his throat as he lifted his head and settled the light on the area she was pointing out. The quake had opened up the vein, exposing what appeared to be an endless green crystalline structure more than two feet long, which disappeared into the wall where blasting hadn't yet taken place.

"Green fire," he whispered hoarsely, reaching out and tentatively touching the nearest emerald crystals.

Cat's laugh echoed in the chamber. "There must be millions of dollars' worth in this one vein alone."

"Look at their color," Slade breathed. "Dark green and clear. Look at this!" He took off his helmet, casting the light directly on the emeralds that glittered fiercely back at them. "They're so clear, Cat. I've never seen anything like this . . ."

She shook her head in disbelief. It was as if the earth had opened up her most precious treasure chest and allowed them to see her finest gems. Reverently, Cat touched one of the crystals. "They're magnificent."

"You're right, they'll be worth millions," Slade confirmed, his voice hushed. "And I'll stake my life on the fact that the emeralds here are of better quality than those of any other mine in the world. I don't believe it . . . This is a miracle, a miracle . . ."

Nodding mutely, Cat agreed. Oh, she'd seen gems in calcite matrix before, but they'd been in single nests once every hundreds of thousands of tons of earth. She'd never seen a long, continuous vein like this. No, this was one of a kind, just like Slade, and his belief that something special—green fire—lived here in the earth.

As if shaking his head from a dream, Slade turned to her. "They're the color of your eyes," he said huskily. "Clear and beautiful and exotic."

Cat walked over and threw her arms around him. Words were useless compared to what she was feeling for Slade. "I'm happy for you, Slade. Your dream has come true. It's paid off."

He managed a soft laugh as he slowly released her. "Sweetheart, when I met you, my most important dream came true." He looked at the emerald vein. "I have you, and we have a mine that's going to yield the world's highest-quality emeralds ever seen by man.''

Cat smiled grimly, looking toward the dust-laden crosscut. ''Only if we get out of here, Slade. I don't want to be a wet blanket, but—''

''I know. Come on, pick up a crowbar. I'm getting a pickax.''

She followed Slade to where the manging wall had fallen. The snapped rock bolts were scattered around like so many toothpicks, shattered by the force of the quake. Slade pointed up at the manging wall and shrugged out of his shirt.

''If you hadn't spaced those rock bolts so closely together, even more would have come down, burying us.''

Cat shuddered. ''We're not out of this yet, Slade.''

''Wet blanket,'' he teased, handing her his shirt and hard hat. In the semigloom his massive chest and shoulders gleamed with sweat as he hefted the ax in his large hands. ''What I want you to do is focus both hard-hat lights here. I'm going to start digging. We can't wait for Alvin to start because we've only got so much oxygen left.''

Cat nodded, standing out of the way. ''Slade, I can take a crowbar and—''

''Not yet. Let me work at this wall, then I'll let you clear away the gangue and I'll go back to work.''

Biting her lower lip, Cat nodded. No holes were visible through the rubble blocking their escape and Cat didn't know how thick the wall was. If too much had fallen down, they could suffocate before getting rescued. As Slade began to swing the head of the pickax into the limestone, she prayed that the rock bolts had prevented a massive cave-in. Each rhythmic swing of the ax echoed throughout the chamber. The limestone crushed easily, powdering beneath Slade's swings. His body looked like burnished metal beneath the light. Sweat ran off the bunched muscles of his back and shoulders, and his dark hair clung to his head as he heaved the pick savagely into the wall over and over again.

How long Slade worked, Cat did not know. Minutes grew into hours, and his facial expression never altered. His jaw was set, lips pulled away from his clenched teeth, eyes narrowed as he glared at the wall that prevented their escape. Cat saw his rugged jeans darken with sweat and cling to his long, firm thighs as he began to make progress into the wall. The limestone was no match for steel and brawn. Each precise swing exploded into the wall, loosening a little more debris, moving them inches closer to freedom. Finally, Slade stopped. He wiped his wet brow with the back of his arm. Dust caked his massive chest, his hair and face.

Cat gave him the shirt so he could wipe his face. She set the lights down, and went to work with the crowbar to clear the gangue out of the way. Slade's incredible strength gave her strength. She knew she could not match his physical power, but she doggedly labored at clearing a space for him to work in. Her shirt clung damply to her body as she lifted some of the larger rocks, throwing them behind her. Sweat stung her eyes and she shook her head to clear them. After half an hour, most of the debris had been moved aside so that Slade could take over.

"You did a good job," he told her, coming up and sliding his arm around her shoulders.

Cat leaned against him and slid her hand across his chest, feeling the mat of wiry hair beneath her fingertips. "Aren't you tired?"

"Not when I consider the alternative," he told her, wrapping his long, callused fingers around the wooden handle of the pick. Leaning over, Slade kissed her cheek, then sought her lips. A satisfied growl rumbled from him as he kissed her quickly and hard. Reluctantly he released her and went back to work.

Glumly, Cat thought about what he'd implied: the air was growing more sparse as time went on. Each breath lessened the oxygen content. Each breath brought them closer to death's embrace. She shifted her attention back to Slade, who had resumed his rhythmic attack against the wall. If possible, he seemed to be exerting even more energy and concentrated power against their foe, death. Huge chunks of limestone flew around him, and sparks flashed as steel bit into rock. The chamber echoed with the tortured crack of rock pulverized beneath his Herculean strength. With each swing of the pick, Cat held her breath. How long could Slade sustain his backbreaking pace? His muscles bunched and released, bunched and released. Looking at his set features, Cat knew she needn't give up hope. Ever.

Five hours had passed and they sat huddled together in the pitch blackness. They had to save the battery-powered light for Slade to work by. The safety lamps required oxygen to remain lit and Slade didn't want their precious supply to be eaten up. The electrical lamps on their hard hats would have to suffice. Cat wiped Slade's shoulders and back with the wet shirt. She splayed her hands on his flesh, feeling an almost imperceptible tremor beneath her palm. He was close to exhaustion. Any other man would have quit hours before, physically unable to go on as long as he had.

"Let me massage you," she whispered, positioning herself behind him. "You're going to get cramps if I don't."

Slade nodded wearily and rested his brow on his arms, which hugged his drawn-up knees. "Thanks," he murmured hoarsely. God, what he'd do for a glass of water right now. He said nothing, realizing Cat had to be as close to dehydration as he was. Her clothes were wet and clung to her like a second skin. He groaned as her fingers worked over his weary, protesting back muscles, helping them relax from the brutal workout he had given them. For almost fifteen minutes, Cat worked out the kinks and knots.

"Thanks, sweetheart," he muttered, patting her thigh.

Cat laid her head on his back momentarily, shutting her eyes. "I love you, Slade. You're incredible."

He snorted softly, rubbing his hand up and down the length of her thigh. "I love you, too. But incredible? Hardly."

"Your strength is unbelievable."

"It's called fear of dying. That's what keeps me going right now."

Cat wrapped her arms around him, feeling the ragged pound of his heart beneath her palms. "You must have moved a ton of gangue from that wall. That's a lot."

Slade knew what she had left unspoken: it was looking more and more as if a huge section of the manging wall had fallen. They were going to be trapped for a long time. Maybe longer than they had oxygen to last them. He wiped the accumulated sweat off his face.

"Come around here. Sit between my legs."

Cat moved carefully in the darkness. She nestled between his thighs, one arm around his waist, and her head resting against his hard, flat stomach. "At least you're with me this time," she uttered tiredly. "Sharing a mine cave-in takes away some of the fear."

Slade curved his palm against her cheek, savoring her warmth and softness. "Not as scared as before?"

"No." Cat managed a choked laugh. "Maybe I'm getting used to them, Slade. I don't feel that overwhelming fear."

He glanced around, unable to see anything. "Yeah, this is my fourth one. They get to be pretty routine after a while. Only one thing occupies your mind, and that's how much oxygen you have left."

Cat pressed a kiss to his slick flesh. "That and water. What I'd do for some water for both of us."

"I'd trade that vein of emeralds for a glass for both of us right now."

She laughed with him. "Amazing how some events in life can put everything into very sharp focus, isn't it, Slade?"

"Yes." Silence settled over them. "Cat?"

She closed her eyes, her arm tightening around his waist, hearing an unexpected tremor in his deep voice. "What is it?" Was he going to tell her that they didn't stand a chance? That most likely, they would die in here together? A fierce love for Slade welled up through Cat like a fist, taking her breath away as she prepared herself to hear those words.

"Marry me."

"What?"

"I know it's a little soon and we haven't talked about it before this, but I want you to marry me." Slade's hand came to rest on her hair. "I can't imagine life without you, lady." There was a long silence and then he felt the wetness of her tears beneath his fingertips. He leaned over, holding her tightly, anguish soaring through him. His voice cracked as he brought her up against him.

"Damn it, I know life isn't fair, but when I've finally found you, it could be too late."

Cat stubbornly shook her head, burying her face next to his and trying to stop her tears. "No, it's never too late—never!"

"I love you, Cat."

"I'll marry you, Slade..."

"You will?"

She managed a half sob and half laugh. "Of course I will!" Cat traced trembling fingers through his sweat-soaked hair, kissing his brow, eyes and finally his mouth.

Savoring her flurry of kisses, Slade held her even closer to him. "It'll be a hell of a marriage."

Cat groaned. "Tell me about it!"

"I'll have your Kincaid stubbornness to contend with."

"You're not exactly a willow in the wind, Slade Donovan," she pointed out archly.

He chuckled, the rumble moving up through his chest. "But we both have a good sense of humor. We know how to take a joke."

"Only because I'm the straight person and you're the comic of our team."

Slade nuzzled his face between her breasts, absorbing her scent. "I need you, Cat," he whispered thickly. "Now, forever. Living with you those months made me realize just how much I liked having you underfoot."

A smile touched her tear-wet lips and Cat closed her eyes, realizing the futility of their situation. "What made you suddenly ask to marry me, Slade?"

He caressed her waist, then settled his hand on her hip. "Sweetheart—" he paused and swallowed "—if I can't break through that wall, I wanted you to know just how damn much you mean to me."

How long they held one another, Cat didn't know. It no longer mattered. The chamber was stiflingly hot and stuffy; the ripe smell of their sweat assailed her nostrils along with the chalky limestone dust that still hung in the air and caked their mouths. Just as Slade took up the pickax and walked to the wall, she heard a distinct drilling noise from the other side.

"Slade!"

He turned, relief etched on his exhausted features. "I hear it . . ."

Cat clutched the hard hat, the light trained on the wall. "Alvin . . . he's coming through. That's an auger bit!"

A grin creased Slade's face as he stepped back and joined Cat against the far wall. He slid his arm around her shoulders and pulled her to him. Leaning down, he kissed her hard and long. Releasing her, he murmured, "Well, gal, it looks like you have to make good on that promise to marry me now."

She laughed, sinking against Slade, dizzy from joy that they were going to be rescued. "You mean asking me to marry you wasn't a sham, Slade Donovan? Some last-minute admission before you said hello to your maker?"

His grin widened against his stained face. "Come to Bogotá with me and find out," he challenged.

When they entered the Bogotá Hilton together, nearly every patron sitting in the lobby turned and gawked at them. Slade grinned at Cat as they came to a halt at the desk.

"I think we're a sight for sore eyes."

Cat grimaced, looking down at her disheveled appearance. "I think we're a sight, Slade." Although they'd washed and changed after they'd been rescued, they had come straight to Bogotá afterward, leaving the clean-up and newly discovered emeralds in Alvin's capable hands.

Slade's eyes sparkled as he took the registration card and signed them in. "We'll buy any clothes we need," Slade said, pulling out his wallet. He gave the clerk his credit card. Within minutes, Slade had the key to their room. "Come on, Cat. You and I are going to take a very long, hot shower. Together..."

From the balcony of their air-conditioned room, a flaming orange sunset bid them good-evening. Cat had groggily awakened from a much-needed sleep and gotten up, wrapping the thick white hotel robe around her. She looked over her shoulder; Slade was still sleeping soundly. A tender smile pulled at her lips as she sat down in the ivory satin settee facing the king-size bed where he lay.

Tucking her legs beneath her, Cat was content to simply watch Slade. She smiled softly. Once they had gotten beneath the hot, pummeling streams of water, their hunger for one another had been tempered. Pure exhaustion combined with the relaxing massage of the water had made them both too drowsy to think of anything else but sleep.

They had curled up in bed on the white cotton sheets, their bodies hot and moist against its cool, crisp texture. Nothing had ever felt so good, and Cat vaguely remembered curving into Slade's waiting arms and promptly falling asleep. Now she looked at her watch; it was almost nine o'clock. They'd slept a long time. Her stomach growled, reminding Cat that she hadn't eaten all day. Quietly, she rose and went to the phone to order dinner.

Slade awoke to the mouth-watering smell of beefsteak. He groaned and rolled onto his back, the sheet covering him from the waist down in twisted disarray.

"Slade?" Cat walked to the bed and smiled down at him, thinking how boyish he looked. She sat on the edge of the mattress, one arm across him, watching him awake. "Come on, time to rise and shine."

Groaning, Slade dragged an arm across his eyes. "What time is it?" he asked thickly.

Cat leaned down and kissed his petulant mouth. "Ten o'clock. Time to get up and eat."

Slade slid his hand up her long, robed thigh. "You have great legs. Did I ever tell you that?"

"I thought all such admissions were given in the cross-cut."

A grin tugged at his mouth and Slade moved his arm and opened his eyes. Cat's hair was long, nearly touching her shoulders, and was shot through with gold from the light above. She looked like a ragamuffin in the oversize robe. "Spunky gal, aren't you?" he challenged, sitting up and leaning against the headboard. The sheet pulled away, leaving him nearly naked, but he didn't care. All of his attention was centered on Cat's shining green eyes. Her smile made him go hard and hot inside.

"You wouldn't want me any other way." Cat patted his flat, hard stomach. "Come on, I ordered us a Texas-size meal. I'm starved."

Slade glanced past her at the sumptuous meal overflowing from the cart behind them. "What? No spotted horse thief? Where's my stewed kidneys? My johnnycake?"

Giving him a playful pat on the hip, Cat rose, laughing. "If you're expecting Alvin's cooking, forget it." She went to the cart and drew up two chairs.

Slade got up and padded to the bathroom to retrieve his robe. He had an odd look on his face as he came back out with it. "Let's trade robes, Cat. You've got mine and I'm sure as hell not going to be able to fit into this one."

Nonplussed, her silverware poised above her thick, medium-rare steak, Cat grimaced. "Oh...sorry. I thought they were all the same size." She got up and came around the table, struggling out of the robe, revealing her nakedness.

"I lied." Slade grabbed her and carried her to the bed.

Cat laughed, throwing her arms around Slade as he settled down beside her. "You're such a joker, Slade Donovan."

Slade's smile grew wide as he leaned over and kissed her laughter-touched lips. "But you love me anyway?" he coaxed thickly, tasting her sweetness.

With a tremulous sigh, Cat slid her fingers across his shoulders. "Yes...yes, I love you anyway."

"Enough to marry me tomorrow morning?" He trailed a path of nibbling, moist kisses from her earlobe down the length of her neck, feeling her pulse flutter wildly at the base of her throat. Her fingers were wreaking havoc on him, too, as she followed the curve of his chest, brushing his nipples.

Closing her eyes, she arched against Slade as his mouth found the valley between her breasts. "Y-yes."

Slade continued his gentle assault. "God, you smell and taste good. Are you sure? You sound a little doubtful."

An exquisite ache was building in her and Cat moaned, her mind fleeing as his knowing fingers gently parted her thighs. "Slade...." His name came out like a breathless prayer. "Love me, just love me. Now. I need you so much..."

With a smile, Slade brought a hardened nipple into his mouth and sucked gently, feeling Cat press against him.

A cry of pleasure tore from her as Slade moved one hand down across her belly, finding the rich carpet below to coax the smoldering fire to life within her. She sagged against him, jolts of such magnitude rushing through her that she was helpless in his arms. The ache intensified and Cat moved against his palm.

"Yes," Slade said in a rough whisper near her ear, "show me how much you need me. Show me, my lovely lady..."

The shattering gift of fulfillment rippled through her, and afterward, Cat lay in Slade's arms, unable to move as wave after wave of melted heat flowed through her. Her lips curved into a smile and she barely opened her eyes. The immense satisfaction on Slade's face reflected how she felt and Cat weakly lifted her arms, pulling him on top of her. "Let me give to you as much as you've given to me," she whispered huskily.

Slade's smile was pure male as he slid his hand beneath her hips and watched her eyes close as he slowly moved into the depths of her warm, rich body. His fingers froze against her hips as her fire touched him and drew him more deeply into her. His breath was torn from him, followed by a groan born deep and low in his chest. Sunlight, she was sunlight on the cool water's surface, he thought raggedly. Then reality became a blur as Slade fell beneath Cat's magical spell. Never had another woman loved him so thoroughly or with such consuming passion. Like the handfuls of warm soil he had held so often in his hand, she reminded him that she was of the earth: warm, fertile and all-encompassing. With a groan, Slade gripped her in release. Sunlight and earth once more touched as he reemerged in the magic that was Cat.

Spent, he lay against her damp breast, aware of the uneven beat of her heart. Sweat trickled down his jaw, but Slade didn't care. Gently, he ran his hand up her torso, and cupped her breast. Cat's fingers moved slowly through his hair, and he closed his eyes in contentment. Words were useless for what he felt toward Cat. Instead, he held her for a long time, caressing her and letting her know just how much he loved her.

Finally, Slade rose. On his return, Cat smiled and curled up again in his arms. He moved his fingers along the satin curve of her back.

"Every time we love, it's better," he told her.

"Every time is like the first time," Cat whispered, kissing his stubbled jaw. "You make me feel like the earth touched by rain and sunlight: a rainbow of colors and sensations."

"You're the earth, sweetheart. Giving and holding the warmth within you and giving it back when I need it."

"I never thought this kind of love or contentment was possible, darling."

"Neither did I."

Slade settled one hand behind his head and stared up at the gray ceiling. "Matt once told me he didn't believe in dreams ever coming true. Kai changed his mind, of course. But in a lot of ways, I was like him. I never thought the woman of my dreams would ever become a reality."

"But you dreamed, Slade. And that was important."

He grinned. "But both of us doubted our dream would come true." He sat up and leaned against the headboard, bringing Cat into his arms. "And we were wrong."

"Men," Cat muttered darkly. "Can't live with 'em..."

"Now, now, be kind and patient to us Neanderthal types. We might be a bit slow, but once we're taught, we come around."

Cat sat up facing Slade. He looked so young. There was a rebellious lock of hair on his brow, as usual, and his cobalt eyes were bright and warm with amusement. "Neanderthal," she chortled. "You're hardly that. A smooth operator would be closer to the truth."

Slade raised his hand against his heart, trying his best to look wounded. "I'm Texan. That says it all."

She gave him a dirty look. "That's barely scratching the surface. Coming out of the bathroom and saying the robe was too small was a rotten trick, Slade Donovan, and you know it!"

A grin edged his mouth. "That was the easiest way I could think of to get you out of that robe and into my arms."

"Did you ever stop to think that asking might have gotten the same result?"

He quelled a smile and shrugged. "I didn't think you'd leave that steak for anything."

"Well, you were probably right. I was hungry."

Slade gave her an impish smile, obviously pleased with the success of his escapade. Cat got off the bed and pulled on a robe. As she handed him the other one, she noted the one-size-fits-all tag on the inside. With a shake of her head, she moved the table. Slade grabbed her hand and pulled her back into bed with him.

"Come here," he growled, wrestling with her until she was effectively trapped beneath him. "I'm not done with you, my proud lady."

Cat laughed, hotly aware of his naked body against her. "Now what have you got cooked up? I see that look in your eyes."

Slade rolled off her and kept a restraining hand on her while he reached in the drawer of the bed stand. "See? There you go again accusing me of being up to something."

Cat waited expectantly as he settled a folded piece of tissue paper the size of a quarter on her robed breast. "You've got that gleam in your eye again, Slade. What do you expect me to think? What's this?"

"Open it and find out. Careful . . . it might bite you."

Meeting Slade's smile, Cat slowly unwrapped the white tissue paper. It crinkled between her fingers. She glanced up at Slade's expectant features. "You're such a rogue, Slade Donovan."

"And you love me for it."

"Yes, I do." Cat pushed aside the outer wrapping. There was a second layer of paper. "What did you do? Spend hours wrapping this?"

"You'll see why," Slade said, his hand resting on her hip.

Cat's eyes widened as she pulled the last of the paper away. There, nestled in the center, was a thick gold ring set with a long, rectangular emerald. She gasped and struggled to sit up. Slade removed his hand so that she could.

"Slade..."

He leaned over her, resting his chin on her shoulder. "Like it?"

Cat ran her fingers lightly over the emerald. "Like it? My God, it's huge and beautiful and priceless! Look at the clarity!" She held it up for him to see.

"Of course it's clear. It's from our mine. The first Verde emerald we discovered." Slade glanced at her, tenderness in his blue gaze. "And it's priceless, like you are to me, Cat."

With a cry, Cat turned, throwing her arms around Slade. "You wonderful romantic. I love you so much!"

Slade held her tightly. "You and I, sweetheart, are going to have one hell of a happy life together. You know that, don't you?"

Cat smiled, kissed his cheek, then eased away from him. Tears made her eyes luminous as she met and held Slade's sober expression. She held the ring between them. "You and I will live life as never before," she promised. "Because now, we've added love to our existence. I'm looking forward to each new day with you, Slade."

His heart wrenched and he cradled Cat's face gently between his palms. "Green fire can't compare to how you've set my soul on fire, my love. You've captured my heart. Forever."

* * * * *

Silhouette Special Edition

COMING NEXT MONTH

#403 SANTIAGO HEAT—Linda Shaw
When Deidre Miles crash-landed in steamy Santiago, powerful Francis MacIntire saved her from the clutches of a treacherous military. But what could save her from Francis himself, his tumultuous life and flaming desire?

#404 SOMETIMES A MIRACLE—Jennifer West
Bodyguard Cassandra Burke wistfully dreamed of shining knights on white chargers. Cynical ex-rodeo star Alex Montana had long since turned in his steed. As they braved murder and mayhem together, just who would protect whom?

#405 CONQUER THE MEMORIES—Sandra Dewar
For social worker Carla Foster it was time to face the music. In an adoption dispute, Drake Lanning recognized her for the singer she used to be, and he vowed to learn why she hid her talent...and her heart.

#406 INTO THE SUNSET—Jessica Barkley
Lindsay Jordan wasn't just another city slicker playing cowgirl, no matter what ornery stable manager Nick Leighton said. And despite his sensual persuasion, she wasn't greenhorn enough to think of riding off into the sunset with him!

#407 LONELY AT THE TOP—Bevlyn Marshall
Corporate climber Keely LaRoux wasn't about to let maverick photographer Chuck Dickens impede her progress up the ladder. But traveling together on assignment, the unlikely pair found that business could fast become a dangerously addictive pleasure.

#408 A FAMILY OF TWO—Jude O'Neill
Hotshot producer Gable McCrea wanted newcomer Annabel Porter to direct his latest movie. But what inner demons prompted him to sabotage her work... and her growing love for him?

AVAILABLE THIS MONTH:

ATTRACTIVE, SPACE SAVING BOOK RACK

Display your most prized novels on this handsome and sturdy book rack. The hand-rubbed walnut finish will blend into your library decor with quiet elegance, providing a practical organizer for your favorite hard-or soft-covered books.

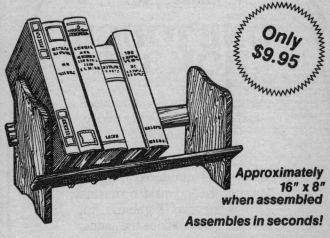

Only $9.95

Approximately 16" x 8" when assembled

Assembles in seconds!

To order, rush your name, address and zip code, along with a check or money order for $10.70* ($9.95 plus 75¢ postage and handling) payable to *Silhouette Books.*

Silhouette Books
Book Rack Offer
901 Fuhrmann Blvd.
P.O. Box 1396
Buffalo, NY 14269-1396

Offer not available in Canada.

BKR-2A

*New York and Iowa residents add appropriate sales tax.